Curse of Ciudad Blanca

Robert V. Wadden Jr.

ISBN: 978-1-62420-510-1

Credits
Cover Artist: Designs by Ms G
Editor: Kitty Carlisle

Printed in the United States of America

One
PLAYA ESTERILLOS, COSTA RICA

The rainy season always made his joints ache. Almost every afternoon the clouds gathered over Playa Esterillos, slowly darkening until the sky exploded with thunder, lightning and rain often lasting all night. Peter loved the pounding rain on the tin roof of his roasting shed and the acrid smell of roasting coffee over the humid air.

When he was not visiting coffee growers in the central highlands he followed the same routine each day. In the warm, dry mornings he stepped out of his compound onto the empty, grey sand beach. He would bring a thermal pot of coffee and lie on his chaise longue reading from his Kindle. Occasionally he entered the warm, calm water. By eleven AM he left the beach to fix a light lunch and check his computer for e-mails. In the afternoon as the humidity rose and the clouds gathered he would retreat to his roasting shed to sample and experiment with the coffee beans he was considering recommending to his clients in the U.S.

The current batch of beans was from the area around San Vito, a town settled in the nineteen fifties by Italian immigrants in the southern mountains of central Costa Rica. The beans were plump with promise; smooth and blue-green. His challenge was to find the ideal roast by roasting small batches to various levels, experimenting with temperature and duration. In his shed he had a small one kilo Diedrich sample roaster powered by propane. Peter spent his afternoons in the shed roasting batch after batch, sampling the results and recording his findings. He loved the smell, texture and sound of the beans as they progressed through the roasting process.

For Peter, coffee roasting was an escape. Immersion in the process let him lose himself in something outside himself. The deep calm he felt as he processed each batch was the result of escaping his own consciousness and savoring the details of the roast. When the results were good, when he had extracted the ideal balance between body and flavor for the particular bean, he felt a deep sense of satisfaction and accomplishment unconnected with the objective importance of well roasted coffee.

In an earlier life, Peter VanOwen had been a lawyer employed by the Los Angeles County Counsel's office. For a while he had a wife and children and a small house in a Los Angeles suburb. A rancorous divorce and early retirement led him to Costa Rica and a stucco house in a gated compound on the grey volcanic beach of Playa Esterillos on the Pacific coast. He had stumbled into coffee brokering more as a way to fill his days than a need to make money. But he had come to love the process and discovered in himself an entrepreneurial side which had lain dormant over his years as a public lawyer. He bought coffee from small growers and sold it to several modest sized coffee shop chains in the United States with recommendations on the roast and brewing. He often travelled throughout the central Costa Rican highlands looking for beans and occasionally travelled to Guatemala and Panama. Several times a month he would drive to San Jose to meet buyers. In between trips he settled into his comfortable daily routine, seldom communicating with any of his old family and friends in California. His simple, isolated life suited him and he rarely felt a moment of loneliness. He loved the tropical weather, green, lush foliage and the easy, unhurried pace of Costa Rica.

Playa Esterillos had its share of American émigrés but Peter avoided them, as well as the nearby surfer town of Jaco with its high rise hotels, surf shops and fish taco joints. He drank at home, not wanting to engage in the banal and self-promoting conversation of the typical American bar in Costa Rica. At 60 he had, he admitted to himself, become withdrawn and introspective.

As he watched the temperature on the Diedrich, Peter heard a car pull into his drive. He walked to the shed window to see a hired van expel a slight man with dark rimmed glasses and ginger colored hair, a man whom Peter had not seen for many years.

Two
LOS ANGELES, CALIFORNIA,
FORTY YEARS EARLIER

Terry Selby first met Peter VanOwen when he stepped into his UCLA dorm room in Sproul Hall and introduced himself as Terry's new roommate. VanOwen was a tall, stocky kid with dirty blonde hair and large green eyes. To Terry he seemed serious and humorless, and as he shook Peter's hand he thought this could be a trying and thoroughly boring relationship. However, Terry was to find Peter was neither entirely dull nor without his uses.

While Terry and Peter never really became friends, they did have their share of mutual adventures, using, buying and selling weed together, exploring late night music clubs and sharing some of the same friends. Peter, or "Van" as Terry insisted on calling him since Peter hated it, was a brilliant student and although he was a philosophy major he seemed to have a greater aptitude for Terry's archeology major classes than Terry himself. Van never refused Terry his help and Terry admitted to himself quite honestly he would never have been admitted to graduate school had it not been for Van's help, especially on the Yucatan field trip. It was Van who had met and introduced him to Zelda.

Zelda Aronson was the most beautiful woman Terry had ever met. At 5'7" she had long dark, silky, brown hair, shockingly huge blue, almost lavender, eyes, pale white skin and long shapely legs. She was also brilliant. Terry could not keep up with her, she made him feel dumb and inadequate but he wanted her more than any woman he had ever met. So did Peter.

Peter had met her during their junior year in a "Language and Logic" class devoted to the study of Wittgenstein. He walked in on them engaged in heated discussion about Wittgenstein's religious faith. Zelda, with her long legs tucked up under her in the little chair in their dorm room, her face flush with enthusiasm and her huge lavender eyes looming behind thick black rimmed glasses, was the most beautiful girl Terry had ever seen, far too beautiful for Van.

Peter and Zelda quickly became close, going everywhere together, to museums and concerts and hikes in the Santa Monica mountains. Whenever he could, Terry tagged along. Unlike Peter, Terry was funny and charming, even if he faltered at discussing Sartre's theory of human consciousness or Leopold Bloom's self-loathing in *Ulysses*.

At the end of Terry's junior year they all went home; Peter to his parent's home in Palos Verdes, Terry to Phoenix where his mother lived and Zelda back to New York to a family she refused to discuss. When they all returned, Zelda had changed.

At first she seemed happy to see Peter, but as the weeks went by she drifted away from him, spending more time alone and focusing increasingly on school. Peter was unhappy with these developments and became a nuisance. He would show up unannounced at her off campus apartment at odd hours, seek her out in the library while she was deeply enmeshed in study, and beg her to go with him on weekend excursions. She finally told him it would be best if they stopped seeing each other and Peter went on a three day drinking and stoning binge. But he left her alone after that.

Terry ran into her one night at a party given by an anthropology faculty member. She was by herself and happy to see someone she knew. They talked and Terry made her laugh.

She got drunk and they ended up in bed at her apartment.

In the morning she was embarrassed and awkward. She gave Terry coffee then told him quite cold-bloodedly she was not interested in getting involved with him or anyone else and she hoped he didn't misunderstand what had happened. She was stiff and cold and clearly wanted him out of her apartment as soon as he could wake up and dress. For Terry it was, in many ways, the best night of his life. He had spent the night with a woman who was unnervingly beautiful, whose intellect he admired, and who, despite being drunk, had been a sensitive and responsive lover.

Terry seldom saw Zelda after that night and on those few occasions when he did she was distant and cool. She and Peter had stopped talking completely, Terry never knew exactly why but he knew Peter was hurt and bitter at the end of their relationship.

At year's end they went their separate ways never to see each other again. Peter, at his parents' insistence to UCLA law school, Zelda back to New York, and Terry, thanks to Peter, to a graduate program in archeology at the University of Indiana.

Three
THE YUCATAN,
FORTY YEARS EARLIER

Terry struggled with his studies but he wrote well and charmed many of his professors. He did have a genuine interest in ancient history and had begun to focus on the ancient civilizations of Central America as a specialty area. Senior year, to his great fortune, he was able to convince a professor to allow him to participate in a field trip to work in the ancient Mayan city of Oxkintok in the Yucatan peninsula.

At the last minute one of the other students became ill and could not go on the expedition. Terry convinced Peter to volunteer instead of going on spring break. Because it was short notice and the expedition was short-handed, Peter, a philosophy major, was accepted.

The expedition camped a quarter mile from the dig site. Neither Peter nor Terry was very impressed by the flat expanse of the Yucatan and its scrubby jungle. But they were impressed with the ruined city of Oxkintok. The site covered almost three square miles of palaces, temples and pyramids set around an arrangement of open plazas. Some of the structures were well over a thousand years old. Part of the site was a labyrinth called "tzat tun tzat" consisting of a small structure with a maze of vaulted tunnels connected by small gates and narrow stairs. The site was open to the public but there were few visitors and many structures had not, or had only partially, been excavated.

The daily routine was coffee and cold cereal with canned milk at daybreak, followed by a brief discussion of the day's assignments by their team leader, then long, hot hours sorting through rubble from the excavations; tagging and labeling pottery fragments, tools and sometimes bones. At midday there was a meal of grilled meat, tortillas and salsa followed by a two hour siesta during the hottest hours of the day, then back to work in the late afternoon and early evening. The day ended with a light meal, cold Morelos and a discussion of the progress of the dig and the significance of whatever had been found. Most nights they were asleep by nine.

On the third day of the fourteen day trip, Peter and Terry were assigned to a small octagonal structure adjacent to a cluster of buildings known as the "Dzib Group." Narrow trenches were being dug by local laborers at the entrance and through the foyer of the roofless structure. Peter and Terry were charged with sorting through the rubble of each layer uncovered by the diggers. They found fragments of pottery and utensils including obsidian knives and pieces of carved stone.

When one of the laborers working inside the structure gave a shout, Peter and Terry ran to the trench. In the rubble was an intact carved stone about three and a half feet in length and a foot or so across. As Peter and Terry carefully uncovered the item they saw that it was a bas-relief. Their first view of it was an intricate carving of an old man with a large nose and sunken cheeks, wearing an iguana headdress and holding an urn or pot. Terry carefully used a brush to remove the dust. The carving was in remarkably good condition. As Terry lifted it from the pile of rubble they saw that the carving was two sided. They turned it over and brushed the dust from the second side to reveal a figure in profile of a hideous creature with an exposed bony spine and skull-like jaguar face wearing a headdress, which appeared to be made of serpents and snails. Instead of an urn, this figure was holding what appeared to be a round ceramic bowl.

"I recognize them both," said Terry "they're major gods.

The old man is Itzamna, a creator god, very old and powerful but good natured and benign. The second carving looks like Yum Cimil, chief god of the underworld and a very unpleasant fellow."

"It's not typical for Mayan gods to be portrayed as dual entities, is it?" asked Peter.

"No, I've never seen anything quite like it."

In the course of that day they found four more representations of Itzamal and Yum Cimil together. They were of varying sizes, one being almost six feet tall and broken into fragments, but all having the creation god on one side of the image and the underworld god on the opposite side. All were found inside the octagonal structure.

"We seem to have found a temple devoted to a dual deity having opposing natures," said Peter as they walked back to camp at day's end.

"The Mayans had a lot of gods with very distinct natures and roles but they didn't see any of their gods having a dual nature and certainly not these two. The Toltecs had gods with dual natures but never the Maya," responded Terry.

"Well," said Peter, "maybe we found something unique which tells us something about the Maya we didn't know, or at least about the Maya who lived in Oxkintok. Maybe when we get these fragments dated we'll have a better understanding of what they mean."

That night they talked with Doctor Frazier, the faculty adviser, about the day's finds. "It's certainly an anomaly in the Mayan world to find a two sided god representation," he said. "Who knows what it means, if anything, but why don't you run with it, Terry, might make a good paper."

That night under a full Yucatecan moon, Terry and Peter drank Modelos and talked about the carvings as a warm breeze swept through the camp from the scrub jungle. "Is it really such a big step from individual gods with unique characters to believing in a divine duality, a dual natured god?" asked Peter, "it might be seen as a type of evolutionary belief, a consolidation of the divine."

"Well," said Terry, "Mediterranean culture went from a multiplicity of gods to a single all-encompassing god. Is that the highest form of religious evolution?"

"No, the Christian god is missing all sorts of qualities its pagan predecessors had. The warlike qualities of Mars and Diana, the venality of Venus, Eros and Bacchus, the fecundity of Demeter, the selfishness and arrogance of Jupiter and the cruelty of Hades, the same with the northern gods who expressed violence and lust. The Christian god is single natured and not in any way like his human creations, even though the Catholics teach that 'man was created in the image and likeness of God.' Of course, you could argue that Satan is the flip side of god that gives him a kind of dual nature and makes him more like his human creations. Of course, to do that you have to ignore the narrative that god created Satan who turned bad of his own free will."

"I don't know, the Old Testament is filled with violent acts by god, cities are destroyed, people are turned to salt pillars and the whole world is flooded. Look what he did to Job! That's a god with plenty of anger issues. And if god created Satan then he gave Satan his free will, so in a way god is the author of evil, at least indirectly."

"But even today, when these acts might seem excessive," said Peter, "we justify them as the righteous acts of a just god. We don't see god as an evil entity like the Mayans saw Yum Cimil, god is 'all good.' Frazier is right you know, there's definitely a paper there that at least might raise some questions about aspects of Maya religious beliefs we haven't seen before."

During the rest of the trip they found no more dual sided carvings. But Peter began to work on an outline of a paper he would write for Terry, who edited it and polished it in his inimitable way. That paper caused a minor sensation and made a small reputation for Terry. On its strength, Terry, who had mediocre grades, was admitted to the PhD. program in archeology at the University of Indiana where he was eventually hired as an instructor. Peter had not seen him since the day he left for the airport to fly to Indiana.

Four
PLAYA ESTERILLOS

It was almost 40 years since Peter had seen Terry Selby but he recognized his college roommate immediately. Selby still had the ginger colored hair, though it had thinned considerably. He was still a short, slender man with prominent cheekbones and almond shaped blue eyes. If anything, he looked thinner and more worn than ever with deep bags under his eyes. The thin ginger mustache he had added seemed ridiculous to Peter.

"I can't say you were someone I was expecting to see Terry. How are you?"

Terry looked at him as if someone had just shined a bright light in his face. "Man, you look like shit, Van, you're so fuckin' old."

"I know, you too, but why are you here, how did you even find me?"

"Ex-wife, first person I talked to. She knew all about where you were. Hey, can we go sit down and have a beer? It's a long flight from home and a long drive from the airport in San Jose and I'm beat." Peter led Terry from the yard into the main house, a simple two story stucco building between the coffee shed and the beach. He directed Terry to a worn couch on the tile floor and went to the adjoining kitchen to grab two bottles of Imperial beer from the refrigerator.

"Nice, man, thanks," said Terry "Look, I came just to see you in this god forsaken place because I really, really need your

12

help, man. I've been having a tough time these past couple years."

"I heard you were teaching at some little college in Illinois."

"No, no, that was a few years back. I last worked at a place in Missouri but I hadn't published anything in years and couldn't get tenure and I had some issues, you know..."

"Drugs, female students?"

"Both, things got screwed up."

"Sounds like you haven't changed that much."

"Look, I haven't worked in almost two years, ok. I've screwed things up, I know. I don't need a lecture."

"Well it's been delightful seeing you again, I hope you enjoy your stay in Costa Rica, it's a lovely country."

"Van, I need your help to get back on my feet, to reestablish my reputation. I spent virtually my last dime to come out here in person to beg you, man."

"So, after forty years you come out of the woodwork to ask me for money?"

"No! I need you to help me write another paper like the one on the dual Mayan gods."

"What? That discovery was a fluke, that paper was a fluke. Do you have some unique artifact that warrants a paper? If you do I'll help you just to get rid of you."

"No, there is no discovery, not yet. But there will be. Something so big it will blow up. I just need to get in on it and I'm almost there. It's the *ciudad blanca*."

"The infamous "white city" in the Mosquitia region of Honduras? Didn't a National Geographic expedition just come from there? Isn't the lost city found?"

"Maybe, we know they found a city there and others have found cities there too. There may be more than one, most likely a lost civilization. The Nat Geo guys didn't do much excavation and they didn't release the location so they can go back and do some real archeology work. We know it's there. We want to get there first. You know Chad Toeb?"

"No, never heard of him. I don't follow a lot of U.S. news here."

"He founded a software company. He's worth hundreds of millions. This is the guy, Van, who wants to launch a new expedition to Mosquitia and they hired me to be part of it!"

"Great, problem solved, you go make discoveries and write a paper on stuff no one has ever heard about before. Your sins are forgiven and you are once again a noted Mesoamerican scholar and you live happily ever after."

"No. Don't you remember who actually wrote the Mayan paper?"

"Okay, I may have made some major contributions back then but I've been a lawyer for thirty-five years while you've been teaching this stuff all this time. Maybe I could help you back then when I was a philosophy student but not anymore, not forty years later. Besides what makes you think you could get me to go to a hell hole like Honduras anyway? I won't even go there on coffee buying trips and they actually have some pretty good coffee there. Terry, we were never real friends and I wrote that Maya paper because I was fascinated by what we found, not as a favor to you. I haven't seen or heard from you for forty years and I am not inclined to just drop everything and run off to Honduras with you and possibly risk my life, out of friendship or any other reason."

"What if I told you by coming with me to Honduras you could see Zelda Aronson again?"

Peter sat silently for a moment, then got up and asked, "Do you want another beer?"

They walked outside with their fresh beers to watch the sunset from the deserted grey sand beach in front of Peter's house. "Not a bad life here, man," said Terry as they walked "you must be doin' alright?"

"I have a good pension and I salvaged what was left of my savings after the divorce, and I make some money off the coffee business, brokering deals between local farmers and co-ops and buyers in the States. I'm okay. What I like most is the quiet and slow pace of living here, and frankly I like being away from the States and the insane politics, greed and dishonesty that just seems to be in the fabric of everyday life there. Where are you staying anyway?"

"With you of course."

"I was afraid of that. Let's get some dinner."

They went to a little Caribbean restaurant on a back road in Esterillos Oeste. They sat silently for a while over plates of fish, beans, rice, fried plantains and two more Imperials. "I guess I better get used to this kind of food," said Terry.

"How soon are you supposed to be in Honduras for the expedition?" asked Peter.

"Three days."

"And is Zelda really going to be there?"

"Yeah, in Tegucigalpa where the expedition is staging."

"Why would Zelda Aronson be there, she's not an archaeologist?"

"Her name is Zelda Toeb now. She's married to Chad Toeb, the guy who is paying for everything?"

"Isn't she a little old to be married to some Silicon Valley wunderkind?"

"Toeb is not so young, he's in his fifties, but yeah she's a little older than he is, but man, she looks good."

"You've seen her recently?"

"Yeah, when Toeb interviewed me along with Doctor DeGroet and Doctor Mellon, she was in the room. So do you want to see her?"

"If your career has hit such a low point, why would they hire you for something like this and more to the point, why would they let someone like me go along?"

"DeGroet loved the Mayan paper, he remembered it, he said it was some of the most original work he had ever seen on the Mayan gods, they wanted someone who thinks outside the box because all this *ciudad blanca* stuff is new and unknown and they thought they could get me for a bargain, hell, they were right, I came cheap. I convinced them you were key to the Mayan paper and they agreed to pay your expenses."

"Is Zelda going on the expedition?"

"Nope, she and Toeb will be there for the orientation in Tegucigalpa, but it's too rugged back there in the Mosquitia and they think the city is pretty far in."

"Well, if it's too rugged for Zelda, it ought to be too rugged for me, I'm older than both her and Toeb and I'm not in any kind of shape to be strolling through the jungle in overwhelming heat and humidity. Zelda was always tougher than me, if it's too rugged for her, it's way too rugged for me."

But, in fact, Peter really did want to see Zelda. He wanted to see her quite badly. He wondered if there was a way to finesse the situation, allowing him a chance to see the woman he had always loved, without going on this damned, absurd expedition.

They finally went to bed. Terry slept in the spare room and Peter lay down and listened to the rain batter his roof. He pulled the covers around him and slept.

He found himself lying in a clearing beneath towering trees. It was dark with just a hint of a moon beyond the canopy above him. He could not move and he spied a creature moving stealthily toward him from the edge of the clearing. The air was heavy and redolent of a sweet odor of decaying flowers. As the creature moved closer he saw it was a jaguar. Peter had only seen a jaguar in captivity at La Paz gardens above San Jose. He had never encountered one in the wild. This one had yellow eyes that gleamed in the moonlight. As it came closer, it came out of its crouch and became bolder trotting right to him. "Don't be afraid of the forest, Peter," the jaguar said to him in the voice of a 19 year old Zelda Aronson, "there are answers there."

"I no longer have questions," he found himself saying. The Jaguar seemed to laugh, baring bright, white, needle sharp teeth.

"You have always been about nothing but questions. Come with me into the jungle and I promise you wonders like nothing you have ever dreamed of if you can accept them. " The jaguar hopped onto Peter's chest with the light adroit motion so characteristic of cats. Despite its agility, he could feel its weight pressing down on him. Its face was right above him now and it stared at him with cold almost reptilian golden eyes. He could smell its hot, sour breath. It flicked its tongue at Peter's neck. "Your sweat tastes good, Peter, your blood would taste better but I'll wait until you find all your answers. "

Peter woke up drenched in sweat. It was still dark outside but the rain had slowed to a light tapping sound on his roof.

In the morning he made coffee while waiting for Terry to wake up. He was exhausted and shaken by the dream that had been intensely vivid. But he decided what he needed to do. He knew seeing Zelda would be painful and there was no hope of any redemption of the lost love of his college years. But something compelled him to see her again, perhaps a hope that somehow he might finally understand how he lost her and what else he had lost along with her.

He would agree to go to Honduras for the expedition so he could see Zelda. He did not see how he could gain access to her any other way. If he went there on his own and could find her she would surely refuse to see him. But after he saw her he would go home. He was not going to the Mosquitia to hike through humid jungles just to keep Terry's academic career alive, he doubted he could survive an expedition like that. If his heart were to give he would rather it happen while he was whoring in Jaco or San Jose.

Five
LOS ANGELES,
FORTY YEARS EARLIER

When Peter first saw Zelda, what drew his attention to her was her eyes. They were huge and vividly lavender. She was pale skinned, long legged and slender but had well developed breasts, rounded hips and a shapely posterior. She was the sort of girl a boy noticed and longed for without knowing anything about her.

Peter's father never paid much attention to him. Leonard VanOwen was an investment banker whose work weeks were usually seventy hours or more. Under other circumstances Peter would have been a mother's boy but she lacked any interest in him. From a very early age he keenly felt the lack of female attention and approval. His high school girlfriend was a plump, wholesome virgin who refused Peter sexual favors beyond the occasional kiss. In three years of college Peter never had a date or found any girl with interest in him. He naturally assumed that a girl as lovely as Zelda Aronson would have no interest in him.

In that first Wittgenstein class something unusual happened. The leggy, shapely coed challenged the instructor's position on Wittgenstein's sense of Jewish identity. She argued articulately and knowledgeably. Peter realized this was one pretty girl with whom he had something to talk about. Having read Wittgenstein's two major published works and his biographical details, Peter chimed in on the discussion. After class he and the girl continued the discussion.

For a time they went everywhere together. They went to museums, saw movies Peter picked and went on hikes and bike rides Zelda picked. They had two sexual encounters, the first of which was a loss of virginity for Peter, but not for Zelda. Both being inexperienced, their attempted couplings were clumsy and unsatisfying. After a while, Zelda expressed her unhappiness with Peter's daily marijuana use. She found fault with his lack of a plan for his life ahead and did not care for his few friends, including his dissolute roommate. Any man experienced in relationships would have seen the problems developing but Peter did not. He was dazzled by Zelda and tried hard to please her but it seemed like the harder he tried the less he succeeded.

That summer after they met, Peter tried to keep in touch and at first so did Zelda. But by late summer she did not respond to his frequent letters, was seldom available when he tried to call and had little to say to him when she was. When school started he sought her out and they went to two campus events together. After the second one he fumblingly tried to initiate sex. Her response, which he realized later she had only been waiting for the opportune moment to communicate, was that she just wanted to be friends, was not ready for a romantic relationship and felt they should see each other less often. For Peter, this was the confirmation of what he had felt all along, that he did not deserve her. She was too beautiful and smart and wonderful for someone like him. The hurt went more deeply than a simple rejection by the only girl with whom he had a real relationship. It went to his own feelings about himself, his unworthiness and unlovability. It confirmed in him every self-doubt and deep seated feeling of unworthiness and self-loathing.

His behavior after this initial rejection had been, he later realized, reprehensible. Convinced there was someone else, he showed up at her apartment at odd hours. He once spent the better part of a night in his car on the street where she lived, waiting to see who brought her home. When he realized there was no one else, his humiliation deepened. It was not another who she wanted more than him, it was only him that she did not want. He asked her out several times a week and increasingly she refused his invitations. Finally, after over a month of this, she told him that she was pained and disturbed by his behavior, they obviously could not be friends and they should not see each other anymore. As difficult as it was for Peter to accept this, there seemed a logic to it. Without sex, without romance, there could be no relationship at all. Zelda was an object of desire, she could not be anything else to him. He could not relate to her without wanting her, could not suppress his sexual feelings, could not deal with the stress of feeling rejected and unwanted which was only accentuated when he was with her.

He never saw her after that. The campus was large and they did not share a circle of friends, so it was not surprising they did not run into each other. After she banned him from her life Peter found himself crying every few days for the first weeks. He lost what he had always wanted, what he most desired, the love and approval of a beautiful woman.

As the months passed, Zelda, or at least his idealization of Zelda, became melded into his psyche becoming a part of his personal mythology. It survived other girlfriends and his marriage to live in his mind simultaneously as a kind of paradise lost and a confirmation of his own inadequacy as a human being.

Six
SAN JOSE, COSTA RICA

Terry seemed shocked when Peter readily agreed the next morning to go to Honduras. Terry's flight left the next day and he had a ticket for Peter, paid for by the expedition, which he frankly had not expected to use. They had reservations at the Sheraton in Escazu for that night and Peter arranged a car to take them up the mountain to the airport in San Jose.

"Pack light, underwear, socks, the expedition is providing khakis and water proof boots to wear in the jungle. They'll provide bush hats too," said Terry. Peter just smiled to himself, thinking that he would not need waterproof boots or a bush hat for the return flight to San Jose he had already booked.

The drive to the central valley took over two hours. They stopped at the bridge over the *Rio Tarcoles* to watch the crocodiles gathered under the bridge. There were over a dozen greenish beige reptiles. A large one basked on the mudflat at the river's edge, opening a huge mouth to reveal large jagged teeth. From there they turned east climbing through lush green mountains, past fruit stands selling mangoes and dragon fruit and roadside *sodas* in cinderblock shacks with signs advertising Cerveza Imperial.

Costa Rica has fewer than five million people but almost three-quarters of them live in the central valley in the mountain range forming the spine of the country. Entering the central valley from the sparsely populated Pacific coast was like entering an alternative world. Although San Jose and the surrounding suburbs boasted a superb climate, beautiful setting and amenities like shopping malls and good restaurants that were totally lacking in Playa Esterillos and environs, Peter disliked it intensely. He came here once or twice a month to meet with coffee buyers but avoided the affluent suburb of Escazu, home to many American expatriates. It was modern, with well-paved roads, gated condominium complexes and homes, American chain restaurants, sleek hotels and a shopping mall that would not be out of place in suburban California.

Instead of the sleek, white rectangle that was the Escazu Sheraton, Peter always stayed at the more modest *Presidente* in central San Jose, a few blocks from San Jose's seedy night life.

Like many Central American capital cities, San Jose was unimpressive architecturally and had no particular historical interest. The districts outlying the central city contained the usual poverty, narrow streets choked with traffic, stained concrete and cinder block buildings, sidewalks teeming with raggedly clad pedestrians, all enveloped with a curiously acrid smell Peter could never quite explain.

When they got to the Sheraton, Peter realized the expedition had only booked one room, either because they doubted Terry would be bringing anyone back or they didn't feel his presence justified the expense of a second room, and that he would have to share with Terry. He let Terry know he wanted his own room in Tegucigalpa.

That night after they had dinner in the hotel, Peter announced he would be going into San Jose and Terry, not entirely sure what Peter had in mind, insisted on going too.

They began their evening at the Del Rey Hotel, grabbing Imperials in the lobby bar amidst a crowd of mostly middle-aged gringos and floridly dressed young women. As soon as they sat down, a woman in a tight, purple rayon dress and another in a ruffled, red, bare shoulder blouse and black mini-skirt came to their table.

"*Hola,*" said each of them as they sat down at their table.

"So this is why you were so eager to get out tonight?" said Terry.

"At my age, after everything I've been through, I just don't want to get involved in a relationship. I can't handle demands, I like living alone and frankly I have nothing to give. The only thing these girls want is money and they are cheap enough for me to afford. So when I come to San Jose, I hit the spots and look for someone I can pretend is special for a half hour or so. It's really the only sexual outlet I can handle these days."

"Jesus, you're pathetic, man."

"Well, what about you, were you ever married? What do you do for female companionship?"

"The beauty of being a professor is the pedagogical privilege of fucking your students. Well into my fifties I was scoring tender little coeds trying to tap into my store of wisdom by tapping my cock. In many ways maybe not so different than you in terms of avoiding involvement but they were acting out of their own free will, not economic necessity, and they didn't cost a dime. Plus the girls were mostly better than what I see here."

"Didn't one of them cost you a job?"

"More than one. An occupational hazard for an academic, at least this academic."

"And you call me pathetic." By this time the girls had moved on and several others had tried to move in, but there were plenty of gringos in the hotel and most of the girls wanted to do a volume business. Peter spotted a girl at the other end of the room he hadn't seen before, signaled her over and bought her a drink. She looked very young, certainly no older than twenty. She had long blonde hair with dark roots, green eyes, light copper skin and heavy eye make-up. She had small breasts but wide, round hips, a configuration Peter liked. He took her upstairs.

The room had a musty smell and the paint and bed linens

were faded. They could hear the busy street outside through the single pane window. "My name is Peter," he told her.

"Elisa," she said quietly.

"Can you take all your clothes off? I'll pay you extra."

"If you wish." But when she did Peter saw the cesarean scar on her abdomen, which immediately evaporated his desire. The girl saw Peter lose his erection and looked at him with confusion and concern. Peter had taken a one hundred milligram Fildena tablet and knew he could get hard again. He grabbed the girl and turned her around rubbing his cock between her buttocks. The girl whimpered, thinking, perhaps, that Peter was going to take her anally. However, once he was hard again Peter entered her vagina and began pumping from behind. The girl relaxed and went limp, supporting herself against the wall next to the bed, waiting for it to be over, but the Fildena was making it hard for him to orgasm. He reached around and grabbed her breasts and pumped harder but his cock remained hard and insensitive, nothing about this situation was going to get him to cum. Finally, sweaty and out of breath, he handed the girl a wad of *colones* and left her. The girl glared at him as he left.

He went back down and found Terry alone at their table, an empty beer bottle in front of him. "Don't care to indulge?" asked Peter.

"I'm short on cash and this really isn't my kind of thing. These girls make me feel sorry for them, not horny."

"I know. That last girl was a sad little teenager with a baby at home, not exactly the fulfillment of the fantasies I had about her. I'm a shit but even though I'm an old man I need some kind of sexual activity, I can't help it."

"If you're so desperate why not get married or shack up? There have to be plenty of little Tica girls, even some real young ones, who'd like to live by the beach with an old gringo who'd take care of them."

"I discovered a long time ago I'm no good at relationships. I like being alone and women don't really like me. It's okay. I've adapted. Let's get out of here. I know a place where you might be able to find something you can afford."

Seven

THE MOLINO ROJO
SAN JOSE, COSTA RICA

It was an old club that had been the hot spot in the 90's but these days was more subdued. An old red painted concrete building on a corner in the *zona rosa,* it contained a stage and plywood bar in a large, dingy, dimly lit cement-floored room smelling of cigarettes, sweat and stale beer. As Peter and Terry paid the cover and entered, two girls were grinding away on the stage to a fuzzy version of Neil Young's "Rock and Roll will Never Die". Peter ordered two shots of *Flor de Cana,* smooth Nicaraguan rum.

The clientele was mostly middle-aged gringos with, unlike the Del Rey, a sprinkling of locals. These were mainly young, well-groomed Ticos in open shirts and tight slacks. Peter's gaze was drawn immediately to a girl by the bar. She had pale skin and, unusual for a Tica whore, her black hair was in a short pageboy haircut. She wore a pale blue off the shoulder blouse with spaghetti straps and leopard print capris with dark blue pumps. She had a slim but curvy body and looked like a young Elizabeth Taylor. She could not have been more than twenty-five.

Peter walked over to the bar and invited her to join them for a drink. When she sat down he saw that she had large pale blue eyes. Around her neck was a silver chain with an exquisite carving of a capuchin monkey face in some sort of pale blue stone. "Your necklace is beautiful," said Peter. When she looked at him her huge eyes looked hostile.

"Thank you, my uncle gave it to me after one of his trips, it is very special, I know." Her English was excellent, barely accented.

"I am Peter and this is Terry."

"My name is Ophelia." Peter got her a rum and she drank it quickly.

"I haven't ever seen you before," said Peter. "I come to the clubs a couple of times a month. Are you usually here, do you go to the Del Rey or Sportsmans?"

"All those places and many others besides. You must have simply missed me. Can I do something for you, Peter?" She looked right at him with a hostile, challenging look in her pale blue eyes. Something about her reminded him of Zelda, which was, of course, crazy.

"*Quanto*?" he asked.

"Depends on what you want. We can start at sixty thousand *colones* for the basics. Everything else is extra." She was matter of fact in her tone, nothing flirtatious or seductive about her. Her price was outrageous for the Molino Rojo but she was special and she knew it. She looked right at him, waiting for his answer.

"Let's go in the back. Terry, I'll see you in a while unless you find someone you like."

"Don't worry," she said mockingly to Terry, "we won't be long."

The rooms at the back of the Molino Rojo were small and stark, lit by a single bare lightbulb in the ceiling with only a mattress and a metal chair on a concrete floor. "I want you naked," said Peter.

"Fifteen thousand *colones*."

"And I want you to kiss me."

"Thirty-five thousand *colones*," she said, her face a blank mask as she began to disrobe.

"What?"

"You want to kiss? You want to be my *novio*? Then you pay!" She looked at him with that same hostile, challenging cast to her deep blue eyes. She was naked now and Peter was shaken by her beauty. Her skin was so pale you could see blue blood vessels in places. She had no stretch marks or cesarean scars. Her breasts were small but firm and pert and her hips and buttocks were curved and round. She had not taken her monkey necklace off.

"Look, I like you, I don't want you to feel like I'm your enemy. I want things to be okay between us," said Peter as he undressed. Ophelia laughed and walked towards him. She pushed him down on the bed and crawled on top of him. She kissed him hard and he felt as if he were falling hopelessly, inevitably, down a dark and bottomless abyss. He had drunk several *Flor de Canas* and before that a couple of beers, he was not entirely sober but the kiss seemed to drive him outside his body, inflicting simultaneously intense pleasure and exquisite pain.

"Now you are my *novio*, do you like it?" She began laughing as she guided his cock inside her. She was amazingly tight. He grabbed her buttocks as she began manically rocking on top of him. Her pale face with the beautiful eyes looked down on him with a faint smile. "You are on a journey," she whispered "you will find what you look for but you will wish you had not." She bent further down and bit his neck hard drawing blood.

Peter came inside her in an overwhelming rush of uncontrollable pleasure mixed with the pain of her sharp bite. He realized she had not insisted on him wearing a condom, nor, despite his many years of whoring in Costa Rica, had he thought to wear one. She looked at him with a crooked smile as she rolled off him. "What did you mean by what you just said?" he asked.

"Aaah, just words of passion. I know nothing about you."

"Your beautiful necklace, where did it come from?"

"From Honduras. It's the monkey god. They used to

worship monkeys there, maybe a long time ago. Maybe they still do. Who knows?"

"I'm on my way to Honduras, with my friend. It's almost as if you knew that."

"Like I said, I know nothing about you, and care even less," she said, licking his blood from her lips. "Ten thousand *colones* for the bite." Peter handed her a roll of bills.

"What did you mean I'll find what I'm looking for but wish I hadn't? What am I looking for?"

"Who knows? Like I said, words of passion, they meant nothing. Maybe you will find god in Honduras?" Peter laughed.

"I doubt I'll find god in Honduras or anywhere else."

"Well, maybe you find the monkey god, maybe the monkey god finds you? I think that's what you want."

"I'm not interested in the monkey god or any other kind of god. I stopped believing in that sort of thing a long time ago. What I do want is to see you again. I want to see you often."

"I am here, or at the Del Rey or the usual places, you know about them, you will find me."

"How about a phone number, so we can make arrangements, maybe go to a nice hotel? I'll pay you what you want."

"No, you will know where to find me or maybe not. I would go with you again but only in the way that I want and yes, you will pay what I want." As if compelled, Peter got down on his knees and began probing her vagina with his tongue, searching out her clitoris. She laughed and leaned back as his tongue worked. It took a while but she appeared to cum, expelling a long, low moan and shuddering slightly. "If you come back from your trip I will teach you ways to please me."

"If I come back from my trip?"

"Who knows? Honduras, they say, is a dangerous place. Lots of murders there. Even the monkeys are evil." She laughed, gathered her money, finished dressing, and left.

Peter went back to his table. Terry wasn't there so he

ordered another rum and waited. There was no sign of Ophelia. Peter guessed she must have left the club as soon as they had finished, perhaps by a back entrance. It wasn't long before Terry ambled in from the back rooms.

"I get, it," said Terry "quick, easy and cheap. Maybe not as succulent as a sweet little coed but at least I can't get fired for it." They drank up and left. For the next few hours they wandered from club to club in the *zona rosa*. They continued to drink *Flor de Cana* as they explored. Peter did not see Ophelia anywhere and neither man saw another girl they cared to go with. It was past two AM before they stumbled back to their room at the Sheraton and collapsed on their beds.

The jungle was insufferably hot and the air was moist and heavy. The vegetation screened out the sky except for a shaft of moonlight thrusting through the canopy off in the distance. Peter was running as fast as he could, sweating, panting and out of breath. In front of him the Jaguar easily loped through the jungle growth. As Peter followed he tripped over roots and branches hit his face. If he fell or stopped the Jaguar would stop, sit, look back and wait until he could start running again. He was exhausted and dripping with sweat, he could feel blood running down his cheek where branches had hit his face. Suddenly the Jaguar stopped ahead of him. He found himself in a clearing illuminated by moonlight. At the far end of the clearing was a limestone altar on which were carved glyphs he had never seen before and did not understand. On the altar sat a blue stone almost a foot and a half in height and about six inches across. The stone glowed faintly in the moonlight. On the pale blue stone was carved the face of a capuchin monkey, angry and fierce looking. He was sure he had seen that carving somewhere else.

Somehow they made their eleven-thirty flight the next morning. They both were badly hung over and Peter's dream had exhausted him. Their plane made the ascent from San Jose, leaving behind the lush, green, central valley of Costa Rica's capital and headed north towards Honduras.

Eight
TEGUCIGALPA, HONDURAS

As she walked through the ornate lobby of the Tegucigalpa Marriott, Zelda felt the gaze of security guards, bellboys and male guests run up and down her body. Not one of them would have guessed she was 57 years old. Thirty years ago the attention would have annoyed her. Now, she found it reassuring. Once, she had resented the implication that her identity was defined by her beauty. Now, she was grateful for the doors it had opened for her. She knew that, ultimately, her successes in life had to do with her ability, not her looks, but her attractiveness had often given her the chance to demonstrate that ability. She was content to accept her beauty was a source of power and she was glad age had not eroded it too badly.

Four years ago she had served as head of a major NGO in Africa, in the course of which she had carried on a two year affair with one of the most powerful leaders of one of the least democratic countries in Africa. That was before she had quit her job in frustration, despite her best efforts, failing to have much impact on the lives of poor Africans. Her first husband had been a highly esteemed academic who was now the president of an Ivy League school. The second was a minor English rock star, then at the zenith of his popularity. Their divorce had been the foundation for Zelda's financial independence, since he had overlooked the need for a prenuptial agreement. When she returned to the U.S. from Africa she met Chad Toeb at a benefit dinner in New York. He was intelligent, confident, dynamic and powerful, all qualities she prized in a man. After a few months of frenetic courtship he became her third husband. Now, three years later, he seemed to have lost interest in the marriage. Zelda had come to understand that he was a man who moved obsessively from one interest to the next and she was no longer that one interest.

She too had become restless and wanted a purpose, which is why she came to Honduras. Thousands of Hondurans and other Central Americans were trying to get into the U.S. to escape the violence and poverty of their homelands. There was a place here for someone to help. She was ready to try again to bring change to a poverty stricken population. Maybe the lessons she learned in Africa might help her here. Maybe she could motivate Chad and some of his Silicon Valley friends to fork over some of their millions to an NGO that would serve Central America.

Zelda hopped the elevator to the third floor where the conference rooms were located. Chad had asked her to sit in on the first staging meeting for his expedition; his current obsession. She dreaded seeing Terry Selby again. She could not imagine why Doctor DeGroet had insisted on including him in the expedition. She was frankly amazed Terry had even been able to get a PhD, much less that he had some sort of reputation which would impress a man like DeGroet.

The conference room contained a large rectangular table around which were assembled an odd assortment of people. Chad was there, his oversized baldhead bobbing slightly as it tended to do when he was fully energized. Next to him sat Doctor Phillip DeGroet, chair of Mesoamerican studies at Brown University. Next to him was a trim, slender Honduran, Arturo Arias-Garcia, who was in charge of the logistics for the expedition. There was also Doctor Hanna Mellon, a respected field archeologist from University College, London. Other than Terry Selby, who sat at the corner of the table next to a stocky, gray haired man, she didn't know the rest of the group.

"Thank you all for coming," said DeGroet in his clipped Dutch accent. "First, let's go around the table and introduce ourselves."

After Arias-Garcia, a dark, slender, shorthaired man with a pencil mustache in a Honduran army uniform said he was "Captain Aramis Cruz-Madrid. I have been assigned by the Honduran high command to provide security for the expedition. I'll be providing a detachment of armed Special Forces troops to accompany you. As you may know, La Mosquitia can be very dangerous. It is a stopover point for drug runners bringing in product from Columbia on its way to the U.S. Also, the local tribes, like the Pech and the Moskito, are not always friendly to outsiders, and there is a constant struggle between poor settlers and larger landowners which is often violent." He turned to the ginger haired man sitting next to him and nodded.

"I'm Doctor Terry Selby, formerly of Indiana University and most recently of Merritt College in Missouri. I've had experience excavating Maya ruins in the Yucatan at Oxkintok."

"And, I might say," interjected DeGroet, "Doctor Selby's paper on some of the finds at Oxkintok is extremely insightful and I hope he can bring some of that same insight into whatever we find at *ciudad blanca*."

The stocky, gray haired man next to Selby now spoke. "My name is Peter VanOwen. I'm not an archeologist at all, in fact I am, or was, a lawyer, and I'm not really sure what I can contribute, but Doctor Selby insisted that I come."

Zelda suddenly understood. If Terry's paper had impressed DeGroet then it must really have been good, and if it was good it couldn't have been Terry's. Peter VanOwen's presence explained that. Peter, whatever else one might say about him, was truly brilliant and original. He had gone on that expedition with Terry and, she was now sure, had written the paper that made Terry's reputation. If Terry had insisted Peter come on this expedition he must be desperate. Hoping, somehow, Peter could duplicate what he had done years ago. Her question was why would Peter VanOwen agree to come on an expedition to a god forsaken hell- hole like Mosquitia? Did he care that much about Selby's reputation and career? Did he care that much about finding the white city?

She had not thought about Peter in years and completely lost track of him. He was a good friend until their friendship had turned romantic and she ultimately ended it because he had become possessive and needy. In the end, as she had gotten to know him, she determined he really wasn't the sort of man she found attractive. When they broke up he had been angry and there was no way any sort of friendship could survive. He was, or at least had been, a brilliant, thoughtful man with little drive or self-confidence. It was hard for her to imagine him as a lawyer. He looked terrible. He had a shaggy, unkempt head of gray hair. His face was wrinkled and jowly with deep, dark colored bags under his green eyes. He was at least 25 pounds overweight and carried a substantial paunch. She knew he could be no older than sixty but he looked ten years older than that.

"Peter is too modest, he was quite instrumental in helping with the Oxkintok paper and has some great insights on early Central American civilization. He also lives full time in Costa Rica and is fluent in Spanish. I'm sure he is going to be a huge help," said Terry.

Zelda found herself smirking. Terry was desperate and she recalled that she had heard he was unemployed, had not published anything in years and been fired from his last job at an unassuming small liberal arts college for an affair with a student to whom he also supplied drugs. It was going to take more than some third rate academic publication, ghost written by a worn out old lawyer, to get Terry a job back in academia.

After the introductions, Doctor DeGroet pulled out a map mounted on a whiteboard on casters. "You may not be aware that Mr. Toeb has managed to surreptitiously obtain for us, at some expense, the LIDAR data that was compiled for the recent

National Geographic expedition. The LIDAR data was gathered by deploying lasers from an aircraft that flew over the area where the city was suspected to be. The lasers can identify manmade structures, which have been completely obscured by jungle. In fact, the LIDAR data identifies a number of sites, including the one the National Geographic expedition visited. While that does seem to be a significant site, we believe there were a number of cities in the region leading us to believe there was a robust and sophisticated civilization. The primary regional center was not the site visited by the Geographic crew but one which we believe is further into the mountains in a large inaccessible valley. That is where we are going, or where we are trying to go.

"We have a charter flight to take all of us who are going from Tegucigalpa to La Ceiba, which leaves tomorrow morning. From La Ceiba we will travel by boat along the coast to the mouth of the *Rio Platano*. We will travel up the *Rio Platano* in motor driven zodiac rafts as far as we can. Once we have navigated the *Platano* to the furthest extent we will establish a base camp. It is our hope that we can connect the base camp to La Ceiba by helicopter. Mr. Toeb has chartered two. They will ferry in supplies and equipment to the base camp and provide emergency medical transport if needed. From the base camp, a group will head into the mountains by foot using Indian guides from the local Pech village to locate the valley where we believe the primary site is located. Unfortunately we don't believe the helicopters can safely fly in these mountains due to dangerous downdrafts and frequent bad weather.

"Captain Cruz-Madrid will command a detachment of Honduran special forces that will provide security. As he indicated, La Moskitia is very dangerous and we all need to be careful from the minute we set foot in La Ceiba. This will be a very uncomfortable and difficult expedition. La Moskitia is remote, excessively humid and hot and plagued by substantial rainfall. The jungle we will traverse is thick and populated by poisonous snakes, insects, hostile local tribes and drug runners.

Mr. Toeb has spared no expense to give us the best of everything but this lost city is lost because it is deep in a largely unexplored wilderness.

"Unless there are questions I'll let you all go so you can receive your medical check in room 718. We will see you in the hotel lobby tomorrow morning. We'll have a shuttle leaving at 11:00 to take you to the airport for the charter to La Ceiba."

Zelda found it all a little boring. The money Chad was spending on this expedition could easily fund a substantial health clinic here in Tegucigalpa where it was desperately needed. She sighed, waved to Chad across the table and went back to her room. She did not notice Peter lurking in the hallway after her.

Nine
ROOM 571
TEGUCIGALPA MARRIOTT

Peter was stunned when Zelda walked into the meeting room at the Marriott. He felt his gut tighten and his bowels become watery at the sight of her, and all the old anxieties and feelings of inadequacy rose. He expected an older, worn version of the girl he knew in school. Instead he saw a striking, mature but youthful looking woman whose long dark hair had no trace of gray, whose face was smooth and firm without wrinkles and whose long legged curvy figure was trim and youthful. It occurred to Peter that she probably had extensive cosmetic surgery as her face had that immobile, plastic look that often results from extensive work. When he heard that the expedition charter would be leaving tomorrow he knew he had just a few hours to find Zelda and talk to her. His flight back to Costa Rica would be leaving later the same morning as the expedition's charter flight. Once he had met with Zelda he would sneak away, maybe check into another hotel, and shuttle from there to the airport after the charter had left for La Ceiba. Only Terry would miss him, but there would be no way to find him and they would not hold the charter for him. Terry would be on his own.

After the briefing, Zelda left the room quickly, not even bothering to say hello to her husband. Peter went down to the lobby and, in exchange for two hundred and fifty *lempiras*, the desk clerk told him that a Zelda Aronson, not, Peter noted, Toeb, was checked into room 571. *Senor* Toeb was in another room.

Peter went for his medical check to avoid arousing suspicion about his impending desertion of the expedition. The Honduran doctor in room 718 took his blood pressure, pulse and a blood sample. He looked quizzically at Peter. "Do you think you are prepared for this journey?"

"I'll be okay," said Peter, knowing it was a journey he would never take.

"Your health is okay for a man of your age so I am going to approve your participation. But I think you are not in the best condition for this expedition. The heat and humidity can be very taxing and you may have to walk through dense forest for many kilometers. The physical exertion may be more than you are up to. It may not kill you but you will find yourself quite miserable. You need to be sure to drink lots of water and to take salt pills. If you can, you should try not to over extend yourself. " Peter nodded and thanked the doctor for a warning he did not need.

Peter went down to the hotel bar; a pretentious "sports bar" with lamps on each table in the form of NFL helmets. He sat at the bar and ordered *Flor de Cana*. A soccer game played on the big screen TV at the back of the bar but the handful of customers were focused on their drinks. After two shots of rum he was ready to go upstairs.

As he knocked on the door of room 571 he felt severe anxiety. He wondered what the point of this confrontation was supposed to be. He wondered why he just did not say no to Terry and allow Zelda Aronson to continue living deep in the well of his consciousness.

The woman who answered the door was stunningly attractive, even in sweats. She frowned when she saw him. "What do you want, Peter?" Her voice sounded tired and resigned.

"You know, I'm not really sure. I guess I just wanted to see you again after all these years. I've missed you and I guess,

I just never understood exactly what happened between us and I've regretted it."

"You smell like you've been drinking," she said, still standing in the doorway.

"Well, I'm nervous. You always kind of intimidated me and after everything and all these years I needed a couple of drinks to calm down enough to see you."

"No need to bother, we don't have anything to talk about. I'm not interested in the past or, to be honest, in you." Zelda felt her irritation rise.

"Why did you dump me the way you did?"

"I'm not sure I really remember, but if I had to guess, you were needy and insecure. You were possessive in a way that was uncomfortable for me and let's face it, you really weren't the kind of man I found attractive. The Peter I remember was smart, very smart. It's what drew me to you in the first place. But you were a dreamer. If you weren't reading, you were stoned, you had no energy, no drive, no confidence, no direction and, ultimately, no point. What did you end up doing with your life? Weren't you going to law school?"

"Yeah, I had a career with the LA County Counsel's office."

"So, decades spent as some anonymous civil servant, pushing paper in a pointless job, accomplishing nothing, not even making a good living for yourself. Actually, it's better than I thought you would do, frankly, I thought you would end up as a stoner doing some menial job to get by and staying stoned every minute you could. Are you happy? Is that what you came to hear? Why I lost interest? Why I broke up with you? Why I never kept in touch?"

"Well, I..."

"The men I am attracted to, the men I married, are ambitious and energetic, good at getting what they want. I never had the sense that you even knew what you wanted much less the drive to get it. And what business do you have traipsing off on this idiotic expedition? An old man like you is likely to have a heart attack before they've walked a mile in this god forsaken Honduran jungle. You are a bigger idiot than I ever imagined. Look, I have no desire to continue this conversation. Please go away and don't bother me again." She turned her back and closed the door to room 571.

Peter, devastated, made his way back down to the bar. This time a Euro league basketball game was on the big screen and there were only two other patrons. He sat at the bar and ordered another rum. He felt like crying but somehow tears would not flow. He had never realized the contempt Zelda had for him. The confrontation brought back memories of the last years of his marriage, a wife that was dissatisfied with their financial situation, found him withdrawn and unresponsive, disinterested in his two daughters, no longer sexually attractive and generally unsatisfying as a husband. Of course, she was right about all of it. Peter had been an appellate attorney in the County Counsel's office and a very good one. The County Counsel's office paid poorly. He had offers to work for several private law firms for a lot more money but turned them down. At one point, when the County Counsel herself had retired, he had inquiries from several County Supervisors about his interest in the job. But he was happy writing his briefs, reviewing trial transcripts and researching issues without the stress of the politics or policy decisions, supervising staff or keeping demanding clients happy. So he never made the money or achieved the status his wife thought he should and she interpreted that as selfishness on his part and a lack of concern for the welfare of his family. He never really had much interest in being a father and his daughters, both now grown, had turned away from him. When his wife announced she was divorcing him, his ego was bruised but he was not surprised and calmly acquiesced to the new reality.

"Ah, *Senor*, you are from the expedition?" asked a slender man in a crisply starched khaki uniform with captain's bars who had slid into the seat next to him. It was Captain Cruz-Madrid, the Honduran army Special Forces officer who would be in charge of security.

"Oh, yes, my name is Peter VanOwen. Captain Cruz-Madrid, right?" He was in his early thirties, a man with light copper skin, a long narrow skull with high cheekbones, a thin pencil mustache and small, intensely dark eyes.

"Yes, I forget what your function in the expedition is?"

"I have none. To be frank, Doctor Selby asked me to come along to help him because I helped him years ago with a paper. But I can't really imagine I could help him now. I'm afraid he's misplaced his confidence."

"Yes, Doctor DeGroet mentioned that paper today, it must have been quite good to attract the attention of a man like that. What was it about?"

"I barely remember it, but I think it dealt with a different approach to Mayan religion based on some artifacts we had found. We surmised that at least some Mayans may have worshipped a primary god with a dual nature, a god that was both good and evil, and that this may have been a type of evolution of religious thought among the Maya who were polytheists who believed there were many gods but each with an individual nature, some good, some bad."

"Interesting, I see you have good taste in rum, can I buy you a drink?" Peter nodded and the Captain ordered *Flor de Canas* for both of them. "Do you think we will find anything as significant in *ciudad blanca*?"

"I have no idea. I know very little about this supposed lost city. I do suspect it is not Mayan and maybe there is a chance we find something that tells us how this earlier lost city civilization influenced the Maya. But who knows? These ruins are entirely mysterious and it doesn't seem as if anyone who has seen them has done any proper archeological work on the sites. At any rate, I'm the last person to really be qualified to shed any light on what we find. To be honest I just came to see an old girlfriend who dumped me back in college and who I just haven't seemed to have gotten over." Peter could feel the cumulative effects of the day's rums beginning to loosen his tongue.

"She is here in Tegucigalpa?"

"It's Toeb's wife. She was at the meeting today. The dark haired, long legged woman sitting by Doctor Mellon."

"Ah yes, I do remember her, very attractive but surely too young for you to have known in college?"

"No, she just looks a lot better than me. She's only a couple of years younger."

"So, have you spoken to her?" The Captain, perhaps also warmed by the rum, was warming to the conversation.

"It went badly, very, very badly, and now I'm just drinking rum and licking my wounds." The Captain laughed sympathetically and they ordered more rums and continued to talk a while about their experiences with women.

"I know a better place than this, do you want to see more of Tegus?" Peter saw no reason not to. After four *Flor de Canas* he was amenable to just about anything. He and the Captain climbed into a taxi in front of the hotel.

Ten

TITO AGUACATE

Tegucigalpa, called "Tegus" by Hondurans, is set in a large valley in the central mountains of Honduras, surrounded by higher peaks not unlike the San Jose, Costa Rica setting with which Peter was familiar. But San Jose, while chaotic and bustling, lacks the armed guards and police patrols that abound in Tegus and the poverty and violence is more visible and threatening in the Honduran city. As the taxi made its way through the traffic-choked streets, Peter was saddened by the trash and tumult. They were passed by pick-up trucks with mounted machine guns full of heavily armed police in military fatigues. There were modern buildings close to the hotel, but as they moved away from the city center most of the buildings were crumbling stucco and the streets were pocked with huge holes filled with muddy water.

Peter was used to Central American poverty. He roamed the adult clubs of the backstreets of San Jose and had visited Guatemala City, a vast and sprawling slum, on coffee buying trips. But something about Tegus felt strangely oppressive. The faces of the people they passed on the streets seemed unsmiling and grim and occasionally they caught a fleeting glimpse of an altercation on the street, a fistfight or a thief running from the merchant he just robbed. Young, tough looking tattooed men in sleeveless T-shirts and baggy chinos roamed in groups. They passed through neighborhoods of large mansions surrounded by high concrete walls topped with barbed wire guarded by armed men, the homes of the wealthy.

The bar, *Tito Aguacate*, known to locals simply as "Tito" was on a corner of two crumbling streets in an older, low rise quarter of the city. It was a plain rectangular structure painted in beige and green with a sagging red tile roof. The interior was white painted plywood with a mosaic tile floor. There were a few tables scattered around and a long white painted wooden bar with a blue glass top. The Captain led him to a table by the wall and they ordered *Flor de Canas* straight up. Although the bar was not crowded, Cruz-Madrid assured Peter that it was usually very crowded and would be filling up as the night wore on.

"My family is very old and very wealthy," said Cruz-Madrid, clearly loquacious from the rum they had consumed. "They own a hacienda outside the town of Ojojona, just south of here, and many thousands of hectares mostly for cattle. My father also has mining interests and owns some agricultural land on the Caribbean coast he leases to American fruit companies. I have four older brothers, so as the youngest son I was told I had to join the officer corps to represent the family interests in the military. Fortunately, my father's influence got me assigned to a Special Forces unit near the capital so I can enjoy Tegus. So you live in Costa Rica? Hard to understand why you would leave the States to go live in a third world country. I got my special forces training at Fort Benning in Georgia. I had a chance to see some of your country. Hell, there, even the poorest live in better places than the middle class do here. Fast food everywhere, chicken for a few dollars, cheap hamburgers, everyone has a car. The double- wide trailers everyone makes fun of there would be middle class homes here. The grocery stores and malls are amazing. When I retire I plan to live in Florida. Why move to Costa Rica?"

"I got tired of my country, and it's changing. The poor are getting poorer and the rich richer, the wealthy control the government to a greater degree than ever. Slowly, we're becoming more like a wealthier Honduras. Our culture is degenerate with popular music and films appealing to the basest instincts. Our educational system is a wreck, only the elites know anything about philosophy and art. Popular music is debased. Students graduate from high school knowing almost nothing. We are ashamed of our history of slavery and genocide of indigenous peoples so we hide it or pretend it isn't true. Many people aren't educated or sophisticated enough to believe or understand scientific or medical opinions. People don't really believe in anything but getting rich and when they understand that's impossible they focus on getting high. All those dangerous drug runners in La Mosquitia we were warned about are bringing drugs to the U.S."

"You say people don't believe in anything, so you have no religion in your country? I thought the U.S. was a Christian country full of evangelicals."

"They're not the majority but their brand of Christianity is curious. They believe it's virtuous to be rich, they hate gays, they think it's okay to murder an abortion doctor. They are for the most part anti-intellectual, don't believe in science, reject the arts and mistrust a government that supplies them with food stamps and health care. In many ways they're far worse than the materialistic fools who spend their lives getting stoned, watching TV and worrying about getting the latest I-pad or smart phone manufactured by drone labor in China. I get that Costa Rica has its problems and its poverty, but I'm an outsider there and I don't have the sense of ownership and loss that I get at home. Staying in my country and watching it wither away was just too painful. I guess I was just born to be an expatriate."

"Peter, Honduras is far worse. You've seen the streets we traveled to get here. My family is one of twenty-five or so that control almost all the wealth. Everyone else has nothing. There really is no middle class. We are the murder capital of the world. Every day in Tegus they take twenty corpses to the morgue. But we do have some beautiful women in Honduras. You shouldn't just drown your pain in rum my friend, you need a beautiful woman to help you forget about *Senora* Toeb." Cruz-Madrid proposed they go to a Palestinian strip club he knew. There, the girls were available to go up to rooms above the club to privately entertain patrons.

El Leon Dorado was in an older section of Tegucigalpa. It reminded Peter of the fleshpots in San Jose. An old building with a sagging roof, concrete floors, plywood bar and a rickety stage on which plump, dark haired women danced laconically amid the smell of stale beer and cigarettes. The only difference was that in this club there were no gringos, most of the male customers had a vaguely Arabic look, without doubt members of Honduras' sizable Palestinian population. Women in tight skirts circulated the room hustling drinks and customers. Cruz-Madrid seemed well known here. They ordered rum and sat a while but none of the women appealed to Peter, who was becoming more morose as he became drunker.

"Zelda, Mrs. Toeb, was so special to me. I always thought of her as the ideal woman, so smart, so strong, so beautiful."

"I see the ladies here have no appeal for you, Peter, but I have a solution, that is, if you are willing to pay. The lady I have in mind is not cheap but she is beautiful and so skilled that she can erase even the most deeply felt sadness. Interested?"

"Sure," said Peter, who was too drunk to care. Cruz-Madrid pulled out a cell phone and dialed. After a brief conversation, he paid the bill and hustled Peter into a cab.

They seemed to drive for hours through neighborhoods of cement block and plywood shacks dark from a lack of electricity. Finally they entered a dimly lit district, which seemed very old. The pavement on the street was worn away in large patches revealing cobblestones over which the taxi bounced mercilessly. The streets narrowed and the buildings on either side were two and three stories tall, stucco with broken patches revealing the underlying adobe bricks. The windows and doors were arched and there were elaborately patterned iron grills on many. Some of the buildings leaned precipitously and most of the tile roofs sagged badly. They pulled up in front of a three- story stucco building with a rectangular front door and Moorish arches for windows. "This is the place," said Captain Cruz-Madrid not moving from the cab. "The woman's name is Jahaira. She will cost you five thousand Lempira but she is worth much more. She is very beautiful, very skilled and very wise. Oh and Peter, there is just one thing."

"Yes, Aramis?"

"She is a *bruja*."

Eleven
LA BRUJA

Peter stood before a huge, heavy mahogany door adorned with worn carvings of pineapples and quarter moons. He applied the wrought iron knocker and a tall, beautiful woman answered the door. By her skin complexion and knotted headscarf he guessed she was Garifuna, a descendant of West and Central Africans and Arawak and Caribe Indians who lived along the Caribbean coast of Central America. Her skin color was clearly African but her face was smooth with round eyes and a straight, aquiline nose. "Jahaira?" he asked. The woman shook her head no and gestured for him to follow. They walked through an anteroom into which a large and beautifully crafted mahogany staircase flowed. On the wall was a portrait of a nineteenth century gentleman in clerical garb. They walked past it into a large sitting room with a huge stone fireplace and worn mahogany floors. To the right of the fireplace in an old wooden carved chair sat a beautiful woman with long jet-black hair and dark copper skin. She wore an elegantly tailored black cotton shirtdress with purple piping, a silver necklace, silver earrings in the shape of triangles, and open-toed, high-heeled black leather sandals. "Thank you Angelica. Senor VanOwen, my name is Jahaira Cristales, I am pleased to meet you."

Peter was finding the situation absurd and awkward. He thought he was meeting a whore but this woman seemed more like some daughter of an old, aristocratic family who was

48

meeting him for tea or sherry. The woman got up from her chair and offered him her hand. She was very beautiful. Not tall, perhaps 5'5" extremely curvaceous and probably younger than thirty. She had large, dark eyes and prominent cheekbones. Her shirtdress was unbuttoned from her neck and revealed a glimpse of firm, round breasts. As he took her manicured hand, Peter could not imagine he was really going to have sex with this woman.

"First, before we become better acquainted, there is the matter of payment, please." Her English was grammatical but her rolled Spanish R's were very distinctive and her accent was thick. Peter quickly dug into his wallet and pulled out the notes, handing them to her.

"*Gracias*, Pedro. Obviously you are fond of rum, can I offer you some?"

Peter, still speechless, nodded his acquiescence and Jahaira went to a carved wooden cabinet against the far wall. "I prefer Barbancourt myself, do you mind? It is more refined and delicate," she said, pulling a bottle of fifteen year old Haitian rum from the cabinet with two glasses. She filled them and handed one to Peter. "You will be leaving on a very difficult journey tomorrow I hear?"

"How did you know about that?"

"I am sure that Aramis mentioned it when he called me." She said, smiling. But Peter had been sitting next to Cruz-Madrid when he called and heard only the briefest of conversations about a friend who desired companionship.

"Well, I'm not going. I just came to see a woman I used to care for and she made it clear she wasn't happy to see me. I just want to go home." He sipped the Barbancourt and, despite all the rum he had drunk that evening, he could still appreciate its richness and delicacy.

"How sad, perhaps the expedition would be the distraction you need to escape your sorrow. The place you are seeking is filled with secrets and perhaps, for the right person, enlightenment."

"What do you know about *ciudad blanca*?"

"Let me show you something," she walked to a desk in the corner of the room, picked up a white limestone carving and walked it over to him. It was a carving of the face of a capuchin monkey, identical to the blue crystal pendant on the whore Ophelia's necklace and the one in his dream. "This came from *ciudad blanca*. The people who built the city worshipped a monkey god. He was a terrible, wicked god but they were close to him, closer than anyone else on earth. They understood his nature and they accepted him in a way that no other people would and so he revealed more of himself to them than he had to anyone else. So many people insist on giving their god the qualities they want him to have, not the qualities they could infer from the suffering and brutality he inflicted on mankind. But the people of *ciudad blanca* accepted him for what he was, a wicked and tyrannical spirit." She smiled at him, a dazzling charming and inviting smile. "But did you come here to discuss ancient theology or to fuck me?"

She led him up the carved mahogany stairs to a bedroom furnished only with a large mahogany bed, a small side table, an intricately carved armoire and a large silver crucifix on the wall. Jahaira pulled off the shirtdress to reveal a simple white cotton bra and panties. She quickly stripped these off and sat on the bed. She had a magnificent body with firm rounded breasts, toned and shapely legs and rounded hips. The sight of her, despite the considerable quantity of rum he had consumed, made him hungry for her, hungrier than he had been for a woman in years. He quickly stripped and sat next to her. She let him kiss her without protest and he gently laid her down and mounted her. His cock was so stiff it hurt and he quickly entered her. He kissed her again and began pumping, she wrapped her legs around him. He felt his body heat up and he began to sweat, his heart was pumping wildly. He exploded inside her and suddenly felt as if he were sliding down a pole. He fell off her and lay on his back. Their coupling had not lasted more than fifteen minutes.

"Aramis told me you are a *bruja*, is that true?" Asked Peter after they had lain together for a while in silence.

"Ha, ha, Aramis is so flattering. I think of myself as more of a *curandera*. I do sell potions and folk remedies and I am known to help people with their problems for a fee. I know something about the beliefs and superstitions of the people and I believe in some of them myself. There is a dark side to nature and to man and I have learned to exploit it. If that makes me a *bruja* then so be it."

"If you are a *curandera* or even a *bruja,* why do you have sex with men for money?"

"Why not? Is it evil? Is it dishonorable? How much money do you think the poor of Tegus can afford to pay me for their cures and love potions? I have no other income. My father's family stopped sending me money a long time ago. I have to live and I have expensive taste in rum. My best asset is my beauty and I choose to sell it, well, let's say rent it, in order to live in comfort. Tegus is full of wealthy men who are willing to pay for the company of a beautiful woman."

"How do you know so much about what the people who lived in *ciudad blanca* believed?"

"My father was a priest. In fact, he was a monsignor when my mother met him. He came from a very prominent family, the Cristales, one of the twenty-five. Yes, I took his name despite the fact that I was born out of wedlock. My mother was a very beautiful woman from a poor, devout family, her father made crucifixes to sell. She was probably what your doctors today would call manic depressive and she went to see my father for counseling. She thought perhaps she was possessed, and she wanted the help and support of a priest. Instead he seduced her. When she became pregnant with me, the family bought her off. They gave her this house, which was one of their original town homes built in 1612. They gave her an allowance to raise me.

My father went on to become the archbishop of Tegucigalpa, the most respected cleric in the country. My mother committed suicide when I was fifteen. The Cristales, though, kept the money coming for a few years."

"I don't get it, what does that have to do with *cuidad blanca*?"

"Be patient, Pedro. It is a long and complicated story. I met my father a few times. He knew who I was, I knew who he was. One time, after he became archbishop, I met with him in the sacristy of the Cathedral of San Miguel the Archangel. I asked how god could have taken my mother for her to die by her own hand so horribly, how he could allow such poverty and suffering and the cruelty of the gangs and of the ruling families, and why he would forbid him from being a father to me or a husband to my mother. He told me that people don't understand God. They want him to be kind and forgiving but that God really wants us to suffer, he created us to see us in pain and that is his pleasure."

"Why would your father think this? It certainly isn't conventional Catholic dogma."

"When he was a young priest my father was a missionary in La Mosquitia. He often visited the Pech tribe in their villages along the *Platano* river. The Pech claim to be the descendants of those who built *ciudad blanca*. My father learned to speak their language and became friends with a Pech shaman who showed him relics from the ancient city and told him about the beliefs of his ancestors. The monkey god was real to them but something happened to my father to make him believe too. It was he who gave me the carving of the monkey god he brought back from his missionary days."

"It's hard to imagine what would make a man of the cloth believe something so radical."

"Is it really so radical, Pedro? If god created everything in the universe then he created all the evil and suffering. And really, Pedro, isn't there a lot more evil and suffering in this world than goodness and happiness? The fact that all life leads to decline and death suggests an evil force at work. Even your Christian god is shown to be evil in the holy bible. Look at the story of Abraham and Isaac. God told Abraham to kill his own son out of love for him, a monstrous thing to do, forcing Abraham to choose between his god and murdering his son, and then at the last moment after Abraham had agonized over what he had been ordered to do, God relented. God destroyed Sodom and Gomorrah whose inhabitants were guilty of things that you and I have just done and will soon be doing again. A little sex was enough to annihilate two cities and everyone in them, including little children and babies? Who were the babies fucking to be so wicked? Except, of course, he spared Lot and his family, but Lot's wife made the mistake of looking back at the cities being destroyed and for her curiosity was turned into a pillar of salt. But two cities were nothing compared to the flood, when god destroyed everything but Noah and his family and a handful of animals. When the Israelites wanted to leave Egypt and Pharaoh would not let them go, god made the poor people of Egypt suffer for Pharaoh's decision, torturing them with plagues and ultimately killing every first born in the land, many of them innocent babies. And poor Job who loved and served god but became his victim when Satan challenged Job's loyalty to god. In order to prove to Satan that Job had not just been bought off with prosperity and happiness, god took it all away. He killed Job's animals, confiscated his wealth and then killed his family all to prove to Satan how loyal Job could be. God not only created Satan, he *was* Satan. Everything that Satan is accused of doing in the bible is really just an act of god. The people who lived in *ciudad blanca* thought of Satan and god as the same entity. The ancient Gnostics believed that too. In the bible, god is quoted in Isaiah 45.7 as saying 'I form the light, and create darkness: I make peace and create evil...' confirming the notion of god as a form of duality. But, in fact, we see little of the good in god as we go through our lives suffering and dying, persecuting each other and destroying the planet. If there is good in god it is reflected in nature, not in man."

"But before we continue this theological discussion, let me get you more rum." She got up from the bed naked and walked out. He watched her lovely naked ass sway rhythmically on her way out. In a few minutes she was back with a tumbler of Barbancourt for him.

"None for you?"

"I have a feeling there is more work for me to do here," she said, smiling and fingering his cock. Peter sipped the rum slowly, savoring it while he continued to admire her naked body. He liked the idea of bedding her again but he was not sure he was up to it. In fact he was beginning to feel a bit woozy and numb.

"The rum is affecting you?"

"Maybe a little, I'm beginning to feel kind of strange." The slap hit him like a brick. He blacked out for a few seconds and, as he came to, he reflected on how much stronger she was than he would have thought. Then she hit him again and he fell back on the bed. He felt numb and paralyzed. He was bleeding a little from his lip. She leaned over him and kissed him on the lips.

"Oh Pedro, will you be my little *puta*? Will you be a woman for me?"

"Whaaat?" he groaned. She stood up, reached into the night table drawer and pulled out a bottle of lubricant and a large plastic dildo attached to a harness. She quickly slipped it on and rubbed it with the lubricant. He lay in bed numb and unable to move. She turned him over on his stomach and he suddenly felt a cold gel being inserted in his anus. "No!" he yelled in terror.

"Quiet *puta*. Your yelling will attract Angelica and she will want to join in, I don't feel like sharing you right now." He felt the dildo begin to penetrate him and he shrieked in pain. "It will hurt at first my little *puta* but you will get used to it, maybe even like it before I am done with you." She pushed into him further and leaned over and bit his neck hard enough to draw blood. He felt like his anus would explode from the pressure and pain but he was too paralyzed to move and resist her. She began to pump rhythmically and reached around to grab his member, stroking it hard as she pumped. The old mattress on the mahogany bed frame creaked loudly as they began moving together. "*Puta,* this comes naturally to you, eh? How many poor girls have you bedded like this? Forcing yourself on them for a few dollars which they have no choice to refuse. How many children have you planted in their wombs only to abandon them? Your cock is a tool of aggression. How does it feel to be the one on the bottom, to be the *puta* yourself?" She grabbed his hair with one hand while continuing to masturbate him with the other. Peter was feeling pleasure and pain simultaneously, he felt himself build towards an orgasm as Jahaira penetrated him more and more deeply. When he came his body tremored as if he were in an explosion. As he came he heard Jahaira laughing.

She pushed him down on his stomach and extracted the dildo from his anus. He was covered in sweat and his rectum felt raw and sore. She climbed off him and he could not resist as she turned him over on his back. She spread his legs and he groaned as she reinserted the dildo in him. She lay over him and he felt her nipples rub against his chest. He realized that the silver necklace she still wore had hanging from it a pendant identical to the one on Ophelia's necklace, a blue stone monkey carving. She kissed him hard on his lips and inserted her tongue deep into his mouth rubbing it against his tongue. She pulled back and began to rhythmically pump the dildo into him. He felt her sweat dripping down on his already soaked body. She looked down at him and smiled.

Her slap felt like she hit him with a board. This time he blacked out completely.

Twelve
LA CEIBA, HONDURAS

Peter awoke in a seat on an airborne plane next to Captain Aramis Cruz-Madrid. His face felt bruised and sore and his anus felt worse. He was hung over from something considerably more potent than rum. Cruz-Madrid laughed. "I hope you enjoyed yourself because you certainly paid the price. You look like shit, Peter."

"How the hell did I get here?"

"We are not really sure, just before the plane was to take off a dark sedan pulled up on the runway, someone pushed you out on the tarmac and drove off. You were still unconscious so we carried you onto the plane. Your old girlfriend was pretty amused."

"Zelda was here? She saw me?"

"Yes, she and Toeb came down to see the expedition off. Your friend, Doctor Selby, was pretty upset until you showed up. Hey, how did you get those bruises on your face? Did someone try to rob you?"

"No, it was that *bruja* you sent me to, she hit me!"

"Jahaira? Why would she do that? Did you try to do something to her? Were you so drunk you got violent and she had to protect herself? I would never forgive myself for referring someone violent to her. How could you?"

"No, I did nothing to her, she attacked me."

"For what reason? And Peter, while you are not a young

man, you are strong enough to defend yourself from a small woman."

"She drugged me. I don't know why she wanted to hurt me. I've never been treated that way by any woman."

"It makes no sense, Peter. I have been to Jahaira myself many times. She is a wonderful woman, intelligent, cultured, funny and charming. She may be a *bruja* but in our culture that is not a bad thing. She is wise and she can cure many things, even a broken heart. That is why I sent you to her. She is not a violent person and she had no reason to hurt you. By the way, are you okay? You look pale and sick and I thought I saw a bloodstain on your pants as we carried you to the plane."

Doctor DeGroet made his way down the aisle, grabbing seats to steady himself. "Mister VanOwen, are you okay? I should have warned you that Tegucigalpa is not San Jose. It is a very dangerous city and no place for a *gringo* to go carousing after dark. I hope you will be okay to proceed on the expedition. Doctor Selby was very concerned about your safety. He tells me you are quite the debauchee. I am afraid you won't have many opportunities for that where we are going and I must warn you that La Ceiba is no safer than Tegucigalpa when it comes to nightlife. Hopefully tonight you will get a good night's sleep, as we leave for *Rio Platano* tomorrow morning." DeGroet tottered back up the aisle. As Peter's gaze followed him he caught a glimpse of Terry Selby in a forward seat.

Peter groaned. "Get some sleep, *mi amigo*," said Cruz-Madrid, "we will be in La Ceiba in a little more than an hour." Peter lay back in his seat and despite his aching face and anus, fell back to sleep.

There was a light rain falling, misting the leaves of the trees around the clearing. He heard a roar in the distance and moved through the heavy growth towards it. He emerged by the side of a roaring cataract; white frothy water rushing down the rocky course. In the trees above he heard monkeys. Downstream, there was a hanging bridge made from rope and vines spanning the rushing water. He moved towards it and felt cool spray as he walked. The heat was oppressive, he was covered in sweat and the spray felt good. From the bridge he spotted toucans in a nearby tree and a flight of scarlet macaws flew overhead. After crossing the swaying bridge he emerged into a dark clearing on the far side of which was a blue stone seat. On the seat was a small capuchin monkey sitting with his head on his hand as if in thought. As he came closer he saw that the monkey's face was scarred and his eyes were bright red. The monkey looked directly at him and screamed.

The plane lurched and bounced, waking Peter abruptly. The plane taxied for a few minutes and lumbered to a stop. The passengers were unloaded down a movable stairway and ushered through a small, empty terminal. A convoy of SUV's was waiting for them.

La Ceiba was primitive. Only the main streets were paved with patched asphalt. The buildings were mostly cinderblock or painted stucco with corrugated metal roofs. In the distance were green forested hills but the salt smell of the ocean mixed with a humid mustiness filled the air. The convoy bounced over potholes and ruts, intensifying Peter's pounding headache. His face ached, his anus ached and every limb of his body ached as if he had been beaten by an angry mob.

The convoy of SUV's pulled into the drive of a surprisingly elegant hotel, the *Quinta Real*, right on the beach. The group waited while Arias-Garcia checked them in and handed out room keys. To his relief, Peter had his own room. When he got upstairs to a spacious and elegant room with an ocean view he looked at himself in the mirror for the first time. One of his eyes was purple and swollen, he had a red welt on one cheek and a purple bruise on the other. His lips were swollen and scabbed where they were cracked. He couldn't examine his anus but he knew it was raw and painful, his underpants were stained with blood. He could not understand why Jahaira, who had obviously drugged him, had done this to him. Worse yet, he now found himself one step closer to embarking on the expedition in which he had never intended to participate. Somehow he had to get out of La Ceiba and back to Tegucigalpa to get home. But his wallet with his credit cards was missing. He would simply refuse to go tomorrow when they left for the docks and somehow he would find a way to get some money to book a flight towards home. He stripped his sweat soaked and filthy clothes, showered and went immediately to bed.

He was soaring over the jungle, below him he saw a city of white stone sprawling in a mountain valley. The people of the city were gathered in a central square surrounding an altar on a pyramid in the middle of the square. A man in a blue monkey mask and scarlet feathers held a sharp obsidian blade. On a wooden post in the middle of the altar a young girl, no older than twelve, was tied. The man in the monkey mask swung his blade and slit her throat. Blood trickled down her body and stained the stone altar. The monkey mask man drove his blade deep into the chest of the girl, reached his hand into the cavity and with a wrench tore her heart out and held it up for the crowd to see.

A loud banging at his door woke him up. He glanced at his watch; it was only just past seven AM, too early to drag his still aching body out of bed. The banging continued and someone seemed to be shouting through the door. He finally could no longer endure the noise and reluctantly pulled himself out of bed to open the door. On the other side was Terry Selby, red faced and glaring. "Our shuttle leaves in half an hour, where the hell have you been?"

"I'm not going, it's that simple," said Peter.

"Look, you made a commitment to me and to this expedition; you're going if I have to drag you." Peter turned to close the door on Selby but he put his foot in the way and pushed himself into the room. "I told you this is my last fucking chance to redeem my career and I need your help, so goddamn it, get dressed and pack and let's get out of here!" Peter started laughing. His head hurt and his bruised face and abused asshole hurt but Selby's sheer, idiotic desperation seemed absurdly hilarious. He wanted to chase off into a hellish wilderness in hopes of redeeming his self-destroyed career and he wanted to drag Peter with him because he knew that career had been fraudulent from the beginning.

"Look Selby, whatever you find out there, assuming there is anything at all, is not going to redeem you from a reputation as a drug user, sexual exploiter, academic incompetent and general fuck up. But even if it were I'm not going to help you. I've already suffered enough on this little adventure. I just want to go home." Selby advanced on him, Peter felt a blow to his face and lost consciousness.

"Hey!" Selby yelled out, "VanOwen has been on another binge and passed out. I need some help getting him to the cars."

Thirteen
TEGUCIGALPA

Zelda sat on the terrace at the Nau Lounge in the Intercontinental, sipping a rum punch and basking in the afternoon sun. A waiter laid down a white rectangular platter of Ahi sashimi garnished with tiny purple orchids. Across from her sat the Deputy Chief of Mission from the U.S. Embassy, Colin Stevens, a tall, slender man in his mid-thirties with unfashionably short sandy brown hair, pale white skin and large, moist brown eyes like those of a baby deer. He was dressed in a brown linen suit, white shirt and maroon tie. The ambassador had been too busy to meet with her but her husband was important enough to get her the second in command. She wanted to discuss the new NGO she was founding to bring medical care to the poor of Honduras. Chad had pledged a substantial sum and she already had feelers out to begin to recruit staff. But she needed approval from the Honduran authorities, needed help finding a location, getting permits and ensuring security. In a country like Honduras none of this was straightforward. She hoped the Embassy would help.

"We'll do what we can but ultimately you'll need some kind of contact inside the Honduran government and once you have found that person it will cost you money to get their cooperation. You can't just go to a window, fill out some forms and get permits. Not here," said Stevens.

"Can you steer me to someone who can help me?"

"That's a problem because the government is in a state of flux and really has been since Manuel Zelaya was deposed back in 2010. The last election was won by the National Party, the traditional establishment party controlled by an elite of a handful of families. Your best bet would be to try to develop some contacts within that elite."

"How do I do that? Who are these elites and how do I begin making contact?"

"Your husband's status may help. They may see you as one of them and that may gain you entry to places you may make contact. Do you see those two men at that table across the patio?" Zelda nodded. "The man in the khaki jacket and blue shirt is Anselmo Ortega, the deputy finance minister. With him is Antonio Cruz-Madrid, the minister of the interior, actually I believe his nephew, an army officer, has some connection to your husband's expedition. They come from two of the elite families who control the government and the economy." While they were watching the table with the two officials, a stunning, dark skinned woman with long flowing black hair sat down at the table with them. She wore a simple purple, cotton shirtdress with open-toed platform heeled sandals ornamenting a pair of shapely bare legs. The two men greeted her effusively and called for a waiter.

"Who is that woman?"

"Well, her name is Jahaira Cristales. The Cristales are also an elite family, one of the oldest and richest, but nobody seems to know if she is actually one of them or really who she is. She's reputed to be a high priced prostitute, not exactly what you would expect from a Cristales. But if she is, her clientele includes some of the most powerful and wealthy men in the country. I've seen her at a number of functions and parties with some impressive escorts." Stevens laughed, "She also has a reputation as somewhat of a *bruja*."

"A witch?"

"Yes, there are rumors that she sells enchantments and

spells and even cast spells on some of the country's leaders." As Stevens spoke, Zelda watched their table. The beautiful dark skinned woman was at ease with the two ministers and they seemed to be trying to amuse her. For a moment it seemed as if the woman was aware of her watching and locked her gaze on Zelda. She felt a chill envelop her body and quickly looked away. When she finally looked back the woman was engaged in an animated conversation with the two middle aged ministers.

"Would a woman like that be the kind of contact I might use to get what I want?"

"To be honest, I don't know a lot about her. Her reputation is a bit unsavory but I see her at some of the most exclusive venues, socializing with some very powerful people. Let's face it, in Honduras being unsavory is not necessarily a disadvantage. But I would be very careful about trusting her; of course, I could say that about almost any one you might have dealings with here." They talked for a while then Stevens excused himself saying he needed to go back to the Embassy for a telephone conference. Zelda thanked him and took a sip from her rum punch. She pulled out her phone to check for messages before leaving to go back to her hotel. She suddenly felt a queasy feeling deep in the depths of her stomach. She looked up to see the woman in purple standing at her table looking right at her.

"*Senora* Toeb? My name is Jahaira Cristales. I wonder, is there something I can do for you?"

Fourteen
SAN MIGUEL, HONDURAS

A cool, marine breeze buffeted his face as Peter regained consciousness. He was aware of a steady, rocking movement, a salty smell in the air and a sore jaw. He opened his eyes to see a green and beige coastline moving by. He was in a boat coursing along the Honduran coast heading south. It was a long shallow draft boat with a central cabin area. He was on the deck in a folding chair. Standing next to him, leaning against the railing, was Cruz-Madrid. "Peter, you are one hell of a carousing wild man. I'm getting tired of having to haul your drunken ass onto airplanes, buses and boats."

"I went to bed at five yesterday, Aramis, and never woke up until Selby came banging on my door. He decked me, that's why you had to haul me on to this boat. Where are we going?"

"To a little Garifuna village called San Miguel on the mouth of the *Rio Platano*. We stay the night there and meet my security squad, then head up the river tomorrow morning in zodiacs. Hey, *amigo*, leave the Garifuna women alone, you will get yourself killed and maybe the rest of us too, and no more liquor, *hermano*, you have got to dry out."

"I didn't carouse last night, I went to bed. Selby shanghaied me. I just want to go home, back to my beach, my coffee trading and my quiet life."

"Ha, too late for that, *hermano*, there is no shuttle service here back to La Ceiba. No telling when a boat going there might

64

come to *San Miguel*, could be months. Hey, I am going to get some coffee. Feel better, Peter."

Peter watched the coastline as they sailed by, perhaps a half mile off shore. Occasionally they passed a fishing village or a small cluster of huts but most of the coastline was empty, overgrown with tangled green foliage. There were long empty expanses of beige, sandy beach. There were inlets filled with mangroves standing in salt water and he could see flights of birds rising above the dense swampland. He saw no boats of any kind. Various members of the expedition circulated on deck but no one spoke with him until Arias-Garcia came and leaned against the railing. "It is a calm and peaceful coastline, is it not, *Senor* VanOwen?"

"I was just remarking to myself on that. Call me Peter. Are we already a long way from La Ceiba?"

"Perhaps twenty-five kilometers, maybe a bit more. You slept quite a while. Are you feeling better?"

"A bit, the cool breeze helps," Peter looked at Arias-Garcia for perhaps the first time. He was a short, slender, light brown man, clean shaven with jet black hair greying at the temples, a cleft chin and pockmarked cheeks. Peter noticed he wore a plain gold cross around his neck.

"You have been through a lot these last few days. You seem to me like a man who is not at peace, someone who has not found Jesus Christ. You know if you meet and embrace god you can find that peace. I was like you when I was younger, I drank, I chased women, I used drugs and ran the street. But when my best friend was shot by thugs, Jesus came to me and took me by the hand and told me he loved me despite all my sins. Since then I have changed, I have found peace within myself and everything I do, I do for god."

"Really, I'm not the carouser everyone here seems to think I am. I admit to a taste for female flesh and a glass of rum occasionally but at home I spend most of my day reading and roasting coffee. I've been viciously attacked two nights in a row and everyone seems to assume I'm some kind of debaucher."

"Have you read the Book of Revelation, Peter?"

"No, my parents were agnostics, I have no religious education, nor any interest in obtaining one."

"John tells us about the Whore of Babylon, in Revelation 17, verse 5, he calls her 'Babylon The Great, the mother of harlots and abominations of the earth', he goes on to say in Revelation 18, verses 7-9 'How much she hath glorified herself, and lived deliciously, so much torment and sorrow give her; for she saith in her heart, I sit a queen, and am no widow, and shall see no sorrow. Therefore shall her plagues come in one day, death, and mourning and famine; and she shall be utterly burned with fire; for strong is the lord god who judgeth her. And the kings of earth who have committed fornication and lived deliciously with her, shall bewail her, and lament for her, when they shall see the smoke of her burning.' " As Arias-Garcia spoke, his voice rose and his eyes glazed, "do not be a king of the earth, Peter, do not lose yourself in the things of the flesh, there will be a cleansing, Peter, that is what John tells us in Revelation, a terrible cleansing and only those who truly love god shall survive the terror. You must learn to love God, Peter, or you will not survive." He looked at Peter meaningfully and nodded, then walked off to attend to his duties. Peter sighed.

The coastline had begun to change. The beaches were gone, now there were more mangroves and small islands began to appear on both sides of the boat. There were more birds and the water had changed from blue green to sienna brown. The boat finally turned west into a broad channel, which gradually narrowed. Aramis came back to sit by him for a while but mercifully Arias-Garcia did not reappear. "We are in the delta of the *Rio Platano*," said Cruz-Madrid, "what you see on either side are islands, this boat cannot go much further without running aground, that is why we stop at *San Miguel* and from there will take powered zodiacs upriver." It began to rain as they talked.

On the south side of the boat they saw a village of

unpainted plank huts with steeply pitched thatched roofs. On the shore were about a dozen dugout canoes. A rickety dock extended out into the water. The boat pulled closer to shore and crewmen extended a gangplank to the dock. Arias-Garcia was running about directing crewmen to start unloading supplies and equipment. On the shore he could see a small crowd of dark skinned villagers. "The Garifuna," said Cruz-Madrid, gesturing, "nobody knows exactly their origin but they are descendants of black Africans brought to the Americas to be slaves, perhaps they are descendants of shipwreck survivors who intermarried with Carib and Arawak Indians. They live a simple, self-sufficient life very much apart from other Hondurans. Jahaira's father, the archbishop, he spent time among them and knew one of their shaman well."

"Wait, she told me it was the Pech Indians and one of their shaman."

"It was both and perhaps others as well. Jahaira inherited from her father a real interest in primitive religions. The Garifuna are interesting in their religious beliefs. They profess to be Catholics but they still observe many of their ancestral West African beliefs and have incorporated them into their rituals much like the people of Haiti and Cuba. They are also expert at using the herbs from the forest for medicinal and magical purposes. Ah, but you will enjoy their food, Peter."

Arias-Garcia yelled for the passengers to disembark into the Garifuna village. Peter had tried to negotiate with the boat captain to take him on as a passenger to the next port of call, but that would be in Nicaragua and the captain refused to take on a passenger with nothing but a promise to pay the fare, so Peter had no choice but to disembark with the expedition crew. The village was primitive with palm thatch roofed planked huts on stilts. The moist, hot air was overwhelming and the entire village smelled of mustiness combined with the smells of goats, pigs and chickens and a faint hint of human excrement. The island on which the village was located was large and heavily forested.

The village itself was ringed with coconut palms and there were small pens containing a few pigs and goats. Chickens wandered everywhere. The villagers were dark skinned and African looking. They wore loose cotton garments in bright colors of red, green, orange and yellow. Many women wore scarves wrapped around their heads, knotted at the front. The villagers stared at the expedition members as they filed ashore. Peter caught a glimpse of Selby ahead of him in the file. They were shown to huts in which they were to spend the night. Peter was to bunk with Cruz-Madrid and Arias-Garcia.

After being assigned to a hut, the first thing Peter did was to enquire if any of the Garifuna spoke Spanish or English. Their chief spoke Spanish and Peter inquired about staying in the village after the expedition left to wait for the next boat. The chief seemed puzzled but explained that boats seldom came to San Miguel, but that Peter was welcome to stay if he could pay for his food and shelter like the expedition was doing. Peter thanked the chief and slunk back to his hut defeated. With no money his only chance of staying fed and sheltered was to stay with the expedition. In the morning he would be going up the Platano with the expedition and there would be no going back. But he vowed he would never help Selby with a paper or anything else.

Not long after the expedition had settled in, the security team arrived on a small Honduran navy patrol boat. There were ten soldiers, small brown men, wiry and tough looking. They wore camouflage fatigues with leather combat boots and black berets. Each one carried an American made M4 rifle and wore an ammunition belt. He watched Cruz-Madrid inspect them and lecture them about the expedition and their role. These were tough veterans who had come from the northern coast where they had been fighting drug traffickers. It may have been Peter's imagination but they seemed disdainful of Cruz-Madrid, the aristocratic officer stationed in Tegus while they operated in the bush.

Arias-Garcia returned to the hut after supervising the supply storage. "Do you think, Peter, that you are a good man?"

"Probably not. I can guarantee my ex-wife, Zelda Toeb and Doctor Selby don't think of me as a good man. I can be selfish and dishonest, I've certainly exploited women."

"If you only found god you would be redeemed. Just learn to love god and develop a relationship with him and you would be forgiven. No matter what you do or what happens to you, the love of god can rescue you. If you don't believe, you must face an inevitable end in hell. Pray with me, Peter."

"Arturo, thank you for your kindness," as tired and sore as he was, Peter knew he would be stuck with the expedition for the next few weeks and he would need the cooperation of the man responsible for its logistics, so he spoke carefully and gently despite his annoyance at Arias-Garcia's proselytizing. "As I look around this world I find it difficult to believe in your god of love. There is so much suffering and brutality and if god loved us so much why would he have us decay and die in such a debilitating and painful fashion, why has he burdened us with disease and natural disasters, why are we humans, made in the image and likeness of god, so brutal to cach other and to other creatures and to the environment itself? I just met a woman who told me god existed but was evil. If I had one shred of evidence to believe in a god at all I would tend to agree with her. But I suspect the heavens are empty and we are just poor biological creatures who evolved from the muck, live at the mercy of the forces of nature and die never to exist again. Pray for me if you like Arturo, I need it, as you say."

"I will, Peter, you are a troubled man but God loves you, you will see, he does love you and all of us." Arias-Garcia got up and left to see to the feeding of the expedition.

Cruz-Madrid was right about the food. Of course, Peter had not eaten in two days and might have found anything delicious. However, the spicy seafood stew made with coconut milk together with cassava bread, mashed plantain and grilled turtle meat made for a sumptuous meal and Peter went to bed saddened but satiated.

He was in an underground vault formed by corbeled arches, there was a blue light emanating from somewhere at the far end of the vault. As Peter moved forward he heard faint drumming. The floor beneath him was fashioned from crude stones, laid without mortar. There were carvings on the walls depicting jaguars, tapirs, sloths and bats and, throughout, white faced monkeys in various poses. Peter moved to the light and saw before him a large carving of a white faced monkey in some sort of blue stone. The light did not seem to be coming directly from the carving but instead from a sort of misty haze surrounding it. As he came closer the light intensified and blinded him.

He awakened with a start. The drumming continued, faint and distant but exactly as he had heard in his dream. For a moment he thought he was still dreaming but he could hear Arias-Garcia snoring and smell the mustiness of the village. He sat up and listened for a few minutes. The drumming was coming from the inner portion of the island, away from the village. Peter got up and looked outside the hut. Off in the distance he caught a glimpse of light through the trees. Without thinking, he climbed down from the hut and began walking towards the light. As he walked it became clear that the drumming sound was coming from the same place as the light. He found himself in a narrow path through a thick growth of tropical forest. Ahead he saw a clearing with a large fire, around which were dancers undulating to the drums. In front of the fire was a low wooden table upon which was laid a small feast of fish, mashed plantains, chicken, cassava bread and a bottle of cheap Honduran rum. Circled around the fire and table were the villagers, swaying and dancing to the rhythm of the drums, passing around a bottle of the same cheap rum. Different dancers would jump in front of the fire, whirl and leap. Women would sway their hips and buttocks as they did a complicated four step dance to the drums. Peter ducked behind a large stand of brush and watched, fascinated, as the villagers danced. Suddenly the drumming slowed and the dancing stopped. The crowd stepped back and a tall, elegant woman in a long dark cotton dress and plain white cotton blouse, who looked surprisingly like Jahaira Cristalcs' servant, Angelica, stepped forward. The crowd began to sing in a language Peter had never heard. The woman did a simple, graceful two step dancc then turned to face the table as the drumming continued. She began chanting loudly as two men brought out a large carved stone statue of what looked like a Christian saint. As the statue emerged in the light it looked to Peter like Saint Francis, portrayed in a loose robe with a rope belt around his waist and a staff. But something was wrong with the statue. The head seemed too big for the body and Peter realized it was blue. As his eyes adjusted to the light, Peter saw that it was the head of a white faced monkey carved from blue stone.

Fifteen
TEGUCIGALPA

The woman looked accusingly right at Zelda. "As a matter of fact," said Zelda coolly, not at all shaken by the other woman's aggression, "I believe there is something you can do for me, and perhaps something I can do for you. Would you have a drink with me?"

"I don't see why not," Zelda noticed that her accent was thick with very pronounced rolled R's. Seen close up she was even more breathtaking than when she was seated across the room. Her hair was shimmering black, her eyes large and dark, her skin, bronze and smooth, devoid of make-up and her compact, curvaceous body well displayed in the simple, purple frock she wore.

"I'm trying to set up an NGO here in Honduras to provide health care to the poor, but I need help dealing with the local authorities. I am told that you are a member of a prominent family and have contacts with prominent people. I am sure that if you could lead me to the contacts I need to get permission to operate, you would be appropriately compensated by the foundation my husband is setting up."

"Intriguing. But first I must correct any false impressions you may have been given. I am a Cristales and, as you say, they are a prominent and powerful family here in Honduras. However, I am illegitimate, born out of wedlock to an ordinary girl and a Cristales who was a prelate and had taken a vow of chastity. As the product of such an illicit union I am unacknowledged by the Cristales family. As to my connections with the high and powerful, yes I can say I know a great many of the ministers and members of the national legislature, who are, of course, either members of, or connected to, the elite families of the country. But my connection is on the unsavory side. I am what we say in Spanish *la zorra* or *la puta*. These men pay me to have sex with them; that is how I know them. That being said, yes I can help you, *Senora* Toeb, and what is more I would like to help you." She smiled her dazzling smile at Zelda as she said this, becoming suddenly a beacon of charm.

"Call me Zelda. Tell me please, how do we start?"

"How would you like to come to my *casa* for a drink? We can discuss this at leisure there and in complete privacy. My driver is waiting outside the hotel, we can be there quickly and I can offer you a homemade liqueur, something very unique I promise you that you could not find here. You may find my home unique as well, it was built in the seventeenth century by the Cristales family as their original town home here in Tegus. It was given to my mother as a settlement for the burden of having to bear and raise an illegitimate child without a husband." Zelda hesitated for a moment, as once again, she felt that dazzling white smile being aimed at her. She had refused Chad's offer of a security guard and she was using regular Tegucigalpa taxis to get around and had no car and driver. Now a strange woman with an unsavory reputation was offering to whisk her off into the darkest recesses of the most violent city in the Western Hemisphere.

"I would be delighted," she answered. Jahaira took out her cell phone and called her driver while Zelda paid the bill and they walked to the front of the hotel. A black sedan moved up to the curb and they climbed in. The car was driven by a tall, dark skinned woman in a headscarf.

The drive took her through parts of Tegucigalpa she had never seen. As always, she found the poverty disturbing as they passed plywood shacks and decaying stucco barrios. They came into a section where the streets were very narrow and the homes were very old and obviously had once been grand. Many of the homes had Moorish architectural touches. There were wrought iron bars on windows in fanciful designs, tiled roofs, and mosaic frescoes in geometric patterns on some homes, arched windows, geometric patterned masonry, Moorish arches and massive, heavy wood doors. Zelda recognized the style from her college days as *mudejar*, a Moorish influenced architecture that had flourished in Spain hundreds of years ago. But these homes were in a state of decay, some were canting badly to one side, tile roofs sagged, masonry was worn and cracked. They pulled up in front of a house, which was both older and simpler than many surrounding it. The house was rectangular and the beams supporting the sagging roof extended out from the walls. There was less ornamentation, a few arched windows with elaborate iron grillwork but no ornamented masonry. The cracked stucco walls revealed solid adobe brick.

They got out of the car, walked through a massive mahogany door and entered an anteroom with a large, carved mahogany staircase. Zelda noticed a picture on the wall of a stern, middle aged man in a prelate's garb holding a curved staff and wearing an archbishop's mitre, probably dating from the early nineteenth century, based on the clothing and style of the painting. There was something vaguely familiar about his dark eyes and narrow nose. "Is that a Cristales ancestor?" asked Zelda, gesturing at the painting.

"Indeed, from a long time ago."

"I do see a family resemblance, I guess you inherited something from the Cristales besides this house." Jahaira took Zelda by the hand and led her past the staircase through an arched doorway into a great room with a huge stone fireplace. Zelda felt a sudden tremor run through her body as Jahaira touched her. She found it both surprising and alarming. Jahaira moved a chair and table across from a large carved, mahogany chair that was already sitting in front of the fireplace.

"Please sit and I'll get us something to drink." She came back with an oval, clear glass decanter filled with a dark liquid and two delicate hand blown liqueur glasses. "These came with the house," she said, gesturing at the decanter and glasses. "Seventeenth century Spanish, brought over by early Cristales." She poured a glass for each of them from the decanter and took a sip. "This is a liqueur I made myself from herbs I learned about from my servant, Angelica. She was the one driving my car. She is a Garifuna, part African, part European, part Arawak and part Carib. She comes from a little village at the mouth of the *Rio Platano* called *San Miguel*. Your husband's expedition is there as we speak."

"You know about that?" asked Zelda startled. She tasted the liqueur, it was curious, both sweet and bitter at the same time. It reminded her a bit of green Chartreuse although its color was darker.

"You and I have a mutual friend."

"Oh really, it would be difficult to imagine who that might be." She took another sip of the liqueur. While the taste was peculiar it made her feel warm and pleasant.

"Peter VanOwen."

"Hardly a friend of mine. Hardly even an acquaintance. Just someone I knew briefly in college. By the way, I really like your liqueur."

"Thank you. I steep over one hundred and forty herbs in alcohol for three months. Many of the herbs are quite rare and hard to get. Angelica's family searches the forest for them and sends them to me. I got the feeling from Peter that you were very important to him, still after all this time."

"Again, hard to believe. How did you come to meet Peter? He didn't come as a client, did he?"

"Indeed, he did, referred to me by another member of your husband's expedition, Captain Cruz-Madrid. I found Peter to be very charming and quite nice. We had a delightful theological discussion and we also discussed *la ciudad blanca.*"

"Oh my god! More nonsense about the lost city. Think, Jahaira, what the money he is spending on that damn expedition could do for the poor of Honduras?"

"On the contrary, that expedition is about to make a monumental discovery and Peter, in particular, will insure that it does."

"What makes you think that? What makes you think any of these myths about a lost city in some godforsaken jungle are anything but nonsense?" As she continued to sip the liqueur, which seemed to taste better and better the more she drank, she found her eyes wandering to Jahaira, running up and down her body and lingering on her lovely face. Zelda was certain she had not ever seen a more beautiful woman.

"The stories about the lost city are more than just myths. You know that a National Geographic expedition just recently found ruins in *La Mosquitia* but what they found just touched the surface. I know because my father, as a young priest, actually saw *la ciudad blanca* and he learned its secrets."

"And what secrets would those be?"

"The most important secrets of all," she said, smiling directly at Zelda who found herself grinning back like a flirtatious schoolgirl.

"Jahaira," she found herself saying, "You are simply the most beautiful woman I have ever met."

"And you are very beautiful yourself. I noticed you at the hotel as soon as I walked into the room. You have a natural grace and confidence I admire." Zelda found herself blushing and feeling strangely excited. She took another sip of liqueur. In the background she heard faint strains of harpsichord music.

"Is that music I hear?"

"Yes, the Goldberg Variations performed for this recording by Andreas Staier, I prefer it to the well-known versions done on piano by Glenn Gould. The harpsichord reminds me of my childhood, there used to be one in this room and there always seemed to be someone playing it. Music seemed to fill the house in those days."

"It's beautiful, I love Mozart." The room was beginning to move around Zelda but she felt a surging sense of wellbeing.

"It is by Bach, actually."

"Could I have another glass of liqueur?"

"Of course, but first I would like to show you a seventeenth century silver crucifix, it is a lovely piece, quite unique. It's upstairs, come Zelda." She got up and once again took Zelda's hand. Once again, Zelda felt a sharp tingling all the way through her body at Jahaira's touch. She led Zelda up the mahogany staircase through a hallway into a corner bedroom. It was simply furnished with a large carved wooden sleigh bed, a heavy carved armoire and a side table. Hanging over the bed was a crucifix that must have been over three feet high in dark ebony wood, on which hung an exquisitely detailed silver Christ figure. Its wounds were excruciatingly detailed and it wore an expression of agony on its silver face. Zelda was beginning to feel a bit unsteady on her feet.

"You're right," she said, hoping she was not slurring her words, "it is exquisite. Are you religious, Jahaira?"

"Yes, very. I may be the most religious person you will ever meet. But my idea of god may be very different than the conventional view. Your friend Peter was quite shocked at my beliefs."

"Did you have sex with him?" Zelda was shocked and embarrassed that this slipped out.

"Of course, but unlike with most of my clients I did what I wanted with him, I like that. Do you want to have sex with me, Zelda?" The ravishing smile was once again aimed at her but this time there seemed to Zelda to be something almost wolfish about it.

"Well, I...," but Zelda knew the answer was yes. She had never been attracted to women. Not that she found it repulsive or immoral, it was simply something she had never felt. She liked men, found them compelling and stimulating, but this, this was something different. Jahaira came close to her, put her hands around Zelda's head and kissed her. Zelda had never felt such profound passion in a kiss and she returned it. Jahaira's tongue forced its way into her mouth and rubbed assertively against her own. Jahaira pulled her down on the bed and they clung to each other continuing to kiss. Zelda felt a hand under her skirt running up her inner thigh and probing her vagina. A sharp jolt of pleasure shot through her body at the touch.

Somehow she found herself naked, she wasn't sure whether she had shed her clothes or Jahaira had undressed her. She sat naked across from Jahaira who was also naked sitting on the bed with her legs apart wearing only a silver chain with a tiny blue stone carving of a monkey as a pendant. Zelda could smell Jahaira's sex and she found herself crawling on the bed towards her open legs, drawn to the warm, musky odor. Her tongue leapt to Jahaira's vagina, searching for her clitoris and aggressively licking once she found it. Jahaira wrapped her legs around Zelda's head in a powerful grip. As Zelda continued to lick, Jahaira moaned in pleasure and loosened her legs to release her. She pushed Zelda on her back and reached over to the drawer of the side table and pulled out a dildo and harness. She quickly stepped into it and stretched out over the prone Zelda, kissing her hard. Zelda relaxed and spread her legs as Jahaira inserted the dildo. Zelda wrapped her legs around Jahaira and they coupled for a long time, kissing as they went until Zelda expressed a suppressed moan and Jahaira withdrew.

Zelda awoke naked in the mahogany bed amongst sweat soaked sheets. It was dark outside and she was alone. Her head pounded and she felt queasy. She thought she remembered having a sexual encounter with Jahaira but she was not sure if it was a dream or really happened. As she lay on the bed trying to get her bearings, Jahaira entered the bedroom. She was dressed in a tight fitting black sheath dress with a V-neck. She looked cool and elegant. "I am sorry that I will have to take the car tonight but, when you are ready, Angelica will get you a taxi to take you back to your hotel."

"Isn't Angelica your driver?"

"At night I only go out with an armed driver, after all this is Tegus. Angelica has many talents but no skill with firearms."

"Will I see you again? We never even got to talk about how you can help me with my clinic." Jahaira bent over and kissed Zelda hard on the lips.

"Of course you will see me again. As to your clinic. I can get you your permits, I know exactly what you need and how to get it. Give me until early next week and I should be able to get you started. How altruistic of you to take time from your comfortable life to help the poor of Honduras." There was something about her tone that made Zelda feel she was mocking her.

"Thank you, I'll pay you what you want."

"I don't want money but I will expect your help when I ask for it."

"My help doing what?"

"Bringing Peter VanOwen to me; if he survives the expedition, I need to see him again but he may be reluctant to see me, I was rough with him the last time we met. But Peter will do anything you ask." Zelda felt a flash of jealousy. She did not want to help Jahaira see Peter and she did not want Jahaira to want to see Peter. She wanted Jahaira for herself.

Sixteen
ON THE *RIO PLATANO*

They gathered at the dock in a warm rain. The party was bigger than Peter had realized. There were the three archeologists, three student interns, himself, Arias-Garcia, Cruz-Madrid, the ten soldiers and a crew of a dozen Hondurans who were busy loading equipment on to a flotilla of eight zodiac rafts with outboard motors gathered at the dock. Peter was directed into a zodiac with Cruz-Madrid, now dressed in green camouflage fatigues like the soldiers, one of the interns, a soldier and a Honduran at the stern controlling the small outboard engine. A small group of Garifuna stood on the shore watching as the rafts pulled out into the channel and headed up river. Arias-Garcia and Doctor DeGroet were in the lead raft.

The channel they followed was surrounded by mangroves. Occasionally they passed an island with tall trees and thick foliage. There were hundreds of birds; blue heron, white egrets and even a few sea birds. From the salt smell of the air they were still at the mouth of the river in its delta. Peter was grateful for the rain poncho and bush hat. Without them he would have been soaked by the incessant rain. The intern was a tall, slender, small breasted girl with short blonde hair named Wendy Dirks. She was an archeology student from Michigan State who seemed excited to be on the expedition. Peter wished he could share her enthusiasm. She immediately assailed Cruz-Madrid with questions about Honduras, its history, government, politics and culture. Cruz-Madrid tried hard to appear authoritative and knowledgeable but Peter could tell he knew surprisingly little about his own country and was bluffing in most of his answers. He suspected Aramis had half-hearted designs on bedding the lanky girl and was trying to impress. In fact, Cruz-Madrid looked completely different in his jungle fatigues, with a .45 stuck in a green canvas holster on his hip, instead of his usual impeccably tailored and starched dress khakis. He looked like a tough but elegant combat veteran, almost heroic in a vague sort of way with his camouflage fatigue cap with captain's bars pushed rakishly back on his head like an early picture of Fidel Castro.

They finally emerged into a wider channel and there were no more mangroves, just tall trees and thick underbrush on either bank. "We are in the main river now," said Cruz-Madrid.

"How long will we be on the river today?" asked Peter.

"Until dark. We won't make the Pech village until late tomorrow so we will probably find a good spot to camp for the night. There is a Miskito village we pass today but I had the feeling Arias-Garcia was not comfortable staying with them."

"What's the problem with the Miskito?"

"Probably nothing. But they are known for not being fond of outsiders. You may have heard that back in 2009 the Miskito in Nicaragua declared independence from that country. Honduras does not bother them much but they would not be very receptive to having Honduran soldiers and a bunch of white men in their village."

"Who exactly are the Miskito?" asked Wendy.

"*Indios*, a local tribe, who, many years ago, intermarried with escaped African slaves and Europeans, perhaps pirates or shipwreck survivors to form a unique culture. Years ago, the English armed them and supported their aggression against other tribes and the Honduran government so they became the dominant group along the coast, other than the Garifuna."

"So interesting," said Wendy.

"What about their religion?" asked Peter.

"Mostly Christian, I think, but much more conventional than the Garifuna."

"So you heard the drums last night too?"

"It was hard not to. I just tried to ignore them."

"What's so unique about the Garifuna religion?" asked Wendy.

"You've heard of Santeria and Voodoo?" said Peter "the Garifuna have a similar melding of Christian and West African religious concepts. Last night I was foolish enough to creep out towards the drumming noise and I saw part of their ceremony. Laying out food and drink for the gods, dancing and singing to summon them. But Aramis, do they worship some sort of monkey god?"

"No, Peter," Cruz-Madrid laughed, "their gods are usually a combination of a Christian saint and a West African spirit, they don't worship animals. You know who is an expert on Garifuna worship, Peter? Our mutual friend, Jahaira. Her father taught her all about them and now she has a Garifuna servant, Angelica, who was a shaman for the village we just left. Jahaira would tell you they do not worship monkeys."

"Who is Jahaira?" asked Wendy.

"A young woman who is the illegitimate offspring of an old and aristocratic Honduran family. She lives in a seventeenth century house in a very old section of Tegus. They say she is a *bruja*, a witch."

"My god she sounds fascinating," said Wendy. "Is she really a witch? Can I meet her when we get back to Tegucigalpa?" Cruz-Madrid smiled.

"I do believe she is a witch, of sorts. Many people go to her for cures of ailments, to solve their romantic problems or to take revenge on their enemies. She has a reputation for being effective. There are even rumors she has cast spells on high ranking government officials but they are just that, rumors. She is a very clever woman and a keen observer of human nature but

I do not believe she has magic if that is what you mean by a 'witch.'"

"What do you believe Aramis, were you raised as a Catholic?" asked Wendy.

"Indeed, most Hondurans and every member of the elite families, are raised as Catholics. My mother was very devout, she made us attend church each Sunday and was always thanking god for the blessings he had bestowed on our family. As for me, I think I stopped believing when I was a teenager and I realized all the things I was dreaming of doing were sins, serious sins. I remember Father Mendoza at school telling us that even to think lustfully of a woman was offensive to god, offensive enough to get us condemned to hell for all eternity. I remember thinking that I could not help having those lustful thoughts, after all I was a teenage boy. So if I was going to hell just for thinking about those things I might as well do them and go to hell for the act instead of the thought. Then my uncle took me to the finest brothel in Tegus and I knew I was right. I just stopped worrying about all those things and live my life as though god does not exist. In the end, why would a god care about love play between men and women much less make it a mortal sin?" Wendy had blushed a bit at what Cruz-Madrid said but she persisted in the discussion.

"What about you, Peter? Did you grow up religious?"

"Not at all, my parents were both professionals, well educated, urban dwellers. They were agnostics, they said, but god or the idea of god played no part in their lives. If they were asked they would tell you that the existence of god could neither be proven nor disproven and that they were open to the possibility of his, its, existence. As for me, I tend to be more of an atheist. When I look at the world I don't see a lot of joy or love. Maybe in books and movies, but not in real life. I see a lot of suffering, poverty, wars, sickness, hunger, earthquakes, storms, tsunamis. If man really were made in the image and likeness of god, then how do you explain the cruelty, intolerance, social rigidity, greed, exploitation and violence that is an everyday part of human society? Is god like that and we are just pale images of what he is? Christians tell us that god is all good and full of love and forgiveness. That just seems impossible to me. So what about you, Wendy, what do you believe?"

"I was raised Presbyterian. We went to church a lot but not every Sunday. Sometimes there were soccer games or practice or family outings that interfered. I played a lot of soccer when I was younger. But I do still believe and stuff. I mean, man was given free will by god and just kind of thrown in to a difficult world. It's obvious god doesn't come down and reveal himself to people like he did in the old testament. He just kind of lets us do our thing and make our own mistakes. The sickness and natural disasters and stuff, I mean I just think that's part of the challenge he's given us. He wants us to struggle and prove ourselves."

From the lead raft, there was suddenly a shout. They could not make out what was being said but those in the front rafts were pointing towards something floating in the water being carried by the current. As it came closer, Peter could see it was a body.

Seventeen
TEGUCIGALPA

It had been twelve days since Zelda last heard from Jahaira. She realized when she returned to her hotel she had no way to contact her. She had no phone number, and no idea where Jahaira's house was located. She was forced to wait to hear from her. Finally she received a message to meet her for lunch at "Caneton," a small French restaurant near the cathedral.

As she waited for Jahaira she was nervous as if she were meeting her lover for the first time. As she thought that, she realized she was meeting her lover for the first time since they had become lovers, if, in fact that is what they were. The restaurant was one she had never heard of and could not find in any guidebooks. It was in a very old building, perhaps as old as Jahaira's house. There were only eight tables crowded together in the tiny dining room. Heavy, rough-hewn beams spanned the low ceiling, stucco walls were painted a light pink. The floor was worn terrazzo. Dim wall sconces provided most of the scant light with each table having a single candle. The waiters wore white jackets with black bowties. Soft jazz played in the background. Zelda ordered a mojito and looked at the menu. True to its name, the menu featured duck prepared several different ways, as well as foie gras and a black truffle salad. The prices would have been high for New York but were astronomical for Honduras. She assumed she would have to pay. The other diners were mostly middle aged and older men dressed in sharply tailored suits of linen or light worsted. At several tables, young, beautiful women sat with the older men.

When Jahaira entered the room most of the men looked up. She stopped at one table on her way to Zelda and greeted the two men like old friends. Once again Zelda felt a flash of jealousy. Jahaira was dressed in a black silk dress flared at the waist and black heels. She was wearing a bit of make-up this time, a little rouge, eyeliner and lipstick. She smiled brightly at Zelda as she sat down and quickly ordered a guaro sour. "You look lovely, Zelda," she said brightly.

"Thank you, I was worried because I hadn't heard from you in quite a while. I wasn't sure what was happening."

"I was busy taking care of your business, *carina*," as she said this she dropped a thick manila envelope on the table. "Inside you will find a license from the Health Ministry for the operation of a health clinic, a proposed lease for an industrial property located in *Barrio Rosales*, one of the poorest neighborhoods in Tegus, a place where people badly need health care. Also, there is a contract with a security company who will provide armed guards. It is the same company that many of the wealthy families use to guard their homes. They can be relied upon. Lastly, there is a permit to convert the industrial property to a health clinic and proposed contracts with a reliable architect to design the renovations and a contractor to do the work at a reasonable price. So you see; I have been busy on your behalf, not neglecting you."

"Jahaira, I'm stunned."

"Do not neglect the security. *Barrio Rosales* is where most of your clients will come from for this location but it is a very dangerous place. You will have gangs trying to extort money for protection. Not all security firms can be trusted."

"Thank you so much, I'll be happy to pay you whatever you want for all this."

"I told you what I want, did I not? I want Peter VanOwen and your help in getting him. Nothing else."

"Why such interest in Peter?"

"Are you afraid I want him as my lover? What if I do? Why should you care? Are you jealous?"

"It's just that he is such a pointless, drab character. I can't imagine why someone like you would find him interesting in any way."

Jahaira ignored her question. "Tegus was founded in 1578. This building we are sitting in was built in 1603 as a trading post for farmers and ranchers to buy goods. It is one of the oldest surviving buildings in the city. It has been used for many things over the centuries. They even say that for a while it was a brothel for the priests at the cathedral around the corner; just an old rumor, of course." The waiter came and Jahaira swiftly ordered a hearts of palm salad and fish quenelles, along with a glass of Sonoma sauvignon blanc. Zelda ordered a duck salad and a glass of Argentinian merlot recommended by Jahaira. In the background a singer sang softly in what sounded like Portuguese, interjected by long mellow saxophone solos. "Aah, Stan Getz," said Jahaira. "I saw him live once in Paris a long time ago."

"You must have had an interesting life, I'd like to hear more about it but, you know, you never answered my question about Peter."

"Yes, I deliberately avoided doing so, *carina*, everything about the man seems to irritate you. Perhaps you still have feelings for him? If he returns alive from this expedition of your husband's, he will have something I want. The fish quenelles here are excellent, by the way, they make them with a white fish imported from Lake Nicaragua."

"What does Peter have that you want?"

"Maybe his cock? Maybe his knowledge of good and evil. Maybe his faith in the redemption of the human race. I'll know for sure when I talk to him." Zelda sighed and played with her mojito glass. "I have told you a little bit about my life," continued Jahaira. "I was illegitimate; my mother was from a poor family. My father was from an elite family but he was a priest who ultimately became the archbishop of Tegus, presiding over the cathedral, which is just around the corner. My mother was a troubled soul and she committed suicide when I was very young. My father abandoned me as a parent but he did not completely ignore me. He taught me many things he had learned in his travels. He found I had, like him, a taste for obscure religions, cultures and rituals. His spiritual beliefs may have been a bit unorthodox but he understood human nature and how it related to our understanding of god. I appreciated that in him, but I never forgave him for refusing to acknowledge me as his child and for abandoning my mother when she most needed him. Even after all these years I am still bitter."

"Where is your father now?"

"Oh, he has been dead for many years."

"I'm sorry to hear that, perhaps if he were still alive you could have found a way to reconcile. He seems to matter a great deal to you still."

"Everything I am, both good and bad, I owe to him. Sometimes I am not sure if I should hate him or love him."

"How sad, how did he die?"

"I killed him," Jahaira said calmly. Zelda did not know how to respond, she assumed Jahaira was joking.

"You mean metaphorically?"

"I mean with poison. Aah, but our food is here now, shall we eat?" Zelda decided to drop the subject. She did not believe for an instant that Jahaira was a murderer. The woman loved to shock and to pose as tough and cynical. If she had poisoned the archbishop of Tegucigalpa, a man from a prominent and powerful family, she would not be sitting at the finest restaurant in town eating quenelles and sipping sauvignon blanc, she would be rotting away in some Honduran prison.

The food was excellent, every bit as good as a top French restaurant in New York. Of course, Jahaira was right about the wine. Zelda was not an epicure when it came to wine but as a woman of wealth who'd had several cultured, wealthy husbands, she had been drinking fine wines for many years and she recognized the Argentinian merlot as superior. Jahaira was a mystery, a beautiful young woman with exceptional taste in food, wine and music, who could navigate the maze of corrupt Honduran bureaucracy with ease yet who was apparently a whore and self-confessed murderer. Even more confusing, this beautiful, accomplished woman was deeply interested in Peter VanOwen.

"When will I see you again, Jahaira?" she asked as she paid the bill and they prepared to leave.

"What you really mean is when are we going to have sex again?" Zelda blushed because that is exactly what she meant. "It seems that everyone wants to fuck me. Sometimes it is a nuisance."

"Well I..." but Zelda's protestation was interrupted by a long hard kiss on the mouth in the middle of the restaurant, which attracted no small amount of attention from their fellow diners.

"Don't worry, *carina*," Jahaira whispered, "you will see me again in the way you wish to see me very soon." They parted and Zelda, swept away by the power of the kiss, climbed into her taxi in a daze.

While they were sitting in traffic on the way back to the hotel, a small motorcycle with two men aboard whizzed past them splitting lanes. Suddenly a half block ahead of them they heard the crackling of an automatic weapon and saw three young men on the sidewalk collapse in a spatter of blood. The group of young men they were with scattered. The motorcycle sped away, splitting traffic. "Aaah, Tegus...." sighed the taxi driver, shaking his head.

Eighteen
ON THE *RIO PLATANO*

The body appeared to be a *campesino,* dressed in rough cotton shirt and trousers with long unkempt black hair. A blood stained bullet hole in his back was clearly visible as the body swept past them in the current, heading towards the Caribbean. Peter found himself unsettled by the sight. "Well, they told us it was dangerous in *La Mosquitia*, a body here or there should not be surprising," said Cruz-Madrid.

"Yes, but I ignored all those warnings because I thought I wasn't going," responded Peter.

"He was probably a settler who had a run in with one of the rich landholders who are beginning to come into the area and cut down forest for timber and to create pasture for cattle. The small farmers who came in first when these lowlands were even wilder are trying to resist, but the big guys bring in hired guns so the settlers do not have a chance."

They had entered a stretch where the river was wider and the mangroves had disappeared. The forest on the banks was dense and the trees were thirty feet tall or more. There were still birds but the seabirds had disappeared. Once they had passed some overhanging branches where capuchin monkeys played. They had seen a small caiman swimming by itself but no crocodiles so far. The sounds of birds and howler monkeys were constant. After two hours in the Zodiac Peter desperately wanted to get out and stretch his legs. He noticed Wendy had not said a word since they passed the body.

"Wendy," Cruz-Madrid said gently "you must be strong, this is a part of the world where people are often cruel to each other and nature can be even crueler. We cannot let that distract us from our mission. Just because we witness cruelty does not mean we have to accept it. I guarantee you everyone in this expedition is only here for the scientific benefits to be gained and we will stick together to make sure that no one is hurt." Peter reflected that even though he was a father with a daughter about the same age as Wendy, it was the bon vivant bachelor, Cruz-Madrid, who had sensed Wendy's distress and tried to comfort her. Peter wondered, not for the first time, at his insensitivity to the feelings of others, something his ex-wife Miriam, and perhaps Zelda, could expound upon in detail.

"Thank you, captain," said Wendy as a tear ran down her cheek "it's just I've never seen a dead person before, outside of a funeral parlor, and he was murdered. I just don't have a lot of experience with death or violence and it's a little shocking, that's all."

"It is why life is so important," replied Cruz-Madrid, "we will all become like that poor *campesino* eventually, whether we are shot in the back or die in our beds. We will end up as lifeless shells, worthless pieces of detritus that will rot back into the earth. I know that sounds harsh, Wendy, but it is why we must savor every bit of the life we have because it ends all too soon and more often than not in pain and suffering. That is why I live the life I do. I know my family is a part of the great injustice that is Honduras and it saddens me, but there is nothing I can do to change things and I am not going to stop savoring life because of the fact there is suffering and injustice I cannot stop." He put his arm around the girl and patted her shoulder and she smiled up at him.

They had passed a few dugout canoes on the river but seen very few signs of human life. Here and there a crude cabin was perched on the banks of the river and once they caught a glimpse of a cleared savannah with grazing cattle, but as they moved west the forest became more and more dense and the only signs of life were the incessant calls of birds and howler monkeys. The rain had slowed down but not stopped and the humidity and heat were intense. As the river widened around a wide bend they saw a village perched on a bluff above a small sandy beach filled with empty dugout canoes. "It is the Miskito village," said Cruz-Madrid. The huts were similar to those of the Garifuna, made from crude wood planks and perched on low stilts with sharply peaked roofs made from palm thatch. From where they were on the river there appeared to be at least a dozen huts, probably more. A few figures were visible standing on the bluff. They were lighter skinned than the Garifuna, with straighter hair. They wore loose, light colored cotton T-shirts and shorts, a few were bare chested in loin cloths. It looked to Peter as if several had rifles. He noticed the soldier in their zodiac check his rifle and bring it up to firing position.

As they passed under the bluff in the middle of the river Peter heard a crisp popping sound and a whizzing overhead. There was splashing in the water beyond them as if someone were throwing small stones.

"*No dispares! No dispares!*" shouted Cruz-Madrid at the top of his lungs. Peter realized the Miskito had been firing at them. The soldiers in the other zodiacs glanced skeptically at Cruz-Madrid but did not fire. "Everyone down," he shouted, "they are warning shots. We do not want a firefight here. Keep down and let us get past them as fast as we can!" Peter glanced at Wendy who was hunkered down in the corner of the zodiac shaking. "Do not worry, Wendy," said Cruz-Madrid calmly, "they are just telling us to stay away from their village. We have more firepower than they do and we can defend ourselves if we have to but there would be casualties on both sides, there is no need for that."

Nineteen
TEGUCIGALPA

Doctor Roberto Castillo was a trim, short, slender, neatly dressed man in his early forties. He introduced himself and sat down across from Zelda in the dining room of the Marriott. There was a coffee pot and two cups on the table. Zelda was enjoying a plate of fresh fruit. There was a basket of coconut bread, *bolillos* and *pan dulce* and two place settings.

"What can I offer you Doctor Castillo?"

"Just black coffee and *pan dulce*." Castillo was dressed in a tan linen jacket, blue dress shirt, burgundy tie and white cotton slacks with oxblood loafers. He was a short, slender man with light brown skin, a thin pencil mustache, neatly trimmed black hair graying at the temples and large brown eyes. As he helped himself to coffee and rolls, Zelda recalled he had an undergraduate degree from the University of Pennsylvania and a medical degree from the University of Maryland medical school. He had interned at Johns Hopkins hospital in Baltimore and for a number of years been in the Honduran Health Ministry, but was now in private practice. He was a member of a prominent family but was known to be a progressive thinker who was concerned with the poor. Zelda was interviewing him to be the medical director of her new clinic. "I must say, Mrs. Toeb, I am very impressed at the groundwork you have done so far. To have licenses, a location and permits so quickly is almost a miracle. I also very much approve of the location. *Barrio*

Rosales is desperately poor and has no access to any worthwhile medical care. I think your clinic will be very busy. It was prudent of you to arrange for effective security, sadly you will need it."

"Well, I must confess, I had some help getting things started. I've worked in Africa for many years but Honduras has been a mystery to me. I would be lost without a guide."

"A most effective guide, I would say. Hopefully it did not drain too many resources from the clinic in order to obtain this assistance."

"Actually, not a dollar. But I wonder if I should be suspicious. Do you know Jahaira Cristales, Doctor?"

"The name is familiar. But I think the Cristales family does not acknowledge her as one of theirs. In fact, if you will forgive me, Mrs. Toeb, I believe the woman is a paid companion."

"You mean a prostitute?"

"Uuh, yes, exactly. I have never met the woman but I have seen her on occasion at parties and in some of the city's better restaurants. She is young and beautiful. But, you are not suggesting she is the one who helped you?"

"I am. She has been indispensable. I truly believe she wants to help the poor and this has been her way of contributing. If nothing else, her notorious profession has given her access to people who can help."

"And she has asked for no money?"

"Not a dime. She only asked that I put her in touch with an old college acquaintance of mine."

"Mrs. Toeb, first, may I say I came here with the hope you might offer me the post of medical director at your clinic. But I must say the involvement of this woman gives me pause. And I must warn you, do not trust her, not at all."

"Doctor Castillo, let me formally offer you the job. You are my dream candidate and we really need you. Look, I've spent some time with Jahaira and she seems like a very cultured and intelligent woman, perhaps bitter about her origins and her father's abandonment of her and her mother, but very genuine and extraordinarily competent."

"What does she say her origins were and who was her father? A Cristales?"

"She told me her father was a Cristales who was a priest and became archbishop of Tegucigalpa. She was illegitimate and...."

"Let me stop you right there, Mrs. Toeb...."

"Please call me Zelda."

"Zelda, there has not been an archbishop of Tegus from the Cristales family in many years, probably over one hundred years. She is lying to you about that."

"Why would she do that?"

"To impress you? She may have some more complicated scheme in which she wants to involve you."

"In her home she has an old picture of a clergyman she says is a Cristales ancestor. There really is a family resemblance."

"But you have no way of knowing whether the picture is really a Cristales ancestor or someone else or someone who is not related to her in any way. Where does she live, this woman?"

"I'm not exactly sure, I've only been there once, but it is in a very old section of Tegus, with lots of houses in the *mudejar* style. Hers is a very old house, three stories with arched windows and wrought iron grill work. She said it was built in 1612, that it was the Cristales' original town home in Tegus and the family gave it to her mother because her father could not acknowledge her as his daughter."

"Fascinating. I know the section of town you describe. It is entirely possible that a home in that quarter could be early seventeenth century and it is even likely once the Cristales family had a house there. They are a very old family, having first settled in Honduras in the Sixteenth century. But I know the Cristales family, my sister-in-law is a Cristales. They have no archbishops in recent memory and they have no scandals of illegitimate daughters popping up out of nowhere. I am not sure about their ancestral home but it seems highly unlikely you were in it."

"She seemed so convincing, I believed every word. Why would she do so much for my clinic without asking for money? I offered to pay her and I would have been generous. Everything she gave me has turned out to be legitimate, none of that was phony. I guess I just don't understand what she is up to."

"Zelda, look. First let me say I accept your offer. I very much want to run your clinic. It is the best chance to give back to my people that I have had since I have been back from the States. You and your husband have great credibility and I believe we can do something very good together. But let me do some research of my own to see what I can find out about this woman. In the meantime, please be very careful in dealing with her, in fact it would be best if you avoided her altogether."

That night while she was on the phone with Chad something occurred to her.

"Chad, you know everything about jazz, right?"

"Not everything, what do you want to know?"

"Stan Getz, he played saxophone right?"

"Yeah."

"Did he ever play in Paris?"

"Sure, so what?"

"When was the last time he played in Paris?"

"My guess is some time in the early 70's, why?"

"Someone told me she had seen him play in Paris, but it had to be more recently than that, she's probably not even thirty yet."

"Sweetheart, Getz died in 1991. She had to have been in diapers or maybe an embryo to have seen Getz at all, and definitely not in Paris."

Twenty
RIO PLATANO BIOSPHERE

The *Rio Platano* Biosphere Reserve is over 350,000 hectares of protected natural habitat encompassing virtually the entire *Rio Platano* watershed. It is the largest contiguous rainforest in Central America with 586 species of vascular plants and 721 species of vertebrates, including spider monkeys, capuchins and howlers, tapirs, anteaters, peccaries, pumas, ocelots, jaguarondis, jaguars, margays and even neo-tropical otters. There are 411 species of birds, and 108 species of reptiles and amphibians including at least seven species of highly poisonous snakes as well as crocodiles and caiman. The area is home to several indigenous tribes, including the Pech and Tawahka tribes and, recently encountered, Moskito.

Arias-Garcia expounded on these details at length as they lay in their tent on a high bank overlooking the river where the expedition had stopped at dusk to spend the night. As soon as they disembarked, the Honduran workers had set up tents, unloaded supplies and started the evening meal. Peter was surprised at how exhausted he was from simply sitting in a zodiac raft for seventeen hours but he responded when he heard the call to dinner. It was just grilled fish the Hondurans had netted on the trip upriver along with the ubiquitous rice and beans and cassava bread brought from the Garifuna village.

The rain had subsided somewhat as the expedition sat on the damp ground with their tin plates eating their fish, rice and beans and drinking filtered water from their canteens. Peter saw Selby across the clearing, sitting with DeGroet and Cruz-Madrid. Doctor Mellon ambled over with her plate and sat next to Peter. She was a solidly built woman in her mid-forties of medium height with dirty blonde hair, pale blue eyes, and a ruddy complexion. Peter was sure she would withstand the rigors of this adventure far better than him.

"How was your trip up the river Mr. VanOwen?" she asked in her slightly fruity south of England accent.

"Surprisingly tiring for a long boat ride, I'm dreading the journey inland once we get to the end of the river."

"It will be a difficult trek. I'm told we will pick up a Pech guide who knows a trail to lead us into the mountains. The Pech send hunting parties up there and they seem to be familiar with the various ruins, including the site the Geographic party found. Phillip seems to think the site we want is further back into the mountains and may not be easily accessible. In any case, all the various ruins are interconnected and represent the work of a single civilization, of that we are pretty sure."

"Do you think that this civilization is pre-Mayan?"

"Of course, there is no way to know given how little information we have, but my gut feeling says yes, at its oldest this civilization is likely to predate the earliest Maya settlements. Of course, there may have been some overlap at some point but in any case we should easily be able to establish the earlier dates of these ruins and perhaps even see if there is any link with Maya civilization. Doctor Selby was very complimentary about your work on his paper on the Oxkintok dig. Obviously religion was a very important aspect of Mayan culture and we do know a great deal about it, but the figures you found in Oxkintok may have represented a rather significant departure from Mayan religious orthodoxy. Doctor Selby seemed to think that your background as a philosophy major gave you a unique insight that an archeologist might not have."

"I doubt that and, of course, I haven't been exposed to

philosophy for decades so even if I once had that insight, I certainly lack it now. I do confess to an undying curiosity about the prevalence of monotheism in the west and polytheism in the earlier religions."

"Yes, the Maya, to the extent we understand them, were polytheists with a very loose hierarchy among their gods. Early western religions seemed to have a stricter hierarchy with Zeus, Jupiter and Thor, or his Germanic counterparts, being chief gods with authority over the lesser gods and more power. Even in Judaism, which, in most people's minds is the source of western monotheism, their religion evolved from an early polytheism derived from Canaanite theologies to incorporate all of the aspects of the multiple gods into Yahweh, all of the aspects except of course for evil. For that they needed Satan, who, while not a god himself nevertheless represents a kind of rival to the one god and the source of all evil."

"Islam had a similar problem in uniting the Semitic polytheist beliefs into a monotheistic one," noted Peter. "There too they had to find a source of evil which is separate from the one god so they came up with Iblis or Shaytan as the evil one. But the problem these monotheistic religions run into is Satan and Shaytan are actually creations of the one god making him the ultimate source of evil. In fact, doesn't the Koran say 'All things are from Allah'? Presumably, that includes evil things as well as good things. Which brings us back around to the Oxkintok figures which incorporated two traditional gods of good and evil into a single god. Was this a form of embryonic monotheism? If it was it doesn't appear to have made its way to the other major Mayan settlements."

"At least not that we know of," said Doctor Mellon. "Oxkintok itself had never been fully excavated and we know there are other Mayan sites that have not been properly explored. But now we head to *ciudad blanca* which is inevitably going to present its own set of unique mysteries. If the occupants of *ciudad blanca* are anything like the other Mesoamerican people, religion played a major role in their lives. We need to find out as much as we can about what they believed and how it affected their daily lives. No mean trick considering we will not be able to understand the writing they might have used, assuming, of course, it is not Mayan." The night was humid and the mosquitos were beginning to gather around them despite the heavy doses of DEET they had all applied at the direction of Arias-Garcia. Peter finished off his rice and beans and the last of his grilled fish and bade goodbye.

"It's been a pleasure talking to you, Doctor Mellon. I look forward to working with you."

"Call me Hanna, Peter, and, oh Peter, I think Doctor Selby feels you are angry with him for some reason, you might want to chat him up and clear the air."

"Thanks, Hanna, I'll do that." As he made his way back to the tent he was sharing with Arias-Garcia and Cruz-Madrid he decided he was no longer angry with Selby. He would do what he could to help him even though it might not make much difference to the career of such a far fallen academic.

As he lay in the nylon tent, bone tired, he heard the rain begin again. At first it was gentle and soothing but after a while it became hard and relentless. Peter was reminded of weekend mornings on those rare Los Angeles rainy days when he and Miriam would stay in bed and listen to the rain on the roof of their little Mar Vista bungalow. Those were among the few moments when they felt close and when the stress and anxiety of his life seemed suspended.

He lay in bed, holding Miriam as the rain beat on their roof. He felt a deep sense of peace, well-being and contentment. His life, which so often seemed complicated and pointless, for the moment felt satisfying. The rain continued to beat harder and harder until it seemed like a series of explosions. Suddenly he was no longer in his bed but falling inexorably through space, down towards the surface of the earth. His heart began beating rapidly and he was filled with terror at his seemingly inevitable high speed impact with the ground. He knew he was going to die. Below him, buildings and geographical features became clearer as he dropped. Suddenly when he seemed only a few hundred feet from the surface he stopped, and floated in mid-air. Below, he saw men dressed in black filling a trench with bodies that had been decapitated. The smell of decaying flesh emanated from the scene. Suddenly he began moving rapidly forward. Below, he saw a woman standing in the middle of a crowd. They were throwing stones at her. Peter saw one hit her head, which splattered like a dropped melon. He continued to move and saw below him a formation of men with rifles advancing behind pick-up trucks upon which heavy weapons had been mounted. Shells began to explode around them, a white gas spread from where the shells had exploded and the men began to fall in convulsions with their skin burning. He moved on and saw a group of Asian soldiers in green uniforms with red bands around their caps. They were in the middle of an agricultural field, it might be soybeans, in front of them a blindfolded man was tied to a stake. The soldiers fired at him and his body relaxed as blood streamed from his wounds. He floated over a bridge in a Latin country from which hung the bodies of many young men. He saw millions living in poverty, starving children, deformed and crippled men and women begging on street corners. Suddenly he hovered over a clearing in a dense forest in the middle of which was a huge monkey. It gestured at him as he hung in the air above it.

Twenty-one
LOS ANGELES, CALIFORNIA

Miriam Griffin sat in her BMW 740, caught in bumper-to-bumper traffic on the 405. Usually this kind of traffic left her stressed out but today she was in no hurry and there was a certain element of peacefulness in being isolated in a metal box with only her own thoughts for company. Her ex-husband used to call this sensation "freeway Zen", a chance for meditation and self-examination through isolation in the midst of an urban wasteland. She rarely agreed with his appraisal of most things but at the moment she understood what he meant.

Unfortunately, the Zen moment was interrupted by the technological miracle of Bluetooth as her phone began to ring and her dashboard screen showed it was her daughter Aileen.

"Hey Mom!" came the voice of her younger daughter, sounding tinny over the speaker.

"Hey babe, what's up?"

"Zach is a shit, he won't go to the agency party with me. Lorraine is going through a horrible break-up and is leaning on me way too much, god! And I'm not going to make my rent this month and I was wondering if you and Paul could help me out?"

"Sweetie, didn't you just have a shoot last week? Haven't you been working a lot lately? What's the problem?" Aileen was a model. Not high fashion, just spreads for Macy's, Target, Walmart and other local stores advertising in the *Times* or doing mailers. She was a beautiful girl, natural blonde hair, blue eyes, that scrubbed beachy look, the all California girl. She worked sporadically but when she did she made good money, or so it seemed, but this asking for cash had become a regular refrain. When Miriam had seen Aileen's name flash on the dashboard screen she'd figured that was what the call was about. She almost hadn't answered.

"I won't be paid for last week for a couple of weeks, you know the payment goes through the agency and they're never in a fucking hurry to pay. I had car repairs and I don't know where the money goes but it isn't much and it just goes."

"Paul is not going to want to fork over any more money for a while, between you and your sister, you're bleeding us dry, or so it seems to him."

"Well, at least I'm not a fucking little drug addict like Leia. Besides, I know Paul hates us." Actually Paul was *not* very fond of his two stepdaughters. He had always been grudging about paying their expenses even though Miriam had made it clear when they married that it was a package deal, her and the girls or nothing. They were beautiful, popular girls and Paul seemed almost to resent that about them. He also resented the fact that Peter, her first husband, had very little to do with them, and he was stuck with their problems, financial and otherwise, since they turned eighteen and Peter's child support checks stopped. He also resented the fact that the girls had never really taken to him. In fact, the girls disliked him intensely and never hesitated to remind her of the fact.

"Hey, I have a crazy out of the box suggestion, why don't you call your father and ask him for some money? I heard his coffee business was doing okay and he has a nice pension to pay his bills."

"Yeah, right, when was the last time we saw a dime from good old Dad? He's living it up in Costa Rica and doesn't give a shit about us. Actually, crazy as it sounds I did try calling him a couple of times. No answer."

"Not even on his cell? That seems odd."

"No, he just doesn't want to talk to me."

"Well, maybe he knew you were going to ask for money. I mean realistically why else would you call him? You know, now that I think about it I did get a call a couple of months ago from some old college friend of his who was trying to find him. He said something about an archeological expedition in Honduras. Maybe that's where he is? Probably not much cell reception in the Honduran jungle."

"Whaaat?" laughed Aileen derisively. "What would Dad be doing on an archeological expedition in fucking Honduras? That's ridiculous!"

"You're right, he probably just doesn't want to talk to you because he thinks you want money."

"Yeah. But seriously Mom, can you talk to Paul about helping me with the rent? I know he can afford it. Please!" Miriam's second husband owned a chain of discount shoe stores. At last count there were over 120 outlets. Paul could easily afford to help but aside from being infamously tight with money he just resented the hell out of his two step-daughters.

"Look, sweetie, I'll try. I don't know how much good it will do but I'll try. Meanwhile you're going to have to start budgeting. You can't just continue to go through life spending every dime as it comes in."

"Yeah, Mom, let me know as soon as you know something. And you know, maybe you should check on Dad. If he's dead, we own a beach house in Costa Rica."

Twenty-two
TEGUCIGALPA

Zelda stood waiting in front of the Marriott in a warm evening breeze as the sun began setting. She had butterflies in her stomach she had not had since waiting for the captain of the state champion basketball team to pick her up for her high school senior prom. When the dark Toyota pulled up, it was driven by a burly man in a dark suit and open collared white linen shirt. She could see the bulge of a shoulder holster under his jacket. "*Senora* Toeb?" he asked as he climbed out to open the rear door for her. She nodded and climbed in, half wondering if this was a kidnapping. She couldn't even be sure if this were Jahaira's car since all black sedans looked alike to her. As the wife of a multi-millionaire in the crime capital of the world she was a prime kidnapping target.

She had not heard from Jahaira since their lunch ten days ago so it had been easy to follow Doctor Castillo's advice to stay away from her. But when she called and invited Zelda to dinner it was impossible for her to refuse, even though Doctor Castillo had called to tell her what he had found. "The last Cristales archbishop of Tegus was Hector Cristales who was appointed in 1827," he had told her. "There has not been a Cristales appointed since, possibly because Hector was rumored to have dabbled in the black arts."

The car cruised through the usual ramshackle Tegus neighborhoods on its way to Jahaira's house. At night, they somehow seemed more threatening. There were groups of young men on the sidewalks, where there were sidewalks, that seemed menacing, but at least this time there were no shootings. The shadows from the sun going down behind the mountains were gone and the city was plunged into darkness. There were no streetlights on the roads they followed but on several streets illumination was provided by flashing blue and red lights on police vehicles.

When they arrived at Jahaira's ancient house, it was dark and she stumbled up the stairs to the heavy mahogany door. Before she could touch the knocker the door was opened by Angelica, the tall, graceful, Garifuna servant. Once again she was silent but gestured to Zelda to follow her. The great room with the fireplace was empty. Angelica gestured for her to sit in one of the large armchairs positioned by the fireplace. Angelica returned with an aperitif. This was different than the cordial Jahaira had given her the last time. It was a blackberry flavored liqueur, not overly sweet or alcoholic but resonant of the flavor of the fruit. As Zelda sipped, Jahaira entered the room wearing her warm, inviting smile and a long, sleeveless dress of green, gold and orange with a plunging neckline, which tightly hugged her curves and strategically displayed her cleavage. Zelda herself had dressed carefully, wearing a short black frock, which displayed her long, shapely legs and slim figure. "*Mi amor*, you look lovely, I am so happy to see you." The words, Jahaira's very presence and the blackberry liqueur all combined to make Zelda absurdly happy and she rose to greet her hostess and embrace her. The embrace turned quickly into a passionate kiss with tongues exchanged. They stood apart holding hands and looked at each other with giddy smiles. Another person had seldom made Zelda so happy.

Jahaira pulled her by the hand to a pair of large mahogany doors at the far end of the room. They went through them into a large, high ceilinged room with a ceiling studded by old, worn wooden beams. A long trestle table in the middle was set for two. Angelica brought a chilled bottle of sauvignon blanc beaded with condensation. Jahaira poured while Angelica came back with two small bowls of soup.

Jahaira raised her glass with a smile, "To Tegus' newest and best medical clinic!"

"I'll drink to that," smiled Zelda as she raised her glass, "what is this soup, it smells wonderful?"

"It is called *sopa de caracol;* a conch soup." There were chunks of tender, sweet conch in a coconut milk broth along with cassava, cilantro, green banana and a touch of crab with spicing Zelda could not identify. "I understand you have a medical director for the clinic now, Roberto Castillo?"

"Yes, he seems very qualified, and a smart, thoughtful man. It doesn't hurt that he comes from a prominent family and his cousin is vice president."

"Second cousin, once removed. Yes, by all accounts he is a very fine doctor. I have never formally met the doctor but I know who he is and I suspect he knows who I am. Have you discussed me with him?"

"Well...." Zelda hesitated, "as a matter of fact we did discuss you." They had finished the soup and Angelica cleared the bowls.

"Did he tell you not to trust me?"

"As a matter of fact he seemed unsure of who you really are. But Jahaira, everything you have done to help me has been legitimate, and besides, I care about you, I don't care who your father really was or what your real name is, I'm willing to accept you for who you really are." Angelica came back with plates of white fish simply poached in coconut milk.

"What, you do not think I am who I say I am, that my father was a Cristales? You think I lie to you?" She was clearly angry and her voice had become louder.

"Look, Roberto, Doctor Castillo, said that there has not been a Cristales archbishop in Tegucigalpa since the early eighteen hundreds and you said your father was a Cristales who was the archbishop. I don't know what to think."

"Were you doing research on me? Checking up on me? Nothing that has happened between us has led you to trust me?"

"Jahaira, you are a mystery. You yourself told me you were a prostitute and Colin Stevens tells me you are some sort of witch and then Doctor Castillo says your story about your father can't be true. Look, I don't care I just want to be around you, with you, okay?"

"*Carina*, I have never lied to you. I may not tell you all the truth but everything I do tell you is the truth. Now eat your fish, I spent many hours teaching Angelica to cook so that everything she fixes doesn't taste like Garifuna food."

"Jahaira, you may be a mystery but you are wonderful and beautiful and I am so sorry. I didn't mean to question what you told me. I do feel as if I can trust you."

"Perhaps Doctor Castillo's sources are simply wrong or they have missed something. Honduran history is not well documented. Perhaps I am just much older than you think I am?"

"Well, you are not two hundred years old, of that I'm sure," laughed Zelda, relieved that Jahaira had cooled down so quickly. In response, Jahaira gave one of her dazzling smiles.

They ate for a while in silence. When the fish was done, Angelica changed their glasses and brought in a bottle of red wine. Zelda glanced at the label and saw that it was a 1995 Chateau Palmer. Angelica then served plates with sliced duck breast, slices of grilled fresh pineapple and fried plantains. "The duck is marinated in sour orange juice," said Jahaira. "It is a technique I borrowed from the traditional Honduran recipe for *carne asada*." The duck was superb, tender, slightly pink inside, and with a lovely hint of sweet and sour citrus that was beautifully set off by the pineapple and slightly sweet plantains.

"You could be a chef, I'm surprised you haven't started your own restaurant."

"Tegus is a limited market for fine dining. Most families that could afford it have their own chefs and don't need to go out often. 'Caneton' is one of the few really good restaurants in the city and it is used for business meetings and romantic liaisons."

"Jahaira, why does Angelica never talk? I've never heard her say a word."

"Angelica has no tongue. It was cut out by a band of Moskitos stirred up by a priest who raided her village. The Moskitos are much more conventional Christians than the Garifuna. Angelica was a priestess among her people and she was known throughout Mosquitia for having remarkable powers. The priest called her a witch and told the Moskitos she was evil and an abomination and must be punished to please god. They thought if they cut out her tongue she could not recite the incantations and spells that displeased their god. She was frightened after that and I took her in and gave her refuge."

"My god, that's horrible!" Angelica had re-entered the room to clear their plates and brought in a platter of sliced fresh fruit; more pineapple, papaya, mango and *maranon,* or cashew apples. She brought out two snifters and a bottle of fifteen year old Barbancourt Estate Reserve and left the room.

"Angelica's story is typical of the violence and intolerance that goes unchecked in Mosquitia and really in other places in Honduras as well. But who is to say that does not please god? I have a feeling that god encourages this type of behavior, so in a way the priest who stirred up the Moskitos to hurt Angelica may have truly been doing god's work after all. What he failed to understand is that if the Garifuna had done the same thing to him, his god would have been just as pleased."

"Jahaira, that's terrible. Despite all the suffering in the world there is just as much kindness and charity in the world as evil and cruelty. How could you believe that about god? If I believed in one, it would surely be a good and merciful one."

"Without some goodness and mercy the cruelty and intolerance would be meaningless. I disagree with you that the goodness in the world is equal to the evil, there is far more suffering, cruelty and intolerance everywhere than genuine kindness and mercy. But without some well-motivated good behavior, the evil would simply be commonplace. There would be no contrast to underline the cruelty. It would just be normalcy. Perhaps even more important," Jahaira paused to take a sip of the Barbancourt, "without some good in the world there would be no hope and really, isn't hope the greatest cruelty of all?"

"I don't know, Jahaira, your view is so bleak; it disturbs me."

"Of course it does. As a non-believer you must find any meaning in the world around you and you have only death and the end of everything to look forward to. If you cannot see good around you, there is no meaning or at least no meaning you would want to live with. I have discovered a god who embraces the chaos of the world, who offers no hope but an ultimate freedom beyond what any other believer or non-believer could ever understand. I embrace the freedom of the chaos and accept the evil of the creator and it sets me free."

"Jahaira, you frighten me."

"As well I should. *Carina,* are you staying the night?" Zelda was instantly happy. "Then why don't we go upstairs?"

They climbed the old mahogany stairs together arm in arm. In the bedroom Jahaira undressed Zelda slowly, kissing her breasts as she undid her bra and laying her naked on the big wooden bed. Zelda trembled as she watched Jahaira undress and straddle her face. Jahaira bent over and began licking Zelda's clitoris while lowering her own pubis over Zelda's mouth. Zelda began licking, slowly savoring the taste of Jahaira's vagina. Jahaira came first, moaning softly. She turned around and lay down on Zelda, kissing her hard while gently kneeing her groin. Jahaira's hand reached down to Zelda's clitoris and began gently stroking. Zelda gasped as she came and Jahaira reached for the dildo and harness in the nightstand drawer. She slowly pushed her way into Zelda, kissing her hard as she entered. She began rocking in slow rhythmic strokes as Zelda whimpered in pleasure. "I'll do anything for you," whispered Zelda.

"Yes, you will," Jahaira said softly. They made love like this all night, it seemed, before an exhausted Zelda finally passed out.

When she awoke, as before, Jahaira was gone. She lay naked on Jahaira's bed, shaking her head and trying to wake up, when Angelica came in with a tray of *pasteles de coco, pan dulce*, sliced papaya and orange and a pot of strong Honduran coffee. She covered herself with the bedclothes as best she could and thanked Angelica. If there was one virtue about Honduras it was the coffee grown in the highlands which was sweet and delicate but with ample body. Zelda had learned to love it, and the coffee she was drinking was some of the best she had enjoyed in the country.

As Zelda enjoyed her coffee, Jahaira entered the room dressed in a simple, black cotton dress, "This morning I am going to the *curandera* shop I own in *Barrio Rosales*, it is my day to administer remedies to the poor of that neighborhood. Angelica is driving me but I have ordered a taxi for you to take you back to your hotel. Thank you for a wonderful evening, *carina*. I will see you soon." She bent down and kissed Zelda hard on the lips and caressed her naked breast with her hand.

Zelda showered in Jahaira's bathroom for the first time. She noticed while there were many glass and ceramic containers on the counter and in the medicine cabinet, none were labeled and none looked as if they were over the counter items.

Awake, fed, showered and at peace after a night of satisfying love making she sat back in the taxi as it meandered through the Tegus streets on the way back to the Marriott. Somehow, the streets looked entirely different than they did the night before or the last time she had visited Jahaira's house. There were no street names or addresses anywhere. She knew she could never find her way to Jahaira's on her own or give directions to a driver. She would have to depend on Jahaira's invitations to continue seeing her. As they drove, her cell phone buzzed and she answered. "Mrs. Toeb?" said a voice on the other end.

"Yes, this is Zelda Toeb, to whom am I speaking?"

"I'm detective lieutenant Anders Parsons, ma'am, Santa Monica police. I'm afraid I have some bad news for you."

"What's the problem, lieutenant?"

"I'm very sorry, ma'am, your husband has been found dead in your Santa Monica condo."

Twenty-three
PLAYA ESTERILLOS

Ophelia pulled off Highway 34 onto a dirt road with a battered sign which read *"Esterillos Este",* and rumbled over a rutted track to a cinderblock wall painted lime green with a metal gate. She got out of her rental car and immediately heard and smelled the ocean just beyond the green wall and the similarly painted buildings behind it. The gate was locked but to a girl who had grown up in the slums of *San Pedro Sula,* picking a lock was no great challenge. She opened the gate, pulled the car into the drive beside the small outbuilding and performed the same procedure on the door of the main house.

She stepped into a large open room with sliding glass doors facing the ocean. On her right was a large open kitchen, beyond which was a sitting area with a worn sofa and flat screen TV on the wall. Below that was an elaborate stereo with a turntable, large speakers and a rack of vinyl records and compact discs. Beyond the sliding doors there was a terrace with chairs and a table, a small yard with a low wall and a gate leading to a dark grey beach beyond which she could see the white flecks of foam on the ocean. To her left was a staircase. She walked into the kitchen area, checked the refrigerator and found eight or ten bottles of Imperial. She checked the other cabinets, finding containers of rice and beans and tinned meat. Finally, she found what she wanted; a liter bottle of *Flor de Cana*, and she poured herself a generous glass.

She walked out on the patio and sat down sipping her rum. Despite the heat, there was a breeze blowing off the ocean and there was no one on the beach within sight. Ophelia stood up and began unbuttoning her blouse, she slipped off her short skirt and shed her panties and bra, walked to the water stark naked and straight into the waves. Having lived in Costa Rica for a while now, she knew nudity on the beaches was frowned upon by Ticos, even those who flocked to the *zona rosa* to purchase sexual pleasures. She also knew she had broken into a house she had no permission to be in and really should not attract unneeded attention. But the breeze, warm water and her own pleasure in displaying her body and shocking onlookers was too much to resist. As she emerged from the water, pale, beautiful and glistening wet, a middle aged gringo walking his dog on the beach gawked at her. She waved and went back into the house to get a towel.

Ophelia Morales was born in a bordello in *San Pedro Sula.* Her mother was a great beauty, her father unknown. She spent her first few years as the pet of the dozen or so women who lived in the bordello, but her mother had more babies, became *gorda,* and got kicked out. They moved to *Colonia Pineda*, one of the poorest slums in *San Pedro Sula,* to a one room stucco shack with a corrugated metal roof. The neighborhood was controlled by the Barrio18 gang. The police were frightened to come into *Colonia* to patrol and never responded to emergency calls. Eventually, Ophelia had five younger brothers, each one with a different father, and her mother was too unattractive and worn even to walk the streets any more so she took in washing for people in the wealthy sections of town. Ophelia did not look like other girls, thanks, no doubt, to whoever her father was. She was pale skinned with large blue eyes and jet black hair. Someone had once told her she looked like a young Elizabeth Taylor, but she did not know who that was. She looked like a *gringa* and the local gang leader fancied her when she was only thirteen, before she was old enough to go and work in one of the fancy brothels. Ophelia had no choice but to submit to Ramon, the twenty-six year old leader of the local Barrio18. While Ramon was lean and handsome, he treated Ophelia like she was a possession and often slapped and beat her.

When her mother died, her brothers disappeared and Ophelia was no longer afraid to run away from Ramon who would surely have killed them. She went to Tegus where she was quickly hired in one of the top brothels in town. She often treated her customers with contempt, especially the older married ones who had wives and children at home. But she did not have to be nice to her clients, since they always came back and asked for her again. Her popularity allowed her to bargain with the brothel owners to limit the number of clients she took per day. Remembering her mother, she always took care to use birth control pills. A few years in a Central American brothel is an education about life and she never forgot any of it.

Ophelia went upstairs to grab a robe from the master bedroom closet and wandered into the study. There was a large floor to ceiling bookcase with books on coffee cultivation and roasting, and dozens of books of fiction. She recognized names she had heard like Joyce, Fitzgerald, Pynchon and Murakami. But these were all in English and she had only learned to read English in the last two years. There were a few volumes in Spanish, with authors like Borges, Marquez, Bolano and Llosa. These too were vaguely familiar names and she thought she would try the Spanish volumes before attempting to read in English. Until a few years ago she could not read at all and she had never set foot in a classroom. She was not even certain that *Colonia Pineda* had a school or that Barrio 18 would have allowed one.

As she walked down the stairs with a volume of short stories by Gabriel Garcia Marquez in hand, she heard a key turning in the lock. A stocky woman with a mop and bucket looked startled when she saw Ophelia. "*Hola*, I am Peter's girlfriend down from San Jose. He told me I could stay for a while when he is on his expedition in Honduras," she said in Spanish. She hoped there was not too much *San Pedro Sula* in her accent. She knew she did not sound like a Tica. The woman nodded and smiled and Ophelia took her book and went out on the terrace in Peter VanOwen's robe. Ophelia smiled to herself, she knew she could stay as long as she wanted. VanOwen would not be back any time soon, if he came back at all.

Twenty-four
RIO PLATANO BIOSPHERE

It was still raining when Arias-Garcia made the rounds to wake everyone up. As soon as they were out of their tents the Honduran crew began packing them up. There was cold rice and beans for breakfast. As they ate, Arias-Garcia produced an unlabeled glass jar, opened it and passed it around with cassava bread. "It is pineapple jam my wife made," he said with a shy smile. Peter helped himself to some on a piece of the cracker-like cassava bread and was pleasantly surprised. The jam was coarse and had large chunks of pineapple. It tasted fresh and tart, livening up what was a dull, heavy and tasteless meal and somehow lifting his spirits. He thanked Arias-Garcia profusely. "God be with you my friend!" said Arias-Garcia in reply, then rushed off to supervise the packing and loading.

The night's downpour had increased the volume and flow of the *Rio Platano,* making their trip against the current slower and more difficult. The rafts were finally loaded with the wet gear and supplies and they set off on the swift moving mud colored river. Peter reflected if the *Platano* were in this state on the way back it would make their trip that much faster.

There were fewer settlements on the banks now. The trees seemed taller and the jungle growth seemed even more impenetrable. Here the river was at its widest and deepest but the rushing current made the zodiacs tricky to control. Peter knew if the raft overturned he had no chance in this current.

Cruz-Madrid was chipper and smiling under his green poncho. Wendy was silent, staring at the banks as though she expected to see *ciudad blanca* appear on them at any minute. "We will be making a stop along the way at *Las Marias*," said Cruz-Madrid. "It is the last town of any substance left on the river. There we will get more petrol and rice and beans, maybe some fresh fruit. The town is mostly Pech, with a few Moskito and some *Ladinos*. Where we stop tonight will be a true Pech village. It is there we will pick up our guides. We will spend the night and the next morning we'll try to go as far up the river as the current will allow before we stop to set up a base camp. From there we go by foot up into the mountains close to the source of the *Platano*. It should be quite an adventure, eh Peter?"

The journey to *Las Marias* was uneventful. The rain stopped and the sun came out behind the overcast for a while. Even before they got to the town they noticed an increase in the number of dugout canoes they encountered on the river. Finally, around a bend in the river they saw a rickety dock and a dozen or so canoes pulled up on the sandy bank. As they got closer, they saw that the town was a collection of plank shacks and a few cinderblock buildings around some dirt paths, housing no more than a couple hundred people. There were no vehicles, other than a few dirty, beat-up motorcycles, no electrical wires or satellite dishes. They tied up the rafts at the dock and Arias-Garcia announced that they were to be back and ready to depart in one hour. Cruz-Madrid went off with his sergeant to talk to the local authorities about drug trafficker sightings. Peter noticed a blue concrete block building with a sign advertising Port Royal, a Honduran beer. He wandered over and found that it was the only tavern in town and had a generator to power the cooler which kept the beer cold. Inside the establishment was a long, heavy plank on sawhorses that served as the bar and Peter relaxed with a cold Port Royal whilst leaning up against it.

A small, lean, dark-skinned, barefoot man in a dirty cotton T-shirt and canvas shorts entered the bar and ordered a beer. He had large, green, feline eyes and moved with small, graceful movements. He looked at Peter and asked in Spanish: "Are you with the expedition?" Peter nodded. "You want the Pech to take you to the white city? I will tell you," he said "the Pech know where the true white city is but they will not take you there. Instead, they will take you to the site where they took the last expedition. It was a city but it is not the true white city. They still worship the monkey god and they wish to protect him and the temple in the true city."

"Well," said Peter, "what can we do to make them take us to the right place?" He had no idea if this man was telling the truth, if he knew what he was talking about or why he would be telling him this. But he was curious nevertheless.

"Are you sure you want to go there? The last group were happy with the ruins they were shown. That is where the Pech will take you."

"But you say the real white city is not there? There is another city, what makes that the true white city?"

"The Pech are the descendants of those who built the white city. Over time there were other satellite cities that were built in the vicinity, a civilization arose, but the original city was the center of worship, the place where the Pech first met their god. It was the largest city, the center of power and the place where the god came to be with them. It was only when the valley became crowded that the other cities began to be built but they always came to the original city to worship."

"How do you know all this?"

"I am half Pech, I know their traditions. I have been to the white city, it is no mystery to me. There have been those in the past who were allowed to visit the original city. Even white men, Spaniards. Go to the shaman when you get to the village, convince him that you are one who is permitted to visit the white city. Tell him to ask the man of the forest." Peter turned to sip his beer and when he turned back the man was gone. He finished his beer and trudged back to the zodiacs just as they were finishing loading up the fuel and supplies taken on in the town.

"Hey, Peter, you missed all the excitement," said Cruz-Madrid as they walked towards their raft, "somebody saw a jaguar right outside town. It is very rare to see a cat so close to a settlement, especially in daytime. Really stirred the villagers up."

Twenty-five
SANTA MONICA, CALIFORNIA

Zelda was shown to a long, drab, rectangular room with a conference table. On one wall was a green bulletin board with a staffing roster and a poster with safety rules. "Please sit down, Mrs. Toeb," said a tall, middle aged man with short reddish brown hair and a faint hint of freckles on his creased face. "I'm detective lieutenant Anders Parsons, ma'am, I've been assigned to investigate your husband's murder."

"You're sure then that it really is murder?"

"He was found in your Ocean Avenue condo with his throat slit. Time of death was approximately seventy-two hours ago. As I understand, Mrs. Toeb, you were in Honduras at that time?"

"Yes, I'm working on setting up a non-profit to provide medical care to poor Hondurans. Chad had provided most of the funding."

"You and your husband reside in Mountain View, is that correct?"

"Yes, that's where our primary home is, that's where my husband's business is located."

"Do you know what he was doing in Santa Monica?"

"I'm not sure. We kept a place here because he had to come down on business so often."

"Did your husband have any enemies? Anyone who might be upset enough with him to want to hurt him?"

"He has an ex-partner who helped co-found his company who got bought out years ago before the company really started to grow. I know he's bitter and still angry at Chad. His name is Dwight Newman and I think he lives in Stockton now, but Chad hadn't heard from him in a couple of years as far as I know."

"I hate to ask these questions, Mrs. Toeb, but what was the state of your marriage? Was Mr. Toeb seeing someone, did you suspect he was involved with someone?"

"Well, to be honest we were growing apart somewhat, spending a lot of time away from each other. I didn't know of any one that Chad was involved with, but to be honest, it's not impossible."

"What about yourself, Mrs. Toeb, are you involved with someone else?"

"No, not at all," she lied quickly, "that's not my style."

"When we checked with your hotel in Honduras they said you hadn't slept in your hotel room the night Mr. Toeb was killed. Can you explain that?" Zelda felt her stomach tighten.

"I spent the night at a friend's house, a woman friend, who has been very helpful in setting up the non-profit. We had dinner at her house and had some wine and it was late and she let me stay the night so I didn't have to try and get a taxi to take me back. Tegucigalpa is kind of a dangerous city, especially at night."

"Can we get a name and a phone number for this friend?"

"Well, her name is Jahaira Cristales, but she has no phone, no cell phone I know of either." Parson looked at her quizzically, his watery blue eyes exhibiting no emotion.

"No phone, what about an address? An address for the place you stayed that night? Anyone else see you there?"

"She has a servant, named Angelica, she saw me there. I...I don't know the address of her house. You have to understand that in Tegucigalpa, in all of Honduras, they really don't use addresses. But I'm sure I can get her to contact you and give a statement, maybe Angelica too. We just had dinner and talked and drank wine and rum. I'm not really a suspect, am I?"

"Your hotel confirmed that you were there early on the morning after your husband was killed. It is virtually impossible for you to have murdered him in Santa Monica and gotten back to your hotel in Honduras the following morning. There are no direct flights from L.A. to Tegucigalpa and neither the airlines, customs and immigration nor TSA, have any record of you having been on any flight that night. But, Mrs. Toeb, who stands to benefit from your husband's death?"

"I don't know. We had a prenup, I don't think I was supposed to get any of his money."

"Mrs. Toeb, the prenuptial agreement only applies if you were to be divorced or separated. Mr. Toeb's lawyer tells us his trust leaves everything to you. He had no children, no other immediate family, only an ex-wife he apparently didn't like very well. You stand to become a multi-millionaire, Mrs. Toeb, they tell us his estate was worth well over two hundred million. So if you ask us whether or not you're a suspect, well, no one else has a motive anywhere near as good as you do Mrs. Toeb. We know you didn't kill him yourself but we can't rule out murder for hire, especially since the person who killed him handled a knife with professional skill."

"Do I need a lawyer?"

"Not my job to advise you on that. It does seem like you can afford one, a good one. Oh, and, Mrs. Toeb, we'd like you to stay in the area until our investigation is done." Zelda's heart sank. All she could think about was when she would be able to see Jahaira again.

Twenty-six
BARRIO ROSALES, TEGUCIGALPA

The *Botanica Dios Mono* was in a small wood frame building on *Calle Verde*. The *Barrio Rosales* was a poor, old section of Tegus made up primarily of unpainted wooden shacks with corrugated metal roofs. There was no park in *Barrio Rosales*, no school, no library, no public square. Most homes lacked electricity and plumbing. The residents went to public taps to get water. The sound of *punta* music, played on tinny speakers on battery operated boom boxes, blared, dirty half naked children played in the potholed, dirt streets. An acrid, fetid smell filled the air, a mixture of charcoal smoke and human excrement. The *botanica* was located between a fruit vendor and *panaderia* on a street of mixed commercial and residential buildings. The line outside the *botanica* was longer than either of its neighbors, mostly women of all ages with children in tow, a few older men scattered into the mix.

Jahaira sat in a back room in a handmade wooden rocker wearing a simple black, cotton dress, her long black hair pulled back. The walls of the room were filled with shelves which contained unmarked jars and vials, some with leafy herbs others with unidentifiable animal parts. Gabriela, the young woman who ran the shop for Jahaira, ushered in a woman with a small boy in dirty cutoffs and white T-shirt, no older than eight or nine. She was older, which in this barrio meant in her forties since few here lived much beyond that. She wore a simple black cotton skirt and a stained white blouse. Her feet were in a pair of badly worn plastic flip-flops. Her skin was dark brown with high cheekbones. Like most people in this barrio she was *indio* or *mestizo*. Her long, coarse black hair was worn in a single braid down her back. "*Curandera*, my son has a sore on his leg that will not heal. It has been three weeks and it still is bad." She pointed to her son's leg, which was oozing puss and was discolored an angry purplish black. Jahaira knew it was infected and that he needed medical attention but there was nowhere for him to get it. She reached to an upper shelf and pulled down a ceramic jar.

"Your son needs to see a doctor but for now use this salve on the wound, rub it on twice a day after cleaning the wound and dress it with a clean bandage. I hope you can find a doctor to help him." The salve was made from the heart of a saw palmetto found in the rainforest on the Caribbean coast, which was ground down and mixed with alcohol. This combination was an effective topical antibiotic but the infection was so far along Jahaira was not sure it would be enough, she knew it was unlikely the woman would find a doctor. She charged the woman one hundred lempira knowing that if she gave the medications away for free her customers would disregard them, but if she charged, even a nominal amount, they would consider them more valuable.

The next customer was a young girl, no older than sixteen. She was thin, with long greasy hair and a gaunt, sunken face. She was pregnant and wanted to abort. Jahaira had a potion for this which she knew would work since the girl was still in her first trimester. This was five hundred lempira, to teach the girl to be more careful in the future.

She was followed by another, slightly older, girl, also slender with thin twig like legs, high cheekbones and almond eyes. She told Jahaira she wanted a man to love her and could she give her a potion to make him want her? Jahaira told her that she could but there was a distinction between love and desire.

Would desire be enough?

"It would," said the girl, "if he wanted me, he would soon learn to love me."

"It does not always work that way," replied Jahaira, "not many men know how to love, but if you learn how to use their lust to lead them where you want, you can get whatever you desire from them, even without love. In any case love is not something you should trust." She gave the girl a powder made from the seeds of a bitter fruit that grew deep in the rainforest. It was a powerful and effective aphrodisiac. She told the girl to dissolve it in a beverage and give it to the man she wished to seduce. Once consumed, even a little stick like her would be irresistible to him.

After she left, Gabriela came in and announced that a Doctor Castillo was here to see her. Jahaira sighed and told Gabriela to show him in. Castillo was a small, slender man with graying temples and tortoise shell glasses with thick lenses. He wore a tan linen suit and a white cotton shirt open at the collar. Jahaira noted with pleasure that he seemed nervous.

"We have never met," he said, by way of introduction, "but we have several mutual acquaintances and, I believe, we sometimes move in the same circles."

"It is my pleasure, Doctor, I am aware of your reputation and, of course, we have at least one mutual friend in Zelda Toeb."

"That is precisely why I have come. As you may know, Mrs. Tocb has hired me to be the medical director for the clinic she is trying to establish. I believe this is a very worthy project and one which I wish to see succeed."

"As do I, Doctor Castillo. I have tried to help Zelda in any way possible. And, to allay your fears, I have not done this for my own gain but to help provide medical care for the poor. I realize my reputation in the circles which you frequent may be a bit unsavory. I have not had the benefit, as you have, of being an acknowledged member of a powerful and wealthy family. My only real asset in life has been my beauty and I freely admit I have taken advantage of it to allow myself to live comfortably. I have no shame about this and make no apology but that does not mean I do not care about the poor and would not do what I can to help them."

"And yet, I find you selling potions to the poor, taking their hard earned money for a few crushed herbs. How is that caring about the poor?"

"If these people had a clinic to provide care, like what Zelda has proposed, they would not need me for medical help. But, do not assume Doctor, what I give them is useless. The folk medicine of the Garifuna and the *Indios* do provide effective remedies for some things. Just because I am not a medical doctor or have a university degree in biochemistry does not mean I have no knowledge of the curative properties that can be derived from the rainforest. I do what I can for these people and I charge only enough to convince them that my remedies have value. In a way, the lustful activities of your colleagues, for which they pay dearly, is subsidizing my service here to the poor."

"*Senorita* Cristales, or whoever you really are, I do not know you and I frankly have no reason to trust you. I have seen Mrs. Toeb holds you in high esteem and you have great influence on her. The woman, despite her best intentions, has no understanding of Honduran culture. She is an innocent who trusts you. Please do not do anything which would interfere with her project, it is of such great importance to the poor here in Tegus."

"You seem to imply that I am some sort of charlatan who is trying to manipulate Zelda. I have not lied to her, regardless of what you may think, and I have helped her and asked only one favor in return."

"And what favor was that?"

"For her to arrange for me to meet again an admirer of hers, that is all."

"For what purpose?"

"Why romance, of course. An older man, much the same age as you, Doctor, who I wish to know much better. A fascinating man with a special gift, quite irresistible to a woman like me who is, at heart, a romantic." She smiled her dazzling smile as if conspiring with Castillo who must surely know what women were really like. "I give you my word, Doctor Castillo, I will do nothing to interfere in any way with Zelda's clinic and I will do as much as I can to help, and I think you know, Doctor, I can help a great deal." The doctor nodded as if this is what he came to hear.

"One thing, *Senorita*, was your father really a Cristales?"

"Oh yes, I remember your sister-in-law is a Cristales. Yes, my father was a real Cristales, but it makes no difference whether or not you believe my story. Now please, Doctor Castillo, as you have seen there is a long line of poor people who wish my help. I have given you my promise, which I do not do lightly. So please leave." Castillo shook his head as if not sure whether to believe her but turned to go. "Oh, and Doctor Castillo, please be sensitive with Zelda when you see her next."

"I do not understand..."

"Her husband was brutally murdered several days ago in the United States, she has left to go back to see to funeral arrangements and assist with the investigation. Curious, I thought such things only happened in Honduras."

Twenty-seven
PLAYA ESTERILLOS

Ophelia liked Peter's house. The beach outside its doors was almost always deserted and she sat out every day puzzling over the stories of Garcia-Marquez. In many ways they were like the stories the women would tell in the brothel in the early afternoon before customers started coming. The stories were about the Quetzal or the monkey god or strange old women who were *brujas* and cast spells on poor unsuspecting villagers or those who angered them. They told about walks in the forest where they encountered talking jaguars or dead people or beautiful naked women who told the future and worked miracles, some good, some not. Ophelia loved these stories. They were an escape from the world in which she had grown up, a world where there was not enough to eat and no bathrooms and there was always noise and crowds and often violence. It was a world where the gangs were kings and they were cruel and unforgiving.

She sat by the beach in Peter's chair, drinking Peter's rum or sipping one of his Imperials, watching the clouds roll by and the tide come in or go out day by day. She did not really know how to cook and there was not a lot of food in the *gringo's* house so she ate at the little local restaurants, the Ticos called them *sodas*. When she walked into one, every male in the house, waiter or guest, looked at her up and down, running their eyes over her body, undressing her in their minds. When they first saw her they seemed to think she was a *gringa,* but when she opened her mouth to speak Spanish to them they knew she was just a girl from the *barrio* and not even a Costa Rican *barrio.* The Ticos all thought they were better than the Hondurans or Guatemalans or especially the Nicaraguans. So she learned that whenever she tried a new place, to speak in English. It was funny that she learned to speak English with little or no accent but she could never lose her *Colonia Pineda* drawl that let every Spanish speaker know this pale skinned, blue eyed beauty was just another *puta* from the *barrio,* which, of course, is exactly what she was.

Or at least, what she had been until the *bruja* showed up. The brothel in Tegus, the *Diamante Azul,* had been the best place she had ever lived at that time. She had her own room, ironically with a large wooden crucifix over the bed she took her customers in. There were clean bathrooms and better food than she ever had. They let the girls go into central Tegus to go shopping some mornings and they would all sit around and laugh and joke until the customers started coming around in the evening. For all this, all she had to do was let some sweaty rich man pin her down and grope and penetrate her for an hour. For this, and the drinks and food the brothel supplied their customers, they paid a lot of money, a small part of which, a very small part, went to the girls. But in the *Colonia* she had been the property of a gang leader who not only took her whenever he wanted without paying her a *lempira* but who slapped and kicked her when he felt like it to show the others he was a real man. In the brothel they had security that would protect her if a customer got too rough without her consent. Her only worry at *Diamante Azul* was what would happen when she began to get old and lose her looks. The oldest girl there was in her early thirties, most were in their teens or early twenties. The day would come when she could no longer work there and she would be back on the streets.

That is why, when the *bruja* came to the brothel and wanted to buy her she did not resist. Ophelia had never believed in *brujas* or any of those stories she loved but knew were not real. But this woman was different and Ophelia knew it from the moment she set eyes on her. She was beautiful, this woman, quite stunning in a very Latin sort of way. She had long, dark, silky hair, dark brown skin that was soft and unblemished, dark eyes and a lovely body with rounded curves. She must have been about the same age as Ophelia, maybe a little older but she had a sense about her that seemed much older. The other girls said she had powers, that she sold potions and had bewitched the ministers of the government. She came with a man one night, a very distinguished member of an elite family. They drank rum in the reception room of the *Diamante* with its plush chairs and flocked wallpaper. The girls were made to parade in front of them so he might choose which one he would go with. The *bruja* gave him advice about which one to choose. When Ophelia came before him she said nothing. She was the most beautiful girl in the house and Ophelia had felt sure he would pick her and she sensed he wanted to, but when he looked at the *bruja* she made a little wave of her hand and he asked for the next girl. But she did notice how the *bruja* looked at her, appraising her and running her eyes over her body. He finally picked Maria, a very young *Indio* girl from the countryside who had only recently come to the *Diamante*. When the man went off with her the *bruja* gestured to her to come over. "*Senorita,* what may I do for you," she asked deferentially.

"Tell me about yourself, what is your name, where do you come from, why are you here?" Ophelia told her everything, that she came from *Colonia Pineda* in *San Pedro Sula*, that she had nothing, had escaped an abusive gang leader, could not read or write, knew nothing of her father. "Ophelia is a beautiful name. Do you know of Shakespeare? Have you heard of Hamlet?" Ophelia had not. "Shakespeare was an *Ingles* who wrote a story many years ago about a prince named Hamlet. In the story his *novia* is a beautiful young girl named Ophelia. Sadly he breaks her heart and she commits suicide because she is so sad. But I would guess that no one breaks your heart, if anything you are the one who does the breaking." She smiled at Ophelia, a smile so dazzling and infectious that it made Ophelia smile in return, an expression that rarely crossed her face.

The *bruja* came back several times by herself and paid the brothel to spend time with her, just talking and answering questions. Then, one day she came and asked if Ophelia would like to come live with her, that if she did, the *bruja* would pay the brothel to release her. She would not be a servant, but a kind of student who would learn the skills and knowledge the *bruja* possessed. She would be a kind of assistant to the *bruja*. To Ophelia this was a difficult decision because the *Diamante* was a good life, the best life she had ever known, and she did not know what life with the *bruja* would be like. But something told her that she could trust this woman and if she went she would no longer worry about what would happen when she became old and lost her looks.

The *bruja* lived in an ancient house in a part of Tegus she had never seen, a district of cobblestone streets and old, tall houses once occupied by the rich but now decayed. She had her own room and, for the first time in her life, her own bathroom. The food was the best she had ever eaten, there were amazing dishes she had never known before. The *bruja* bought her beautiful clothes, the finest she had ever owned. In the cellar of the old house was a workshop where the *bruja* prepared remedies and potions to sell in her *botanica*. She taught Ophelia how to prepare the simpler ones and lectured her about the properties of dozens of herbs and seeds. She told Ophelia stories about the people of the Mosquitia who believed in an evil monkey god who loved seeing people suffer. She gave Ophelia a lovely necklace, real silver with a blue stone carved like a monkey. "It is so we do not forget the monkey god," the *bruja* said, smiling when she gave it to her.

Then one day, after they had been sitting and talking while drinking a homemade liqueur the *bruja* had made herself, she kissed Ophelia. It was not a sweet kiss between sisters but a hard, passionate kiss like you would give your lover. It surprised Ophelia but she did not dislike it. When the *bruja* kissed her again she found herself kissing back and before she knew it they were in the *bruja's* bedroom doing things Ophelia had never done before. She had been a *puta* but not once had she ever thought about a woman in that way. In the *Diamante* there were girls who did that sort of thing and no one cared, but Ophelia had never even been tempted. Not that she got much pleasure from the men she had known. In her view you had sex to get something in return. She let Ramon take her because he protected her from the other gang members and from anyone else. At the *Diamante* she let the customers take her to have a clean place to live and food to eat and some spending money. And even here, she gave herself to the *bruja* for her room and board and clothes and her monkey necklace. But she had to admit that this was different. The *bruja* knew how to pleasure her and for the first time her practical lovemaking was enjoyable as well as profitable.

For two years she was the lover of the *bruja,* who taught her how to read Spanish and speak English, gave her books and taught her potions. Then one day she asked Ophelia to go to San Jose, Costa Rica.

Twenty-eight
RIO PLATANO BIOSPHERE

The river narrowed and the current became faster. The trees on either bank seemed taller than those further down river, so tall that the river was covered in shadow most of the day. They began to encounter large rocks in the river. Peter marveled at the skill of the Honduran pilots as they managed to steer around the rocks in the ever increasing current. He told Cruz-Madrid about the little man in the bar in *Las Marias*. "Probably just some drunk, too many *cervezas*," said Cruz-Madrid. "It is my understanding that the Pech are thoroughly Christian and they no longer have shamans. But we do know that the site the National Geographic expedition found is not the only one in the area and there may be a bigger find somewhere close by. The LIDAR data confirmed that. If the Pech really do know how to get to it we need to find a way to persuade them to take us there. "

"He said to tell them to ask the 'man of the forest 'and that I was some sort of special person to whom they would be willing to guide there."

"Well. That seems unlikely."

"Don't a lot of these indigenous cultures believe in half man, half animal forest creatures?" asked Wendy, who had been following their conversation.

"But the Pech have supposedly abandoned those superstitions and converted to a conventional Christianity," replied Cruz-Madrid.

"This village is pretty deep into the forest, maybe they didn't get the memo?" said Wendy. As they wove their way through the burgeoning current they saw macaws, green parrots and flocks of unidentifiable birds that squawked loudly as they settled in the trees. They looked closely for the telltale movement of tree branches that signaled the presence of monkeys and occasionally saw groups of spider and white faced monkeys playing in the tree tops. They heard the low-pitched growling grunt of howler monkeys but saw none. Suddenly they heard a call from the front raft that they were approaching crocodiles in a calm pool-like stretch of the river. Peter had seen them often on the *Rio Tarcoles*, north of his Costa Rica home, but here they were right on top of the rafts. Peter lost count after twenty. Most were semi-submerged, a few were on the rocky bank, basking in the sun. The crocs paid no attention to the rafts and they left the calm stretch through a channel in a barrier of rocks, back into a narrower and faster section of river.

They did not stop for lunch, but ate cassava bread and tinned meat on the rafts as they traveled. By the time they saw the Pech village in the distance the sun was going down. It was on a bluff above a sandy stretch of beach in another calmer, pool like stretch of river. There was no dock, just a line of dugout canoes drawn up on the sand. Peter was stunned at the crudeness of the huts. They had steeply peaked thatched roofs with walls of sticks laced together with vines. Some of the structures were just pavilions with no walls at all. As the rafts were pulled ashore it was obvious they were expected. A welcoming committee of bare chested men dressed only in baggy shorts came to meet them. Arias-Garcia greeted them and spoke with an elderly man who seemed to speak Spanish. He motioned for the expedition to follow him as they walked into the village. Peter was greeted by an overwhelming smell of overripe fruit and human excrement. In the huts they passed they saw women and children with long, straight black hair dressed in faded cotton shorts and T-shirts. They were shown to a group of huts at the edge of the village farthest from the river. Peter ended up in a hut with Cruz-Madrid, Arias-Garcia and Doctor DeGroet, all three of whom immediately left him and went off into the village together. As he waited for them to get back he spotted Selby arranging his gear in a hut across from him. He got up and walked over. "Hey, Terry, look I just wanted to say I'm not angry, I'll help you if I can." Selby looked at him, peering over his glasses.

"And, I'm sorry I dragged you into this man, it was really selfish, I was, am, desperate, and in the end I'm not sure we'll find anything worth writing about. It all looked different before we got here. Now, in this fucking jungle, so far away from everything, I gotta tell you I'm kinda freaked out. This is not like Yucatan where every night we went back to the camp, had tacos and drank Modelos and shot the shit. This is heavy shit and you're only here because I shanghaied you. God I'm not sure either one of us will make it out and we haven't even started the hard part yet."

"I know, but what's done is done and well, this is sort of an adventure and it has been interesting, sort of."

"Yeah, I guess. Hey I never did find out how it went with Zelda."

"It was a disaster in every way conceivable. Totally humiliating."

"And back in Tegucigalpa, at the airport, was it Zelda who did that to you or did you just go on a bender in a tough town?"

"Neither and I don't even know how to explain it. But I met a woman who beat the shit out of me for no reason. She was someone Cruz-Madrid knows, a real Honduran beauty but strange as hell." They were interrupted by Doctor DeGroet coming into the tent.

"Aah, Mister VanOwen, there you are. I was just looking for you in our hut. Can you come with me? The village *Wata* has requested that he speak with you."

"The what?"

"*Wata* is what the Pech call their shaman. Follow me,

please. Captain Cruz-Madrid told him your story about meeting a man in *Las Marias* and it got the *Wata's* attention. By the way, he speaks Spanish, not many here do." DeGroet led Peter through the village to a hut at its center, which looked no different than any other hut. "He wants to talk to you alone," DeGroet said, gesturing towards the door." Peter walked into the hut.

The hut had a strange herbal smell to it. It was sparsely furnished with a bed mat made from river rushes, a small, crude wooden table and a basket of clothes in the corner. An old man was seated on a stool behind the table. He was short and slender with long, white hair, deeply brown, wrinkled skin, high cheekbones, narrow almond shaped eyes and thin lips. Peter noted immediately that he wore a rawhide necklace with a blue stone monkey pendant identical to Jahaira's and Ophelia's. "So you are the one," he said, more as a statement than a question. "Once, a very long time ago there was a white man, a Spaniard, who came to us like you. He was a Christian priest but he understood our beliefs."

"I thought the Pech were Christians."

"Maybe in *Las Marias* but not here. We worship the old gods here, the same as our ancestors who built the white city. Our god has not been kind to us, our numbers have dwindled, we have many enemies, but our god still comes to us and talks to us and whether he favors us or not we know his power and we fear his whims."

"He comes here to this village?"

"No, he comes only to the white city and few of us have seen him, he sends to us the man of the forest who tells us what the god wants."

"Have you seen the god?"

"Only once at the white city after we had taken the mushrooms. He came to me as a Jaguar and we spoke. But that is not important. I have spoken to the man of the forest and he has said you are one like the Spanish priest who must be taken to the white city."

"Why?"

"It is what the god wants. I am not worthy to ask 'why?' He wants you to go there and we can help you find it."

"The white city, the real white city? Not the place you took the others?"

"We never take outsiders there, and it cannot be found unless we lead you and we will."

"But why me?"

"I cannot answer that. But from time to time the god will command someone to be brought to him. They say he gives them a gift. A terrible, wonderful gift. He is the creator and the destroyer and he can do as he wills. The last one was the Spanish priest. You need not worry, the priest came back full of wonder and fear but he was safe."

"How long ago was this?"

"You mean in your years? I have no idea. The Pech do not conceive of time as you do. We do not measure it as you do. I only know that it was before I was born."

Twenty-nine
TEGUCIGALPA

The plane descended to Tegucigalpa nestled in a high valley among green clad mountains. Zelda had called an attorney who called the Deputy District Attorney in charge of her husband's murder case. She was finally given permission to leave the country to return to Honduras. The D.A. had determined that there was no evidence to link Zelda with the murder and no justification to detain her. The only evidence they had was some surveillance footage from the lobby of the condo building showing Chad and a dark-haired woman going into the elevator together. The face of the woman could not be seen in the video and no witnesses could be found who remembered her. The condominium unit itself had been swept clean of any forensic evidence, as had the body. The wound did show an expert stroke with a short, sharp blade, probably a switchblade, but no knife had been found. Zelda had been genuinely surprised when she heard that she was Chad's primary heir and she suspected that surprise had helped to convince the detectives she had nothing to do with the murder. She never really had thought about his estate since he was younger than her and, if she were honest with herself, she never really expected the marriage to last either one of their lifetimes. She would have expected Chad to give most of his money to charity. In fact, according to Chad's estate planning lawyer, he did make some minor bequests to charities but most of the money went to her.

While she was in Santa Monica, staying in a hotel because the condo was a crime scene, an unfamiliar number appeared on her cell phone. "*Carina*," said the voice on the other end, "I am so sorry for your loss, what a shock this must have been for you."

"Jahaira, how did you know?"

"We get international news even here in Honduras, my love, when an important man like your husband dies it gets attention. Will you be able to come back to Tegus sometime soon?"

"Yes, my attorney cleared it with the D.A. I'm not a suspect so I'll be leaving next week. There is a lot to do on the clinic, I'm eager to get back. How are you?"

"Busy as always. Were you planning on staying at the Marriott again?"

"I suppose, do you recommend someplace else?"

"*Carina*, why not stay with me? You will probably need to get a car and driver because I am usually using mine but that will still be cheaper than staying in a hotel and using taxis. I can help you find a good driver, one who can provide security for you as well as driving."

"Jahaira, I would love to stay with you, thank you for offering. I can't wait to get back."

"Just call back on this number and leave your flight information when you get it. I'll have you picked up at the airport."

As she recalled this surprising conversation the black sedan pulled up to the curb. This time Zelda recognized the driver and stepped immediately into the car. The ride, as always, seemed to meander through unfamiliar streets as if the route to Jahaira's house were always different. After Los Angeles and Santa Monica the poverty in the streets was jarring. Scrawny dogs wandered stiff legged on side streets, young boys in ragged T-shirts and shorts played soccer barefoot in the streets, women lugged children and baskets of fruit, tough looking young men in sleeveless T-shirts and baggy shorts roamed in packs and glared at the dark sedan as it passed. It was late afternoon and the sun sinking below the mountainous horizon cast shadows in the streets. As they neared Jahaira's house the streets narrowed, the torn pavement gave way to ancient cobblestone and the tall houses blocked the light. Beige, lime green and pink stucco on the old buildings gave a fairy tale look to the street. Here there were few people on the street and no shops or vendors, just the blank facades of old houses with their Moorish filigree and empty arches. Something about the district made Zelda shudder.

As she approached the familiar mahogany door it was opened by Angelica who gestured her in. She went through the now familiar vestibule with its portrait of a long forgotten Cristales cleric into the great room with its large fireplace. Angelica took her bags and left the room. On the table by the fireplace was a note with Zelda's name on it:

"Carina, welcome back to Honduras! Please make yourself at home, I am out on business but will return and meet you for dinner at home.

If you need to freshen up do not hesitate. Angelica can make you a drink if you like. She understands enough English to tend to your needs but

really, my love, you must start learning Espanol.

Love,
Jahaira"

When Angelica returned to the room, Zelda asked to be shown to her room. To her surprise and delight she was shown to Jahaira's own room where her luggage was laid out. A dresser against the far wall stood empty with the drawers and shelves left open for her use. She undressed and used the large shower in the bathroom. Was she really moving in with a woman? Was she really moving in with a lover so close to the death of her husband? She felt guilty that there was no remorse for Chad. In fact, she felt nothing other than confusion at why anyone would have murdered Chad and in such vicious fashion. Why would anyone slit his throat? Her world had changed so quickly. Now she was moving in to a house in a strange country with a woman she barely knew and had been told not to trust. Yet she felt she was on her way to discovering a new way of life. After showering amid the strange unlabeled containers in Jahaira's bathroom she carefully unpacked her suitcase and put the contents away in the empty dresser.

After she dressed and unpacked she began exploring the house. It was much larger than she realized. Jahaira's room was at the far end of the house just beyond the landing. The stairs went up to a third floor which Zelda guessed was Angelica's living space. The hallway outside Jahaira's bedroom door ran the length of the house and Zelda counted six arched doorways to bedrooms off the hallway. She peeked into one and saw that the furnishings were covered with sheets and the room was filled with dust and cobwebs. At the end of the hallway, on the opposite side of the house from Jahaira's bedroom, were double doors in an archway. She went through and found herself in a hexagonal solarium with tall, arched windows and a domed ceiling. The windows were covered with wooden frames carved in geometric designs. The floor was covered with mosaic tile in a radiating geometric design. It was a lovely room with afternoon light filtered by the window screens filling the room. There was no furniture and Zelda wondered if the room was ever used.

She went downstairs and entered the great room. For the first time she noticed a pair of double doors to the right of the large fireplace. Behind them was a large library with tall mahogany bookshelves. The shelves were filled to overflowing with books. Many of the volumes were leather bound and appeared to be quite old. Arched clerestory windows let in light from above. In the middle of the room was a large wooden trestle table. Several books lay scattered on the table. All of the volumes on the table appeared to be extremely old with worn leather binding and yellowed pages. She looked at their titles, one of them was "*Libro De Los Muertos*," another "*La Busqueda de Satanas*" by Leandro Cruz and the last one "*Creencias Religiosas del Pueblo Pech*" by Hector Cristales.

In the corner of the room was a small arched door. She opened it and found a narrow stairway leading down. She descended the stairs in the dark but found a light switch at the bottom. When she switched it on, the light revealed a large workshop with bell jars full of dried herbs, terrariums of scorpions and reptiles including frogs and snakes. There were Bunsen burners and various glass and ceramic vessels, mortar and pestles and bottles of unidentifiable liquid. The entire scene made Zelda uncomfortable so she quickly retreated up the stairs after turning out the light. She remembered Doctor Castillo saying Jahaira was rumored to be a *bruja* and this workroom looked very much like the lair of a witch.

Zelda left the library, returned to the great room and sat. Almost as if on command, Angelica brought her a drink, a rum punch made with white rum from Martinique, simple syrup and fresh lime juice. As she sipped, Jahaira walked in smiling. "Welcome back to Tegus, *carina*, I hope you made yourself comfortable."

"I did, thank you, I've already unpacked and showered, I am glad we're sharing a room," Zelda smiled as she said this. Angelica slid silently into the room with a rum punch for Jahaira.

"Zelda, I am so sorry for your loss. It must have been a shock for him to have gone so suddenly and, so violently. I am glad I can be here to comfort you."

"To be entirely honest, Jahaira, I really don't feel anything. I know I should, I know I should miss him and grieve but I just don't feel a thing. Do you know he left his entire fortune to me? It almost makes me feel guilty, I wasn't such a great wife and now, thanks to him, I'm incredibly wealthy."

"I think it is normal at this stage to feel numb. But you never asked him for his fortune and you did not marry him for his money, did you? Why should you feel guilty? Use his money for good and for your own satisfaction, that, I am sure, is what he would have wanted. " Angelica came in and gestured towards the dining room. The table was set for two with the usual antique china with its Moorish designs and the elaborate hand blown crystal. Angelica brought in two crystal bowls filled with white fish *cerviche* made with avocado and green chiles.

"I had a conversation recently with your Doctor Castillo," said Jahaira, "he seemed to think that I would take advantage of you in some way. I tried to assure him that was not the case, I am not sure if he believed me. I have planned a day for us together tomorrow, *carina*. They have started construction on the improvements to the clinic so we will stop by there to see how things are going, Doctor Castillo will probably be there as well. Then we will shop in an open air market and have a real Honduran lunch. Then we go to my *botanica* so you can see the health care the people of *Barrio Rosales* are receiving now and you can see what a *curandera* really does." Angelica brought in the next course, grilled snapper filet with *buerre blanc* and a Caribbean rice and beans dish cooked in coconut milk. They drank a crisp, dry Chilean sauvignon blanc with the fish. "But tomorrow night I have, shall we say, a 'date', and I will have to be gone for dinner and the rest of the evening."

"Jahaira, you don't have to do that anymore."

"Oh but I do. I make no money off the *botanica,* it is my personal charity, I can only support myself by sleeping with the rich and powerful. As you can see, I have expensive tastes and a comfortable lifestyle which I have no other means to support. Besides, it is not so offensive as you imagine. I dress up, look beautiful, allow some middle aged rich man to wine and dine me then I let him do what he wants. Most of them have little stamina so the ordeal does not last a long time and these are well groomed men with acceptable personal hygiene. They may get a bit sweaty and out of breath but I can always shower afterwards." Angelica cleared their plates and brought in coconut flan garnished with sliced fresh strawberries.

"Jahaira, I'm rich now, incredibly rich, I can support your lifestyle with ease. Besides, you are supporting me now, feeding me and letting me stay in your house, you should let me contribute, let me support you. You don't have to have sex for money anymore."

"But if I let you support me, is that not exactly what I am doing?"

Thirty
RIO PLATANO BIOSPHERE

The river had become impossible. The rafts were getting caught in the current, banging into rocks and swirling around in circles. The recent rains had swollen the river and the rafts were gradually moving up in elevation against the descending water. Arias-Garcia finally signaled to land at a rocky beach in a relatively calm bend in the river. The adjacent forest looked exceedingly thick but the Hondurans immediately went to work with machetes to clear room for the tents. This was to be the expedition's base camp for the duration. DeGroet let them all know there would be a meeting that evening before dinner.

Peter was exhausted from being buffeted around by the current, his stomach was queasy and he really wanted a drink. Cruz-Madrid seemed to sense his discomfort and produced a silver flask. As Peter sipped, he realized it was *Flor de Cana,* smooth and rich on his palate. As soon as his tent was up he went in, still grasping Cruz-Madrid's flask, and unrolled his sleeping bag to lie down and quickly fell asleep.

He awakened with a start and the sense that he was being watched. As his eyes cleared he saw a young man sitting cross-legged across from him. He realized it was Pravia, one of the Pech guides they had picked up at the village. He was the younger one who spoke Spanish. The older guide, Yauwi, spoke only Paya, the ancestral Pech language, but knew the forest far better than his younger colleague. Pravia smiled at Peter as he sat up and rubbed his eyes. Pravia was small, perhaps 5'6" with long dark black hair, dark brown eyes and a round, plump face which was at odds with his slender, almost gaunt body. "*Hola, Senor* Van, you know you have a meeting soon?" he said in his halting Spanish.

"*Gracias,* Pravia, why are you here?"

"To see what makes you different."

"Different from what? If I am different it's probably because I'm a bit worse than my fellow man."

"You have been chosen to go to the *ciudad blanca*, the first one in many years, that makes you different than the other outsiders we meet. The last one was a *ladino*, a Christian priest who seemed to understand our beliefs and the significance of *la ciudad blanca*. The *hombre del bosque* told us to guide him there and he came back in a state of shock."

"How long ago was this?"

"It is impossible for me to say, we Pech do not perceive time as you do. You see time as based on the solar year, you see it as linear and one dimensional. We see time as multidimensional and based on cycles which are both natural and supernatural and occur simultaneously but interrelatedly and overlap. You, *Senor* Van, are part of a cycle, a cycle which is turning, just as that priest, Father Cristales, was a part of the same cycle. Somewhere, each of you have or will enter the seams of the cycle and emerge transformed but still a part of all other aspects of time."

"None of what you just said makes any sense to me and I was once a philosophy major."

"Do not be afraid, there may be terrible powers abroad but you have safe passage for now. Anyway, it is time to go to your meeting." Pravia got up and opened the tent flap for Peter and they walked together to Doctor DeGroet's tent where the expedition was gathering.

DeGroet sat on a folding campstool surrounded by the other members of the expedition sitting on the floor of the tent.

"Mister VanOwen, thank you for joining us, we were beginning to worry about you," he said in his clipped Dutch accent.

"Sorry, I was just getting a lesson in the Pech concept of time from Pravia here."

"Then without further delay let us get started. Tomorrow we start in the morning on foot to go further inland with our Pech guides. We will be splitting up the expedition. Myself, Doctor Mellon, Doctor Selvy, two of the interns, Wendy Dirks and Paul Salman, Mister VanOwen, Captain Cruz-Madrid and four of his men, six of the Honduran workers, and of course Pravia and Yauwi will head out on foot towards the white city. The rest will remain here in the base camp. We were hoping to get resupplied by helicopter before we left but there is simply no spot level enough that we can clear to allow one to land, so we will have to send some rafts back to *Los Marias* to bring back supplies. Perhaps in a week or so we will have a landing site cleared. We will have to travel light. Pravia says that it is approximately six days by foot to the valley in which the true white city is located and he is not sure how to get into the valley but thinks that Yauwi knows how. Once there, we will size up the extent of the excavation to be done and begin work. We will send back one of the Pech guides to lead a group to resupply us from the base camp and we will try to work this way as long as we can, depending, of course, on what we find. Any questions?" There were none and the group broke up to return to their tents. Peter walked back by himself and carefully packed the gear he would need for the trip. As he did so, it began to rain again, pelting the tent with hard drops. As he slipped into his sleeping bag he reflected on how far he had come from his seaside home and how absurd Pravia's discussion of him as "different" sounded.

Peter found himself slipping downward, on one side of him was a Los Angeles street scene with parking meters and awnings, Mercedes and BMWs parked by the curb, on the other side he saw the ocean by a gray sand beach lined with coconut palms, directly below him he saw impenetrable jungle and heard the cries of toucans, macaws and howler monkeys reaching up to him. He descended right into the brush and came out into the elegant dining room of a restaurant in which was seated a smiling Jahaira Cristales. Across from her sat a handsome middle aged man in antique clerical garb who was crying.

Thirty-one
LOS ANGELES

Miriam and her husband sat at a table in a small North Hollywood club called the Alley Katt. Miriam nursed a large goblet of white wine of unspecified origin and Paul drank a Seagram's and Seven. The club was a modest place with red vinyl chairs, an old oak bar and walls lined with sound insulation. The tiny stage at the back of the club had a piano and stand-up bass with three music stands. "How much are they paying her for this?" asked Paul.

"Honey, what difference does it make?" responded Miriam, "this is what she has chosen to do and she should have the chance to do it."

"At some point she has to realize she needs to make a living. Do you really think pursuing a career in a dead musical genre is going to get her anywhere? Look around. Does it look like this place is booming?" Throughout the small club there were a dozen or so, mostly middle aged, patrons nursing drinks. Before Miriam could respond, four musicians came out on the stage and began tuning their instruments. There were three black men, one on trumpet, one on bass and the other on tenor saxophone. The piano player was a young white guy with dirty blonde hair. Miriam had met them all but could not remember their names.

They soon launched into an instrumental version of a song they called "Blue in Green." The music was quiet and moody.

When they finished there was scattered applause. Someone at the bar called out, "Ladies and gentlemen, Leia VanOwen!" Miriam's older daughter walked onto the stage, a short, slight, elfin figure with long brown hair and big green eyes. She was wearing jeans, flats and some sort of flowing, long sleeved blouse. Leia stepped to the music stand at the front and grabbed a microphone. After a few words of introduction she began singing a version of "Skylark." Her voice was thin with limited range, especially in the lower registers, but her pitch was good and her phrasing superb. She paused throughout the song to give each musician some solo time. They were all good but even Miriam recognized that the trumpet player was extraordinary, his tone was pure and he managed to push the melody to strange and uncommon places. At the end the crowd applauded enthusiastically but Miriam could not help but think that it was more for the trumpet player than Leia. This perturbed her all the more because she suspected he was sleeping with her daughter.

The set continued with a song called "Small Day Tomorrow", followed by one called "Wheelers and Dealers," "The Look of Love" and others. After almost an hour she ended the set with, "A Nightingale Sang in Berkeley Square" in which Leia's voice hit some nice high notes. The band put down their instruments and Leia went to sit down with her mother and stepfather.

"That was a lovely set darling!" said Miriam as Leia sat down. With her maternal powers of observation she noted that Leia's eyes were slightly glassy.

"Thanks Mom, seems like things are coming together."

"How long before you expect to make any money doing this?" asked Paul.

"I don't know, Paul, jazz is a limited market, even the established musicians with reputations don't make a lot. I'm not in this for the money."

"Face it, Leia; jazz is dead, look at your audience here tonight. It's just gonna get worse as these old timers die off, you won't have any audience left," said Paul.

"Paul has a point, honey, maybe you could move into something more popular, some kind of rock or maybe sing in shows or something, like you did in 'Jesus Christ Super Star' in high school. This music has no future, nobody cares about it."

"Maybe not but I do, and so do Trevor and the rest of the band, and there are other musicians out there who care. This is roots music and it's a huge part of American musical heritage." Miriam remembered the trumpet player's name was Trevor Clarke.

"Yeah, I hate to be blunt but you're old enough to support yourself now and you can't expect your mother to keep supporting you while you pursue something so impractical," added Paul.

"Dad would have appreciated what we're doing."

"If Dad wasn't M.I.A. Has your father ever heard you sing?" asked Miriam.

"Not since I've been doing jazz, not since high school really."

"Your father loved jazz, that doesn't mean he loves you, at least not enough to be around occasionally," said Miriam.

"Speaking of Dad, has any one heard from him for a while? I tried calling last week but some woman, girl actually, answered and said he was away on some sort of fucking expedition in Honduras. She said she was his girlfriend but she sounded about my age."

"I told your sister some old friend of his called me to find out how to contact him. The guy said he was an archeologist and he wanted your father's help on some sort of expedition. That must be where he is. As for a young girlfriend, it's probably some street whore he picked up. Hell, in a poor country like Costa Rica even an old broken down loser like your father can buy himself a young girlfriend for a few bucks." Leia cringed at her mother's tone and once again reflected that it had been her mother's harshness which had helped chase her father all the way to

Central America.

"That's so ridiculous, how could Dad help on an archeology expedition? Are you sure he hasn't been kidnapped or something?" asked Leia. Paul laughed.

"If he was, the kidnappers are going to be very disappointed there's no one to pay the ransom," said Paul.

"Paul, that's really not funny, if they couldn't get ransom money they would kill him," said Leia.

"Honey, I hate to say it but you wouldn't even know the difference if they did. It's not like he's any part of your life." The table went quiet after that comment by Miriam. The band members were starting to congregate on the stage, the trumpet player raised his hand as if to signal Leia they were ready. "Look, sweetie, Paul and I can't stay for the second set, we have a thing to go to. I hope you understand." Leia nodded and got up to return to the stage. As Paul and Miriam left, Leia was doing a slow, bluesy rendition of "Saint James Infirmary."

Thirty-two
TEGUCIGALPA

They spent the entire night, it seemed, making love. Zelda was exhausted when Jahaira got her up in the morning. They had breakfast in the dining room, fresh fruit and *pasteles* along with strong Honduran coffee. Jahaira was dressed in a black shirtdress and black high heeled platform sandals with her hair pulled back and secured with a hand tooled leather strap. Zelda was in a peach colored cotton skirt and a white cotton blouse with tan sandals. As always her dark hair was long and loose.

After breakfast they climbed into the dark sedan driven by Jahaira's male driver. They drove through the narrow cobblestone streets of Jahaira's neighborhood with its decrepit Moorish mansions and emerged onto dirt roads in neighborhoods of cinderblock houses with rusty corrugated metal roofs. They quickly found themselves at a checkpoint manned by Honduran soldiers in camouflage uniforms, armed with assault rifles and wearing Kevlar vests. The soldiers made them open the doors and trunk. The officer in charge spoke briefly to Jahaira in rapid fire Spanish. The officer nodded to Jahaira and they closed the doors and drove through the checkpoint. "This is *Barrio Rosales*," said Jahaira, "the checkpoint is more to keep the residents in than visitors out, but they always check for guns and drugs and they always warn you before you enter."

"What do they warn you about?"

"Gangs, this *barrio* is controlled by MS13, the authorities cannot control them in the *barrio* so they try to keep them in. You will never see a police patrol in this *barrio*."

"Are we in danger?"

"No, MS13 knows me. Years ago they tried to collect protection money from my *botanica.* When I refused they threatened me. Shortly thereafter their *jefe* died. It may just have been a coincidence but since then they have been afraid of me. It does not hurt that the locals support me. I have provided them with the only health care they have ever had and I help them with their other problems as well, as you will see."

"So for the clinic security will be a real problem here? "

"Without question, which is why I have recommended a very good security firm to provide armed guards. However, it might be wise, at least at first, to pay MS13 something. Otherwise they may frighten the residents from using the clinic." They pulled up in front of an old concrete building that had once been a clothing factory but had long sat empty. It was one story with high ceilings and was almost forty thousand square feet, more than Zelda needed for the clinic but with room for expansion. There were trucks being unloaded and workers milling about the site. There were a half dozen armed guards carrying rifles. A light blue Mercedes was parked alongside the building. As they walked in they saw partitions being erected, electricians working on wiring, plumbing fixtures piled up ready to be installed. Ahead of them they saw Doctor Castillo speaking with a foreman. When he saw them he stepped towards them and offered his hand to Zelda.

"Senora Toeb, I was so devastated to hear about your husband, please accept my condolences," he glanced at Jahaira who smiled back at him, "Senorita, a pleasure to meet you again." They walked through the ongoing construction with Doctor Castillo pointing out which areas would be examination rooms, laboratories, X-ray rooms and the main waiting room and lobby. Castillo mentioned that he was interviewing staff and had found several Honduran doctors who were willing to work part-time at the clinic. It was hard to find RN's and trained nursing staff and he believed the clinic would have to do some training on its own. The work would be at least another month to complete and probably longer. Getting equipment and medical supplies would also be a challenge and take additional time. However, he believed they could start treating patients even before much of it arrived.

Zelda was ecstatic, the clinic was moving much faster than she had ever hoped and she felt convinced Castillo was the right man for the job. He was already under salary, and a Honduran bank account had been established with the money Chad had contributed. She could already see it would take much more money to keep the clinic running at full capacity and she planned on contributing it as soon as she had control of her inheritance. Best of all, Castillo and Jahaira seemed to be cordial with each other which pleased her immensely as she saw the three of them interacting frequently in the near future.

When they finished their tour Zelda thanked the Doctor profusely and Jahaira gave him her hand. They piled into the dark sedan and headed for a nearby *Mercado*. It was nestled between *Barrio Rosales* and the neighboring district serving both. They got out of the car and entered a maze of open air stalls hawking mangoes, pineapples, cashew fruit, melons, guavas, papayas, onions and yams. There was a poultry stall with scrawny chickens displayed, a bread vendor with small loaves of crusty bread and a selection of *pan dulce*. Another stall featured goat meat, the unsavory looking carcasses covered with flies. There were also stalls for ceramics, leatherwork, hand woven textiles, woodcarvings and shoes. Zelda was overwhelmed by the color, variety and smells of the place as well as the crowded aisles and noise of the vendors. Jahaira carefully picked over fish at one stall, buying filets of a Caribbean white fish. At another stall she bought strawberries grown in the local mountains and mangoes from the lowlands.

On a nearby aisle Jahaira pointed out a group of young men in white cotton sleeveless shirts and baggy khaki pants. These, she told Zelda, were MS13 members and each day they chose a different aisle of the *Mercado* to collect protection money from the vendors. There were no police to be seen anywhere in the *Mercado*. Jahaira and Zelda crossed over into the aisle with gang members so Jahaira could purchase platanos from a vendor she favored. As they passed them, the MS13 members stood aside respectfully for Jahaira to pass and nodded to her. Noting Zelda's surprise, Jahaira explained; "They are not going away and neither am I so we have learned to accommodate one another over the years. This is their territory but it is also mine."

They returned to the car with provisions and Arturo, their driver, took them into *Barrio Rosales* to a narrow dirt road lined with shops in cinderblock buildings painted various pale, pastel shades of blue, violet, pink and green. Arturo let them out and drove back to Jahaira's house with the purchases from the *Mercado*. Jahaira led Zelda down the street to a small restaurant with bars on the windows. Jahaira greeted the owner like an old friend and they took a table, with Jahaira ordering *carneada*; steak marinated in sour orange juice with seasonings, along with rice, beans and fried plantains. The restaurant's cinder block walls were painted aqua inside, the floor was cement and there were rickety Formica tables and old wooden chairs. On the walls were posters for Honduran pop groups. The proprietor treated Jahaira like a guest of honor. Port Royal beers were brought out without being ordered, as was a basket of tortilla chips and hot bean dip topped with white cheese. Several people came up and spoke with Jahaira in Spanish. Zelda noted they all addressed her as *Curandera*. The food was delicious but heavy and the beer made Zelda feel sleepy. She had, after all, been up half the night making passionate love with the *Curandera*.

"After we eat, my work begins. My *botanica* is on this street a few doors away and they are already lining up to see me. Until your clinic is open I am the only one who provides any sort of medical care to this *barrio,* and spiritual support as well. The priests of the new religion provide little."

"New religion?"

"The Catholics, Christians, Evangelicals, these are religions brought by the Spaniards and those who came after. They replaced the old religion while enslaving and exploiting the people in its name."

"Was there one main religion in Honduras before the Spanish came?"

"Once upon a time, yes. *La ciudad blanca* was the religious center of the country and all the tribes looked to it for spiritual guidance. But when that city was abandoned the different tribes fell to their own forms of worship and then came the Spaniards who brought Christianity along with disease and death. The irony was that while the old religion was a religion of misery and the new religion was one of hope it actually brought as much misery and suffering as the old religion ever did."

"Jahaira, how do you know these things?"

"Well, my father was a priest of the new religion who became a believer in the old religion. He went to *la ciudad blanca* and met with the priests of the Pech who live deep in the forest and still cling to the old religion. Something happened on his visit to the old city that helped him understand the nature of the old religion and its god. He did say that the old god was not displeased with the new religion and my father, even as his beliefs changed, never felt the need to abandon his priesthood."

"Why do I get the feeling that you don't believe in anything yourself?"

"You mean like you?"

"Yes, I was raised by secular Jewish parents who were atheists. They didn't believe in anything other than being Jewish in a cultural sense. But you do what you want, you don't seem to live by any rules. It's hard to believe that you believe in anything."

"The fact that there are no rules is the rule. You define belief as faith in a logical system designed for man's ultimate benefit as controlled by a kindly and loving god. Religion has always functioned as a vehicle for man's search for meaning. But this type of belief is based on hope. It implies facts for which we have no evidence, only our fervent belief that our purpose here must be for good, that our creator is good and that his purpose for us is for our good. I do not believe in any of that, my love."

"Then what do you believe, Jahaira?"

"That man was made to suffer, that moral order does not exist, that chaos reigns, and that these things are as god intended." Jahaira smiled her dazzling smile and Zelda shook her head.

When they finished eating they walked down the street to a lime green wooden building next to a *panaderia* with a small hand lettered sign in the window, which read "*Botanica Dios Mono.*" The front room contained a counter with various bottles and boxes. A plump young girl with dark black pigtails sat behind the counter. "Zelda, this is Gabriela who runs this place for me, Gabriela, this is my close friend Zelda who will be opening up a clinic in the barrio very soon we hope." Gabriela took Zelda's hand and nodded. They went into the backroom which contained a rocking chair, a small table and a stool. Jahaira sat in the rocking chair and motioned for Zelda to take the stool.

Gabriela brought in the first customer, a stocky, square faced woman in her late twenties. She was barely pregnant, with three children to feed all by different men, none of whom were around in any sense. She wanted to lose the child. Jahaira nodded and said nothing. From an upper shelf she took down a glass vial containing an amber liquid. "This will rid you of your child safely, because it is so early. This woman," she gestured to Zelda sitting on her stool in the corner "is opening a clinic near here. There you will be able to get birth control pills to protect you from this happening again. You cannot feed your children now, you cannot have more or they may all starve." The woman nodded, paid the requested four hundred and fifty-thousand lempiras, and left, thanking Jahaira as she went.

The next customer was a pimply-faced boy, no older than nineteen. There was a beautiful girl he wished to pursue but she had no interest in him, could she help? "How much do you have?" she asked. The boy had only one hundred thousand lempiras. "For five hundred thousand lempiras I can give you a potion that will make her want you more than any man she has ever known. But I cannot make her love you. That is beyond my power. Only you can make her love you by being the man she wants in her heart, by caring for her, by treating her with affection, by being proud and confident and strong. So if it is sex you want, go find more money and I will help you, if it is love you want you are in the wrong place."

"Why Jahaira, "said Zelda, as the boy left, head hanging, "I would almost take you for a romantic." Jahaira smiled her dazzling smile and said nothing.

The next customer was a worn, haggard woman in her late twenties wearing a white cotton, embroidered, sleeveless blouse and black cotton skirt. She had a young boy by the hand. He was nine or ten. He looked pale, was covered with a thin slime of sweat and had dark circles under his eyes. The boy was sick, the woman said, and had a bad fever for the last three days. Jahaira looked him over and told the woman, "You know I am not a doctor, your boy is very ill. It could be dengue, yellow fever, zika or even typhoid or malaria. His fever is a symptom of all of these and I have no way to tell which." She walked over to a stepstool and reached to an upper shelf bringing down two glass vials, one a thick amber color, the other clear. "This can reduce his fever," she said holding up the vial with the amber liquid." It is made from the liver of a tree frog and will work on any fever. This," she said, holding up the clear vial, "is an antibiotic made from the pollen of a flower found in the rainforest. It will not help against malaria or zika but it can weaken the other diseases.

It may help, but you should understand he is in real danger and needs a doctor, if there is any way you can get him to a clinic or hospital. You can have both for one hundred thousand lempiras." The woman began to cry.

"I have no money, just fifty thousand for food, if I give you that my family will not eat anything."

"Then pay me later, when you have some money. If they do not work at all then you owe me nothing. It is important to eat and I am in no danger of going hungry myself." The woman looked at Jahaira and smiled through her tears. "Just remember what I told you about finding a doctor, what I have given you does not guarantee that he will get better." The woman nodded and left. Jahaira looked at Zelda and smiled. "You see how badly they need your clinic here? Once upon a time they would come most often for poisons or curses to punish their enemies, not so much drugs to cure their ills. But now that the gangs are here they go to them to do ill to their enemies. They are cheaper and just as effective."

The next customer ushered in by Gabriela was a woman in her early thirties. Her eyes were red and her face creased with sorrow. She was painfully thin and looked as if she had not changed her clothes in weeks. A vague odor of decay seemed to follow her into the room. "*Curandera*," she said "my daughter of twelve years died last month. She was my *Tesoro,* a beautiful, intelligent child, I could have asked for no better. We were so close. Since she became ill and died I have not been able to stop crying, I feel no desire to eat, or to go on living. I want to kill myself but the priest said that is a sin and I would go to hell. Can you help me?"

"Well, on the street they sell drugs that can make you happy or at least make you numb. I do not usually deal in recreational drugs. If I did, the gang bangers would probably shoot me. But is that what you really want? Among the elites and the *gringos* they prescribe drugs that supposedly make you feel better, less depression, less anxiety. Maybe if those feelings have no relation to your life and are not a response to anything real they are useful. But the feelings you have are natural, you lost a child who was dear to you. What kind of monster would you be if you felt nothing? In my life I have, more than once, lost a love, I know the sadness that comes from out-living someone you are close to. Grief is part of being human, which, when we feel it, becomes a part of who we are, part of our consciousness. So too, the struggle to overcome despair and grief becomes a part of who you are and brings you both strength and resignation, which itself is a kind of strength. There is nothing I can give you that would cure your grief and that is as it should be. You will see, *madre*, time will help assuage it and you will go on with the struggle of your life. You do not need a drug or an easy cure, you need to accept your own humanity of which grief is a natural part." Zelda looked at Jahaira as if seeing her for the first time. This woman who posed as such a cynic was really kind and wise and strong, especially when it came to the poor and oppressed. Zelda was not sure she had ever met anyone so wonderful.

Thirty-three
RIO PLATANO BIOSPHERE

Peter awakened to the sound of raindrops plopping monotonously on his tent. He felt a deep sense of anxiety in his gut as he realized that today they set out on foot to find *la ciudad blanca*. The journey terrified him. They were on their way to penetrate on foot deep forested areas, ascend to higher altitudes and encounter the snakes, spiders, leeches and discomfort of the Central American wilderness. They would be dealing with excessive rain, and never ending heat and humidity. Even the raft trip they had just finished had exhausted him. He was an old man, in poor shape, about to brave some of the harshest wilderness in the new world. Even as a boy and young man he had not cared much for hiking and camping.

Arias-Garcia was in the tent. He seemed to be arguing with Cruz-Madrid. "Aah, *Senor* VanOwen, you are awake," said Arias-Garcia. "Let me warn you now as I have been warning the Captain, the deceiver is out there in those hills, you will encounter the master of lies on your journey, I feel certain. Are you prepared, *Senor,* to deal with the father of evil? Have you found god in your heart? Because only god can protect you from the evil out there."

"Look, Arturo," Peter said gently, "I really don't think I believe in evil at all. Men make choices out of self-interest. We treat each other badly for some sort of material or psychic gain. Nature is random, we can't always control her forces whether they be earthquakes, volcanoes, harsh weather or disease. None of these things are evil. They just exist. There is no such thing as abstract evil, just an ongoing struggle to survive among these very impersonal forces that sometimes work against us. We have rules because it helps us survive. It helps us avoid chaos. We make violence a crime as a form of self-preservation, to bring peace and stability to our human societies."

"Yet we still have war," said Cruz-Madrid, standing there in his Special Forces camouflage, "we have capital punishment, we have not outlawed violence, just institutionalized it. Societies like the Maya and Aztecs ritualized the most horrible types of violence as an essential part of their religion."

"But was that really evil?" asked Peter. "War, capital punishment, even ritual sacrifice is supposed to have social benefit. Can striving to achieve social benefit really be considered evil?"

"Well," said Cruz-Madrid, "it depends how you define 'evil' if you..."

"STOP IT!" Bellowed Arias-Garcia, "the deceiver is out there, there can be no doubt. While you debate the meaning of evil, the father of lies is coveting your souls! He is in these hills, I can smell him, feel him and you are at risk, I cannot emphasize enough, you are at risk! *La ciudad blanca* is the gateway to hell!"

"Well," said Cruz-Madrid, "it is a good thing Peter and I are going, our souls were lost long ago, so we have nothing to fear." Cruz-Madrid and Peter smiled at each other and left for breakfast.

The usual rice and beans were served along with some tinned meat that had been grilled over a fire, weak coffee and fried plantains the Honduran crew had picked in the forest. They double-checked their packs and set off into the jungle led by the two Pech guides. The first two hours were brutal as there was no trail and the expedition was forced to hack their way through thick undergrowth. Even Peter had been given a sharp machete to clear away vegetation as they passed. Future resupply groups would be passing this way and they wished to leave a discernible path for them. Around noon, the group stopped to eat and rest in a clearing beneath a grove of very tall teak trees.

"The size of these trees indicates that we are in virgin forest. In the lowlands no teak trees this size would have survived logging," said Cruz-Madrid.

Peter was exhausted. The going had been slow but his arms ached from swinging the machete and he was soaked with sweat. The rain had stopped but the humidity had not. Their lunch had consisted of cassava bread and dried fruit. There would be no more food until they camped that night. After an hour break they started out again behind the Pech guides. Within a half-hour they emerged onto a vestigial trail.

The younger guide, Pravia, came back to talk to Cruz-Madrid. "This trail is used by drug traffickers. If they see you and your soldiers they may become alarmed. You should have your men on full alert while we use their trail. There is a place, about an hour's walk from here, where they have a small landing field that will be the most dangerous portion of the trail if they are expecting a shipment. Once we pass that we should be safe." Cruz-Madrid trotted off to brief his four soldiers.

From here the trail seemed to lead over a series of ever higher ridges with narrow valleys in between. The terrain was intensely green and, except for the incessant call of birds, very quiet. They passed the area Pravia had identified as close to the traffickers landing field. The trail there was wider and clearer than at any place they had been. They passed several side trails that were also well cleared. Within twenty minutes of passing the area the trail went back to being narrow and cluttered with growth. Pravia made a sign to Cruz-Madrid that they were clear of the danger zone.

Peter noted it was becoming cooler as they increased elevation. When they reached the top of a ridge they could sometimes see ahead of them three tall peaks looming in the distance, shrouded with mist. Somewhere among those peaks was their destination. The forest was beginning to change. The trees were taller and there was less undergrowth. At one point they surprised a group of spotted deer grazing on grass along the trail. The deer raised their heads in alarm and trotted back into the dark forest as they approached. There were monkeys in the trees but it was only the rustling of the branches that alerted them to their presence. They occasionally heard the low growl of a howler monkey but saw none.

It was just as dusk came upon them that they found the first ruins. They were in a narrow valley between ridges. A stream rushed down from a small waterfall off the next ridge. By the side of the stream a mound rose, covered with vines. Yauwi stepped forward and slashed at the vines with his machete revealing a bas relief of a jaguar preparing to leap. It was carved into a soft limestone pedestal and the overgrowth had probably kept it from weathering beyond recognition. DeGroet, Mellon and Selby all ran forward to examine it. The jaguar was not realistic but highly stylized. However, it was not done in a recognizable style. It was clearly not Mayan. The head was oversized, as were the paws, while the body was slim and delicate. It had something unrecognizable held between its paws. As they looked around they saw a few similar mounds and some low structures covered in vegetation. To Peter's great relief, DeGroet announced they would camp here for the night.

Pravia told them the National Geographic team had also passed this site but the large city they had reported on was at least a day and a half further. DeGroet surmised, as they ate their freeze dried beef stroganoff, that this had been a hamlet in the political sphere perhaps of a greater city. Whether that greater city was the one the Nat Geo team had discovered or existed elsewhere was one of the things this expedition might determine. DeGroet emphasized that either way this was an unknown civilization, clearly not Maya, and a wonderful opportunity for truly original and significant scholarship. Peter was happy when the group decided to turn in. His legs were stiff and every bone ached from deep within. He could only hope the next day would be easier. Once he was in his tent he quickly fell asleep.

He found himself on a narrow trail in the dark. Ahead of him was a large jaguar loping through the jungle. At first he thought absurdly he might be chasing the cat but he quickly realized he was following it to safety and if he could not keep up, he was in great danger.

When they broke camp the next morning they found jaguar prints running through and around the camp, but the soldiers on duty said they saw nothing.

Thirty-four
JACO, COSTA RICA

Ophelia sat at a corner table by herself in an American restaurant called Kokomo's on the main drag in Jaco. She had seen him come in with a group of young gringos. He must have been twenty-five, a surfer type, over six feet tall with a blonde buzz cut. The group noisily consumed mojitos in copious quantities. They seemed to look over at her periodically and become noisier. Ophelia ignored them until the young gringo staggered over and sat down across from her.

"You're beautiful," he said, only slightly slurring, "where you from?"

"No place you have ever been my friend, and you should consider yourself lucky."

"You 'merican?"

"No."

"C'mon talk to me, tell me 'bout yourself." Ophelia considered that finishing her hamburger was not worth putting up with mister buzz cut who showed every indication of becoming physically belligerent. She signaled to the waitress for her check and swallowed the last of her Imperial. She had no desire to make a scene or to draw attention to herself. She made a mental note to herself to, in the future, avoid Jaco; a city of bars, surf shops and prostitutes. She paid her bill while buzz cut implored her not to leave. Her car was parked on a back street so she was forced to leave the lights and traffic to go around the corner. It was already dark and there were no streetlights.

She was almost at her car when she heard, "not so fast bitch," from behind. She whirled around to see buzz cut looking angry and ready to strike.

"I tol' you not to leave bitch, I wasn't through talking to you. C'mere!" He lunged forward ready to grab Ophelia's arm.

She quickly stepped back and drew a small switchblade from her pocket, releasing the blade. He grabbed her shoulder with his left hand and, with his right hand, went for the left hand in which she held the blade. Her stroke was quick and he pulled back, squealing in pain as his arm dripped blood. Ophelia stepped forward, going after him, he lunged again for the knife but she ducked away and cut his side. His billabong T-shirt was soaked crimson where she cut him. He looked at himself and ran at full speed back to the main drag. Ophelia quickly jumped into her car and sped away, using the back streets until she came to the main highway and headed for Peter's beach house.

When she got there, she poured a tall tumbler of *Flor de Cana* and sat on the patio watching the phosphorescent tide. There were fireflies fluttering about and bats maneuvering among the trees. She took a long sip of the rum and sighed. A girl, especially an unusually pretty girl, growing up in *Colonia Pineda* had to know how to use a blade and she knew how to use one pretty well.

She had been surprised when the *bruja* had asked her to go to San Jose. "I want you to look for a man for me, one who likes the *putas*," she had told Ophelia. She would be given money but it would be good for her to turn a few tricks just to help her blend in to the whole *Zona Rosa* scene. So she went, her first ride on an airplane, and landed in this strange city, not as big or as decrepit or as dangerous as Tegus. She found a room in a small *pension* and began the circuit of bars in the *Zona Rosa*. Unlike in Tegus most of the customers were gringos, especially in places like the Del Rey, the Molino Rojo, and the Neruda. The man she was looking for would show up at one of these eventually. The *bruja* described him as a gringo in his sixties, of medium height with gray, receding hair, a potbelly and long sideburns. His name was Peter and he spoke Spanish correctly but with a heavy accent.

The life in San Jose was very different than it was in Tegus. It was not safe to be a streetwalker in Tegus; the gangs would target you and take whatever money you earned, if they did not hurt you badly. In Tegus, the high end girls were all in brothels and their customers were mostly wealthy Hondurans, there were few gringos. In San Jose brothels were illegal, so the girls worked the clubs which teemed with gringos and wealthier Ticos. You worked on your own and kept what you made. A lot of the girls did drugs and partied hard when they were not working. They made a lot of money but they spent it just as fast. She felt safe in most parts of San Jose. There were places to avoid at night but there was nothing like the violent chaos of Tegus or of her home city San Pedro Sula. She missed her life with the *bruja,* in her big house with good food, no tricks to turn and her only task to study English and help the *bruja* with her herbs and medicines in the basement workshop. But life in San Jose was not altogether bad and she savored her independence here.

She had been in San Jose a few weeks and had turned a few tricks, mostly out of boredom, because she had enough money from the *bruja.* When she saw the man, she was not sure why but she knew who he was right away. She did not have to make an effort to gain his attention, his was riveted on her as soon as he saw her. Men often reacted to her like that but seldom with the alacrity and intensity as this Peter. She owned him the minute he saw her. He was a *putero,* like many she had known in Tegus, a man hungry for female flesh with no sensitivity to, or interest in, the person within the flesh. Yet there was something about him that attracted her and made her wonder exactly what it was in him that so interested the *bruja.*

After her encounter with him she reported it to the *bruja*

the next time she called. Ophelia had a cell phone and the *bruja* called every few days. The *bruja* asked a great many questions about him, his looks, his attitude, whether or not he intended to proceed on the expedition the *bruja* told her he would be going on. "You have done well, my sweet one, I will be the next one to meet *Senor* VanOwen. You stay in Costa Rica for a while."

San Jose was beginning to bore her but she did as she was told. When the *bruja* called her the next time, she was happy to be told that she had a job for Ophelia in Los Angeles and she should book a flight out of San Jose in one week.

Thirty-five
RIO PLATANO MOUNTAINS

The constant, disturbing dreams exhausted Peter almost as much as the daily trek. They continued to gain elevation day by day. On the fourth day out they found themselves in a saddle between ridges in a forest of huge conifers. There was no underbrush as the conifers blocked out all light. The forest floor was littered with pine needles and cones. The acidic needles acted as a prophylactic against undergrowth on the forest floor. In the darkness of this forest the air was surprisingly cool and a broad flat path wandered through the trees. They could hear ahead of them the sound of rushing water but above that there came the cries of children laughing and shouting. Peter was sure the inevitable madness from the isolation and fatigue had overtaken him and these were auditory hallucinations. But in fifteen minutes they walked into a clearing with three solidly built wood plank houses next to a roaring mountain cascade. Playing among the pinecone littered yard were three children, two young girls, perhaps ages nine and twelve, and a boy who could have been no more than seven. The boy wore bib overalls and a plain blue cotton shirt. The girls were dressed in plain, pale blue, cotton dresses down to their ankles and each had a small white cloth pinned to their hair. A small hound dog raced towards the expedition, barking manically as the children turned to stare.

A tall, bearded man dressed like the boy stepped out of

one of the houses. Phillip DeGroet trotted forward and addressed the man. "Greetings sir. We are an archeological expedition searching for the *ciudad blanca*. We mean absolutely no harm."

"I didn't suspect you did," said the man. "You are welcome to camp here for the night if you like. We may try to change your mind about what you seek though." People had stepped out from the other houses. Among them were several women dressed like the little girls. Peter immediately noted a lovely blonde, blue-eyed young girl in her early twenties. The plainness of her attire only accentuated her beauty. Peter glanced at Cruz-Madrid who winked and licked his lips. Peter smiled.

The bearded man introduced himself as Aldor Hostettler. He and the others were the descendants of an Amish colony that had been established in the 1970's. Their parents had finally given up and returned to the United States but Aldor and his friends and their wives had only known Honduras as home. So three couples, the Hostettlers, Stolls and Troyers, stayed in Honduras when the others returned and they had been moving progressively further and further away from civilization. "This place," said Aldor "is a fine place, there is good water, it is not too hot. We are far away from all the corruptions of your world. We are even further into Mosquitia than the drug runners come. We raise goats and sheep. We have vegetables and fruit trees and we live well. But I will tell you, we cannot go any further into the mountains. There is an evil there that makes the modern world seem benign. The place you are seeking, this white city, is a terrible place and you must stay away."

The expedition was shown an area to pitch their tents and the principles, including Peter and Aramis, were invited to dine with the family elders that night.

The dinner was outdoors at a large wooden table in the clearing between the houses. There was, of course, to Peter's great disappointment, no alcohol. They served a delicious goat stew along with freshly made corn tortillas. There was fresh guava juice to drink, sweetened with honey, and fresh fruit for dessert including cashew apples, raspberries, tiny wild strawberries and soursop. The men sat at the table with the expedition members, DeGroet, Selby, Mellon, Cruz-Madrid and Peter, while the Amish women served. Cruz-Madrid joked and laughed with the young Amish girl whose name was Karen. She laughed and blushed at the attention. Peter wondered if her father, sitting at the table, had noticed.

DeGroet went on at length about the purpose of the expedition and the importance of *la ciudad blanca* to the history of Central America. "Have you talked to those Pech guides you are traveling with?" asked Jakob Stoll, Karen's father.

"Of course," replied DeGroet, "and with the shaman in their village as well."

"I did get the impression," interjected Peter, "that they still worship the old gods of *la ciudad blanca*. They also seem to believe in someone they call the *hombre del bosque,* some character who lives in the forest and communicates with their gods or god."

"Ah yes, we know the man of the forest, we know the Pech cling to their old beliefs," said Aldor, "their 'god' is really Satan himself and his presence in these mountains is solid. Our faith keeps us safe and strong, but the Pech have invited Satan into their village. I strongly urge you to stay away from this white city. It was the place the Pech learned their devil worship and the stench of it and the presence of the great deceiver are strong there." Peter grew tired of this talk and excused himself to head back to his tent where he fell asleep immediately.

The jaguar sat in front of him. Peter could smell its peculiar feline muskiness. "Almost there, Peter," it said in a tone that seemed sympathetic. "The great one will greet you with a gift and quickly you will see its benefits. Your life henceforth will be different in ways you cannot imagine." In the distance he heard thunder and he looked to the sky. When he looked back the jaguar was gone.

The thunder awakened him and he was surprised to see

that Aramis was not in his sleeping bag. The dream, as they all did, had exhausted him. He lay there for a while stretching his aching limbs. Suddenly Cruz-Madrid crawled into the tent. He smiled broadly and held his finger up to his lips. He was asleep before Peter could utter a word.

The next morning they were given a breakfast of corn meal mush and goat milk. Karen served Cruz-Madrid and smiled at him with every serving. They said their thanks to the Amish settlers who renewed their warnings, and set off.

The hike that day was mostly uphill over endless switchbacks, through more pine forest, crossing dozens of streams. By mid-afternoon it started to rain hard but they pressed on. By early evening they were on the crest of a forested ridge. Pravia took a few of them down the western slope of the hill a bit, where it gave way to sheer cliffs overlooking a deep valley with tall, white, limestone cliffs. Four or five waterfalls fell into the valley and it looked as if a small lake lay at the bottom, which was green with forest. "Below," said Pravia, "is *la ciudad blanca*. Now, we just have to find a way down."

Thirty-six
TEGUCIGALPA

Zelda rented an office in a tall building in downtown Tegus. She was sorting through the bills for the clinic construction when she found invoices she did not recognize. There were statements for food, supplies, fuel, canoes and even a bill for a helicopter rental. She called the accountant Chad had hired to manage the cash flow for the clinic and asked him where these bills had come from. "Senora, have you forgotten the expedition your husband funded before the issue of the clinic had even been raised? That was his reason for coming here to Honduras in the first place." Zelda had forgotten. The clinic, her relationship with Jahaira, Chad's murder, these had overshadowed the reason why she herself had come to Honduras. To her, the expedition had always been a folly and she saw no reason to continue it.

"Shut it down," she told the accountant.

"It is not that easy," he replied. "We have people in the field who cannot be readily contacted. We have a base camp on the *Rio Platano* and logistics people in La Ceiba. We have a helicopter under contract. First thing we must do is pull the group out of the jungle before we can shut down the base camp or the support people in La Ceiba. We cannot leave them hanging, we cannot jeopardize their safety."

"So how do we shut it down?"

"We need to send out a party to recall the archeological

group. The base camp can be contacted by radio but the archeological group is outside radio contact so they have to be located by following their trail. Once they are back we shut down the *Rio Platano* base camp and get them out of the jungle and back to La Ceiba. Then we can fly them all home. It could take five weeks, maybe more."

"Do it, get that party out as soon as possible, I don't want to spend any more money than necessary on this charade."

That night, over dinner, she recounted her conversation with Jahaira. "Why are you so against this expedition, *carina*? Is this not what your husband wanted to do? Do you not dishonor him by abandoning a quest he thought was important?"

"I always thought it was a ridiculous idea, a kind of boy's adventure magazine lark that Chad became momentarily obsessed with. I don't think it provides any honor to his memory and I don't want to see money syphoned away from the clinic. Anyway, why do you care?"

"I have told you before that I am familiar with the *ciudad blanca* and its mysteries. I believe your late husband's expedition has the potential to find many things of value."

"That's right, you said your father had been there. Why didn't he get an expedition going? He was a powerful and influential man from a wealthy family. He could have launched an effort."

"I told you he was a man of the cloth who wore his vocation like a cloak. Underneath he truly believed in a god which was far different than the Christian god but for him open expression of such notions would be blasphemy."

"But what does any of that have to do with *ciudad blanca*?"

"It was during his visit to that place that he came to understand the reality of the true faith, but for the rest of his life he had to hide that understanding or risk losing his position. He may have been an apostate but he liked his comforts and the power and prestige of being archbishop and did not want to jeopardize them because of his true beliefs. He was just as happy to see *la ciudad blanca* remain hidden in the jungle. But, there are many truths to be found in *ciudad blanca*, your late husband's expedition has the potential to publicize some of those truths which is why I would like to see it continue."

"Jahaira, I rarely disagree with you but on this I really do. If what is out there is so valuable then eventually someone will find it. With Chad gone, the money is mine and I just don't see the usefulness of spending millions of dollars, which is what this is costing, on something with such an abstract value, if any value. I'm sorry but I have already given direction to terminate the expedition."

"How long will it take to stop it?"

"I was told five weeks, maybe more. The group in the field cannot be reached by radio. The base camp will have to send out a party with a guide to recall them."

"You realize the field group are almost at the *ciudad blanca*, they are perhaps a day or less away."

"How could you possibly know that?"

"I have sources that have been following the expedition closely. What is most important to me is that Peter VanOwen is allowed to reach the site. However, it sounds like your search party will not reach the field group before they get to the city. They should have at least a few days and perhaps more than a week in the city before they can be reached. That should be enough time."

"Enough time for what, Jahaira?" Jahaira smiled as if smiling to herself at a private joke.

"Aaah, time to find the meaning of life, right?" Zelda's face took on a sour expression as if she had just tasted vinegar. "Is Peter really so bad, Zelda, that you find discussion of him unpleasant?"

"Yes. Peter was one of those men who treat a woman as if she weren't quite human, as if they were an icon, something foreign and unknowable, do you know what I mean?"

"I know exactly what you mean. An American writer, Katherine Anne Porter, once wrote that 'woman has been symbolized almost out of existence. To man, the myth maker, her true nature appears unfathomable, a dubious mystery at best.' Men have iconized women out of existence as human beings. Men like Peter cannot relate to women as people, at least not attractive women. And really, hasn't western culture reinforced this with movies and advertisements, popular music, perpetuating this impenetrable mystery that ultimately robs us of our humanity and individuality? Yes, your friend Peter seems very much of that ilk of men."

"Then why so much interest in him?"

"Because he is about to discover the meaning of life, that's why." They continued to talk into the night, sipping snifters of Barbancourt until finally they went up to bed.

Jahaira leaned over and kissed Zelda hard on the lips, grabbing her hair and pulling her down underneath her. Her hands worked quickly to remove Zelda's nightgown and she scooted up to squat over Zelda's mouth. Zelda's tongue emerged quickly to pleasure Jahaira as she rocked over her. Zelda loved Jahaira's aggression, which she interpreted as extreme desire for her. The more forceful Jahaira became, the more submissive Zelda felt. She had never been so relaxed and secure with a man. Strangely, sex with Jahaira allowed her to fully realize her femininity in a way she never had before. After Jahaira came, she quickly strapped on her dildo and entered Zelda who was still on her back. Jahaira wrapped her arms around Zelda's neck and kissed her hard while she pumped. Zelda grabbed Jahaira's buttocks and wrapped her legs around her. The passion continued for almost two hours. Both were exhausted lying side by side covered with each other's sweat. "I love you," sighed Zelda, "like no one else."

"*Mi amante tu eres mi vida*. Zelda, marry me."

Thirty-seven
RIO PLATANO MOUNTAINS

Yauwi knew the way down into the valley. What had once been a trail was now a crumbling series of switchback limestone ramps. There were places where it had completely fallen through, leaving gaps that seemed impossible to negotiate. The crumbling limestone made for perilous footing, especially for those with heavy packs, the weight of which provided downward impetus on the steepest slopes. Peter's legs ached and felt rubbery after days of hiking and the straps of his pack chafed his sweaty chest.

As they descended, the air became warmer and vegetation sprouted along the trail sometimes blocking it. The soldiers and Honduran workers had devised a wooden trellis they carried with them to bridge the gaps in the switchbacks. Cruz-Madrid walked alongside Peter and helped him around the spots where larger limestone rocks became impediments. He seemed excited and exhilarated at being so close to the expedition's goal. Selby, Mellon and DeGroet walked together behind Yauwi and Pravia at the head of the group. They came to a flat stretch of trail under a narrow archway of trees interwoven with vines, some of which stretched across the trail and had to be severed with machetes. They stopped at what looked like a thick tree trunk covered with vines. Pravia hacked away at it to reveal a limestone column, three feet thick, covered in carvings of spider monkeys, howlers, squirrel monkeys and a fearsome rendering of a capuchin scowling and baring its teeth. "A signpost," said DeGroet.

The next stretch of trail was a long, steep, incline. Its surface was a bed of crumbling limestone rocks. The party proceeded slowly, carefully picking their way down the rocky slideway. Peter was having a difficult time maintaining his footing. He slipped several times, once bruising his right hand as he thrust it forward to prevent himself from falling on his face. Suddenly he felt his feet sliding forward and the weight of his pack pull him backwards. The trail was so steep he began to slide downward quickly, vainly trying to grab at the crumbling trail surface to stop his slide. He began yelling as his slide took him over the side of the trail. He landed with a hard thump on a lower section of switchback having fallen over ten feet. On the limestone cliff wall next to his landing place was a worn carving of the fearsome capuchin with characters in the form of geometric shapes carved underneath.

The expedition hurried as fast as they could down the treacherous ramp to get to him. Peter felt as if he could not move or breathe. Cruz-Madrid was first to reach him and carefully examined him before turning him onto his back. "Breathe deeply," he told Peter, "I think you may be okay but the air has been forced out of you." Peter did not feel okay but was able to begin breathing normally again. They stripped off his pack and shirt to reveal a welter of bruises along his chest and stomach. DeGroet and Selby, however, seemed more interested in the carving than Peter.

"They seemed to have had some type of writing," said DeGroet of the geometric characters below the monkey carving, "but it is not pictographic and is unlike anything I have ever seen. Sadly we may be dealing with a literate society whose writing could take years to understand, if ever. So much knowledge out of our reach, it is painful."

"The capuchin monkey theme has already recurred twice," said Selby, "it seems to be important. But the monkey, which most of us find small and cute, seems to be fierce and hostile. Surely they couldn't have been afraid of the actual monkeys. Yet something in their culture led them to idealize the capuchin as a fearsome monster." Peter groaned and wondered if he had broken a rib. Cruz-Madrid told him no, they did not appear broken, just badly bruised. The group took a break as Peter recovered his wind and tried to pull himself together. Through the trees at the edge of the trail the valley lay below them. Pravia pointed out what appeared to be a large green covered hill at the far end of the valley.

"That is the main temple, a pyramid, the biggest structure in the city," he said. Peter was certain he saw Selby lick his lips as if preparing to devour a feast.

The rest of the climb down into the valley was without incident. It was late afternoon by the time they arrived at the valley floor among a stand of huge tropical cedars. Immediately they found traces of stone paths or roadways underneath a layer of vegetation. They quickly found walls and foundations covered with overgrowth. As they proceeded into the valley they encountered a broad creek. The green piles lining the creek proved to be buildings, some quite large. DeGroet had decided they would start at the temple since they had limited time and resources to deal with the extensive ruins they were now encountering. The temple, he reasoned, would be one of the most important buildings in the city with a good chance of revealing something about the rituals and beliefs of the city dwellers.

The way to the pyramid was choked with vegetation. The Honduran crew and Cruz-Madrid's soldiers wielded their machetes to carve a way forward. They skirted a small lake fed by the creek they encountered. At the far end of the lake the pyramid loomed like a green hillock covered in growth. Peter lagged to the back of the group, his exhaustion outweighed only by the intense pain from his bruises and sore ribs. He was relieved when they finally arrived at a clearing near the temple and began setting up camp. The next day they would begin clearing the vegetation from the temple structure and excavating.

Thirty-eight
LOS ANGELES

Zelda and Jahaira sat in a conference room of the Santa Monica police station at a table with Detective Lieutenant Parsons. Jahaira verified Zelda's story about spending the night on the evening Chad Toeb was killed. The detective nodded.

"We never really suspected you of actually committing the murder, Mrs. Toeb," he told them, "to be honest we did think it was possible that you could have hired someone to do it, after all you stood to benefit from his death more than any one. But we can find no evidence of any outstanding payments or cash transfers from your accounts, nor any since you began managing the estate's money. You seemed genuinely surprised that you were the only heir to your husband's fortune and you have a record of being a sterling citizen with no serious legal problems or debts, and certainly no criminal record of any kind. You also have a comfortable personal income independent of your husband, nor could we find any indication of serious marital discord that might have motivated a vicious killing like this. In short, Mrs. Toeb, we don't think you are much of a suspect in this crime and we are looking elsewhere for a suspect. One thing you can help us with, Mrs. Toeb, and let me put this as delicately as I can, was your husband romantically involved with anybody you know of? Did he ever patronize prostitutes?"

"Oh my god, why do you ask? I certainly never knew Chad to have anything to do with hookers, and no, I really had no idea that Chad could have been seeing anyone else. That really wouldn't have been like him."

"Your husband was last seen on a security camera in the lobby of your condo building going into the elevator with a young woman who had short black hair in a kind of page boy." He showed Zelda a still black and white photograph of Chad getting into the elevator in their condo lobby. All you could see of her was her back and the back of her head. "Her back was to the camera and she did seem to be with Mr. Toeb, although perhaps that's wrong. She was young and shapely and presumably pretty and not particularly well dressed so we thought she might be a prostitute. Otherwise we don't have a shred of evidence. The place was wiped clean by a pro, and whoever handled the knife that killed him knew what they were doing. We don't know of any hit woman who looks like the lady on camera and we really can't find anyone who wanted him dead. We are totally at a standstill on this case. I can only apologize for our lack of progress, Mrs. Toeb. We're baffled."

"As am I, lieutenant. Chad had enemies but no one who would be violent and really no one who would benefit from his death."

"Other than yourself?"

"Yes, other than me, and I would never kill someone over money, even if I didn't have a cent, which I do, and did before Chad was killed."

"Does the woman in the photograph look at all familiar to you?"

"She doesn't look like any one I know, not remotely. I am sorry, Lieutenant, this whole situation is just surreal to me." They took their leave of the Lieutenant and Zelda called an Uber to take them to her lawyer's office to discuss Chad's trust. Jahaira had insisted on signing a prenuptial to emphasize to Zelda that her money had no relation to her desire to marry her. Two hours later they traveled to the downtown County Courthouse to get a marriage license, then back to Zelda's Santa Monica condo which was no longer a crime scene. They carefully dressed and did their makeup. The wedding was scheduled for sunset in the Zen garden courtyard of Yamashiro restaurant, high in the hills above Hollywood.

Neither of them had family. Zelda's parents died several years ago and she had no siblings. There were several cousins back in New York but no one important enough to invite. Jahaira had already told Zelda the story of her parents' demise, her mother from grief and madness and her father by her own hand. Zelda was not sure she believed either story but it was clear enough Jahaira had no one worthy of attending her wedding. The only other attendees would be a retired judge who was performing the ceremony, a young trumpet player, named Trevor Clarke, and a *congero,* who Jahaira had insisted on hiring to provide the only musical accompaniment to the nuptials. They both chose white silk dresses, not identical, but similar. Zelda's, a sheath hemmed just above her knees, sleeveless with a white mesh bodice. Jahaira's skirt flared slightly at the waist and ended mid-calf. They both wore white, patent leather spike heels. "Are we crazy?" asked Zelda as she stared at Jahaira.

"Of course we are," laughed Jahaira, "but we are the most beautiful crazy women in Los Angeles, are we not?" They went downstairs to climb into the large black limo to take them to Hollywood and their future.

Thirty-nine
LA CIUDAD BLANCA

They started work in the cool of the morning while mist rose from the lake. No one bothered Peter, who, because of his injuries from his fall the previous day, was allowed to sleep late while the others began carefully clearing brush away from the base of the pyramid. He awoke to the sound of machetes hacking at vines and branches. The pyramid was quite large with a height they estimated at almost two hundred feet and base measurements of about seven hundred and fifty feet on each side. It was constructed from limestone blocks. On the side facing the lake there appeared to be a broad stairway leading to a platform, which may have been used for sacrifices and other public ceremonies. The initial clearing was focused on the base of this stairway. In the next day or two trenches would be dug in the ground surrounding the pyramid to locate detritus.

Peter stumbled to the mess tent. The only one there was Cruz-Madrid who was nursing a cup of coffee. He pointed Peter to a covered bowl of fried bananas and a dish of rice that had been the expedition's breakfast. Peter helped himself and poured the last of the coffee into a tin cup. "How are you feeling today, Peter?" asked Cruz-Madrid.

"Really quite awful, my side is black and blue and it aches when I breathe, otherwise my whole body is one dull aching mess. Where is everyone else?"

"They are all working on clearing the temple. I have never seen such excitement, you would think they just found the Holy Grail!"

"Why aren't you out there helping?"

"Well, they commandeered my men, so they have plenty of hands. Really, this sort of hard work is not my thing and I guess that ruins do not excite me much."

"As a Honduran, aren't you interested in your national heritage?"

"Well, it is not really my heritage. My family were Spaniards who came over after the conquest. These ruins are more the heritage of the *Indios* who lived here before my people came. It is not anything we had much to do with, it is a Honduras that no longer exists, except maybe in the imaginations of people like Jahaira."

"What do you mean?"

"Our friend Jahaira has a fascination with the ancient traditions of Honduras and perhaps in particular the Pech. Maybe it is a *mestizo* thing trying to derive pride from the ancient traditions of *Indio* ancestors, maybe a reaction to the Hispanic domination of modern Honduran culture and how we demean the *Indio* culture as primitive and ignorant."

"I thought Jahaira was a Cristales herself?"

"Her father, yes, but her mother was clearly not. She once told me her mother was part Pech, which may account in part for her fascination with their beliefs. Her father, too, spent time in *La Moskitia* and visited the Pech villages. Even though he was of pure Spanish descent he was fascinated with their culture and a student of ancient religions. She told me he even wrote a book about them."

"Did you ever meet him?"

"My relationship with Jahaira was strictly, shall we say, professional, so we did not meet each other's parents. But I do know some Cristales and none of them could ever figure out exactly who her father was. They thought she was a fraud."

"Do you?"

"Actually, no, Jahaira may be devious and really just a high class and expensive *puta,* but when she talks about things that mean something to her, I think she is honest. I think the Cristales family do not want to admit to their relationship with her and would say anything to discredit it."

The front of the base of the pyramid and the first tier of steps had been cleared, as well as a pathway all around the structure. DeGroet, Mellon and Selvy had been surveying the area around the pyramid. Peter and Aramis heard an excited shout. They ran from the mess tent towards the temple.

Wendy was running towards them. "They found an entrance!" she shouted, "at the back of the pyramid, a stairway leading down, underneath," she said breathlessly.

They ran to the side of the pyramid facing away from the lake. The three archeologists stood there looking at a rectangular opening in the base. There were the remnants of stairs going down towards an aperture choked with rubble.

"From now on," said Doctor DeGroet, "the focus of the excavation will be right here. Let's see if we can penetrate the interior of the pyramid."

Forty
LOS ANGELES

No one went to Yamashiro for the food. L.A. had dozens of Japanese restaurants with better food. But the view was spectacular and the restaurant itself had charm and ambiance. It was built in 1914 in the Hollywood hills as a private residence by a pair of eccentric brothers with an extensive collection of Asian art who intended it to be a replica of a palace in the Yamashiro district of Japan. The brothers spared no expense in importing craftsmen from that country to fashion the finishing details. It was a large rectangular building with a pagoda style blue tile roof set around a courtyard with a Zen garden. The floors were burnished wood tiles and the interior walls dark stained wood framing rice paper. In some places ink drawings adorned the rice paper panels and here and there were alcoves with brass Buddhas. On a clear day, a patron sitting by a front window could see all the way to the ocean and, at night, the Los Angeles basin spread below like a twinkling fairyland, a dream city glowing with possibilities.

Miriam, Paul and Aileen passed through the bar and foyer of the restaurant to wait for their table. They caught a glimpse of a wedding party, including musicians, coming through the door behind them.

"Hey, Trevor!" shouted Aileen. The tall black man looked over and waved. He walked over, gesturing the two women with him to follow. There was a tall white girl and a shorter, bronze-skinned, dark-haired girl. As they got closer, Miriam could see the tall white girl was no girl at all, probably just a few years younger than herself, but she had some artful and expensive plastic surgery done and looked good for her age. The other woman was shorter but much younger and a real looker. She appeared to be Hispanic or Native American or something, probably twenty-five or twenty-six with high cheekbones, large dark eyes and a voluptuous figure.

"Hey, Aileen. I want you to meet my new friends, Jahaira and Zelda. They are getting married here. They hired me to play for their wedding. Jahaira, Zelda, this is Aileen VanOwen and her mom Miriam Griffin and her stepdad Paul Griffin. I play in her sister, Leia's, band."

"A pleasure to meet you," said Jahaira, "you would not by chance be related to Peter VanOwen, who we both know?"

"That's my dad," said Aileen, "but I haven't seen him in forever. In fact, I don't even know where he is now. Some girl answers his phone and says he's in Honduras on some expedition. That seems so ridiculous."

"Aah, but it is true, both Zelda and I saw him just before he left. We live in Honduras. He is fine, but the expedition is out of communication range for the moment. He will be back very soon sincc my fiancé has pulled the plug on the expedition. Her late husband had financed it. I am sure we will see him when he gets back to Tegucigalpa. I promise to tell him to call you as soon as he can."

"Well, it might be nice to know he was all right," said Aileen, overwhelmed by the wealth of information just provided and the realization the two women were the ones getting married. "Anyway, congratulations on your wedding, best of luck."

They sat nursing their drinks with little to say to each other. Aileen, as always, was having both money and boyfriend problems. Miriam was not eager to say anything that would touch off a torrent of complaints from her daughter, which might worsen the already sullen mood of her husband. She liked the restaurant, she liked the view, she liked the pale blue drink that tasted vaguely of pineapple, and she wanted a quiet, pleasant evening unmarred by whining, complaints or quiet, passive-aggressive hostility. A stream of music, which sounded faintly familiar, interrupted her thoughts.

In the courtyard, the couple they had met were being married, each woman dressed in white. The older, taller woman had long legs and a graceful figure with long dark hair. The judge finished taking their vows and Trevor Clarke began playing a sweet rhythmic version of "The Look of Love" with almost perfect tone. Miriam knew that was why the sound was vaguely familiar, Trevor Clarke's clear clean style was distinctive. She noticed on the far end of the courtyard a *congero* provided a complex Latin beat. The two women danced slowly, barely moving, holding each other tightly. When the song ended, they kissed, a long passionate, sensual kiss that made Miriam wince. She was all for gay marriage and had a few gay friends but she was glad her daughters were heterosexual. There was enough drama with their boyfriends than to have to deal with gay subculture and the stigma. However unfair, there still was a stigma in their circle of friends that would create far more stress than she could bear.

The couple broke apart and held hands for a few seconds. Then the trumpet player started playing a fast *punta* rhythm and the shorter dark girl stepped forward and began dancing, moving her hips rapidly with quick short steps. The *congero* increased the rhythm and the trumpet player followed suit. The girl began twirling and jumping as she danced. Miriam was transfixed. The girl's dancing was free, joyous and celebratory in a way Miriam had never seen and certainly had never felt herself. The tall white girl seemed a little lost, just kind of dancing in place while her partner danced joyously at an ever-faster pace. Everyone in the restaurant who had a view of the courtyard had stopped eating and talking and watched as the beautiful dark girl twirled and rocked her hips at the same time. She was a lovely dancer, moving her body in perfect rhythm, graceful, unselfconscious and uninhibited. When the music and the dancer had stopped, there was a smattering of applause throughout the restaurant, which the girl acknowledged with a nod of the head. The party then went off to have their dinner.

Forty-one
PLAYA ESTERILLOS

Ophelia was getting bored. The books that VanOwen had were boring. She did not understand them. She was running low on *Flor de Cana*, she no longer felt comfortable going into Jaco, which anyway bored her. She thought about going back up to San Jose but really what was there but a bunch of *putas* and horny gringos, in her opinion the worst kind of a bad lot. At the little market where she shopped they had told her about a new beach-side restaurant at Esterillos Centro. She decided to try it and have a few drinks before coming back and sitting on the beach to watch the bats.

To reach Esterillos Centro you turned off Highway 34 down a rutted dirt road. She went all the way to the beach where she could see the white ribbon of froth that was the surf line. She turned right and parked on the sand across from an open palapa filled with tables. In front there were perhaps two dozen gringos playing a game where they threw horseshoes at an iron rod in the ground. To her dismay she saw the place was full of gringos. She almost turned around and went back to the house. But these seemed like a different breed of gringo from the surfer punks in Jaco. They were mostly middle aged and mostly male. They were all in shorts and T-shirts. Most of the men had substantial bellies. Many had graying hair and sideburns. She could hear a band playing loud rock music, a song she remembered from her days in the brothel, something about a hotel in California. As she approached, she noticed a table of women. They were all middle aged and every one had short hair. Two of them were tall and lean with leathery skin and silver hair. The rest were wide hipped and *gorda*. She realized these were American expatriates, Americans who lived here permanently or at least most of the time. As she walked past the horseshoe players she got the usual horny stares, but there was something else, a sense that she was unwelcome as an outsider. She decided she would at least order a drink and subject them to her presence for a while.

The bald proprietor was one of those Ticos who had been to America, spoke colloquial English and thought he knew how to deal with gringos. She sat at a table   in the back, away from the horseshoes and close to the band where no one else was sitting. The band finished the hotel song and began a song about a slow ride, repeating the lyric over and over. She did not care much for the jazz and classical music of which the *bruja* was so fond, she preferred *punta* and *cumbia*, but this was far worse.

When the *bruja* asked her to go to Los Angeles she was excited. The only time she had ever been on a plane was the flight from Tegus to San Josc and the only place she had been to outside of Honduras was Costa Rica. Los Angeles was a great city, far greater than Tegus or San Jose, but she knew she was not going there to sight see. The flight had been long and boring despite, or perhaps because of, the attempts of the man in the adjoining seat trying to flirt with her. By the time she got to L.A. she was tired and the airport there was disappointing. The San Jose Airport, though much smaller, was nicer and cleaner too. She rented a car with the credit card the *bruja* had given her and drove to a large hotel by the airport. From the sky, L.A. had appeared enormous, stretching for countless miles but she seemed destined to be confined to a small corner of the massive city.

She ordered a Pilsen and the whole grilled snapper from the bald proprietor. As far as she could see, the crowd of gringos was only drinking beer, no one had food. The proprietor, whose name was Chris, asked her in Spanish where she was staying. In her clear, unaccented English she replied that she was staying in Peter VanOwen's house in Esterillos Este. He nodded, clearly confused as to whether or not she was or was not a *gringa* herself, and went off to place her order.

She liked the hotel room at the Airport Marriot in L.A. It was big and clean with a nice firm mattress, and clean sheets and a clean bathroom all to herself that maids would clean every day. She could order food from room service and they brought it right up to her. She got a steak, a baked potato, a salad and, because they had no good rum, a bottle of Johnny Walker which she had tasted once when a client brought a bottle to the *Diamante Azul* to share with the girls. So, the *puta* from *Colonia Pineda* was now lounging in her palatial L.A. hotel room drinking Johnny Walker and watching some sort of American police drama on television.

From time to time, the gringos playing and watching the horseshoes would yell triumphantly, usually after a clink of metal on metal. She was aware of furtive stares directed her way. Men checking her out, undressing her in their minds, women, hostile and disapproving. Finally a tall, thin, leathery *gringa* with short grey hair walked unsteadily over to her table.

"Why don't you get yourself back over to the Cocal, this isn't your crowd," she said, referencing the oceanfront casino, bar and hotel that was the epicenter of Jaco prostitution. In fact, she knew some of the girls who came down on weekends from San Jose to ply their trade, and had shared a drink with some of them in a Jaco bar before her run in with the surfer gringo.

"I am sorry, but I am not a *puta* and have every right to be here even if I were," she replied in unaccented English. "I am here to house sit for my boyfriend, one of your own as it happens, Peter VanOwen, while he is in Honduras."

"Oh him, saying he's your boyfriend doesn't mean you're not a hooker, everyone knows about him. For an old loser like him to end up with someone like you there has to be money changing hands. You heard me, you're not welcome here, and stay away from the men or you have a serious problem."

The plan Jahaira had given her was simple. The *bruja* told her where in Los Angeles she needed to go and wait for the man. She described him, short, bald, with a large head, broad shouldered, clean-shaven. She would inspect the lobby of the condo complex for cameras, wearing a hat, wig and sunglasses, so she would know to keep her face away from their range. The man would be in a bar in Century City at about six the following evening. She would pick him up there, offer to go home with him and go back to the condo. She would take care of her business and leave the condo complex using a utility exit from the basement. From there she would walk the ten blocks to the Expo line station and take a circuitous route on light rail to the green line from which she would take a bus back to her hotel. She would fly back to San Jose the next morning, rent a car and drive to VanOwen's beach house. Unlike most plans, this one worked exactly as envisioned, no complications, no unanticipated changes.

As she ate her snapper Ophelia watched the tall, leathery *gringa* wobble her way back to her table, occasionally flashing a dirty look back at Ophelia. When the *gringa* got back to her table she said something and the other women laughed. Ophelia sighed, finished her fish, and left as quickly as possible.

Forty-two
LA CIUDAD BLANCA

All of the workers were now clearing rubble from the opening at the back of the pyramid. It appeared that there had once been a stairway down the opening but time, and perhaps earthquakes, had collapsed the staircase and clogged the opening with rubble. DeGroet and Mellon speculated that the space below may be a burial place for a king or high priest. Such places were often a rich source of archeological material, often giving rise to sculptures and pottery of high quality. The dark, relatively dry atmosphere of such spaces helped preserve artifacts.

Peter and Aramis had little to do. Cruz-Madrid's *Flor de Cana* was long gone and their subsistence was primarily rice, beans and whatever bush meat the soldiers might bring down when they were not helping clear the opening in the pyramid. "What will you do Peter, when you go back to your seaside house?"

"Same as before. Buy and sell coffee, spend days by the beach. Go into Jaco or San Jose for whores."

"You can't live without women, can you Peter?"

"No, can you?"

"Never. My mother was a great beauty. She was always going to parties and gatherings. Even as a married woman with children she had many admirers and, sadly, I am fairly sure she cheated on my father. She had little time to spend with her children. When I was ill or bullied at school or unsure of myself in some way she was never there to give me support or love. I never really felt worthy of her love and I always craved it. When I was sixteen, my uncle took me to an elegant brothel in Tegus. It was the first time I felt loved by a woman. I was too young to understand they were doing this for money and they were so attentive and gentle with me knowing that it was my first time, that I took it for real. It gave me a sense I could relate to a woman and it made me appreciate the power of a woman's body. It is still something I crave on a daily basis. Maybe I am still just looking for *amore de mi madre*, *mi hermosa madre*. I cannot say I have ever found it."

"I know, I feel like I've spent my life searching for approval from women and never finding it. I became a lawyer instead of a philosophy professor because my mother's idea of success demanded a six-figure income. A procession of girlfriends, from Zelda on, found me less than satisfactory. My wife divorced me because she felt I wasn't providing for her and our daughters as well as I should. When I passed up promotions to continue doing the work I loved she was furious. I always felt her disapproval and disappointment. The whores in Jaco and San Jose are better looking and the only thing they want from me is money and not much of it. When I am finished with them I can walk out the door with no obligations."

"But the bond between men and women is sacred, which is why god created holy matrimony," said Arias-Garcia, who had taken a break from running the camp to eavesdrop on their conversation, "what you are talking about corrupts and defiles that bond. The Apostle Paul wrote in his epistle to the Hebrews 'Marriage is honorable in all, and the bed undefiled, but whoremongers and adulterers, god will judge.' You are defiling yourselves, and your time to make things right with god is running out." Before either of the astonished friends could reply, they heard a shout from the pyramid and ran back to the excavation site to see what was happening.

The last of the rubble had been removed from the opening.

Mellon and DeGroet were standing by the entrance peering down at a dark void. "Clearly there is some sort of chamber below. The stairway leading down has collapsed but maybe we can rig a pulley system to lower people and equipment down," said DeGroet.

"First we need to establish how far down the chamber goes and whether or not the floor is flat. I mean it's possible this was just a garbage dump under the pyramid. If we're going to take risks we need a better idea of what's down there," responded Mellon.

"Perhaps if we can send a strong light down on a pulley we will have a better idea, but I have to say, I doubt this is just a rubbish bin under such a major pyramid," answered DeGroet. They both knelt down by the opening and peered down into the darkness. Selby and Peter joined them. Peter dropped down to a prone position with his face over the edge of the opening. He was sure he had caught a glimpse of some sort of movement.

They suddenly felt a rolling sensation and the earth began to move. DeGroet, Mellon and Selby scrambled back away from the opening but before Peter could get up, the stone lip of the opening collapsed under him and he went hurtling head first into the darkness.

Forty-three
TEGUCIGALPA

Zelda and Jahaira lay naked on top of her heavy mahogany bed. Their bodies glistened with sweat after almost two hours of lovemaking. Zelda could still taste the salty residue of Jahaira's vagina and her own vagina was sore from the relentless pounding of Jahaira's dildo. "I still feel guilty over feeling so little grief at Chad's death, especially considering the grisly way he died. Have you ever lost someone?"

"Yes, I've lost several people, my mother and father, of course, but also several lovers and a husband."

"You were married before?"

"I am sorry I did not tell you before, *carina*, but it never really came up and never seemed like the right time to tell you. In any case, it does not really matter, he is long ago dead and you are now the person in my life."

"That's a lot of loss for someone so young. What happened to your husband?"

"He died. Really, *carina*, I do not like to talk about it. All I am saying is I know loss and one feels it differently every time. Perhaps your marriage with Chad was already in a state of decline and you had already started dealing with a type of loss before he died, so the impact was not so great."

"Perhaps, I'm not sure. What was your husband like? And you married a man, do you prefer women now?"

"He was very handsome and very bright. I liked the way

he looked at the world. He was young when I married him but he was a good companion for our entire marriage. After he was gone I vowed never to put myself in a place where I was vulnerable to such a loss. As to preferring women now, yes I do. When I was younger I did not mind so much the tendency of men to try to dominate both sexually and within a relationship. I admired their vitality and I felt flattered by their lust. But after a while I wanted to be the strong partner, the one to dominate both in bed and in the relationship. It was harder to do with men. Women are more sensitive and pliable, they understand the female body so much better and, in their own way, they are really more sensual than men, so many of whom are really just alley cats in pants."

"I guess you broke your vow by marrying me. Does it bother you at all that I am so much older?"

"I do not intend to lose anyone that I care for, not ever again, and as I have said, I am not nearly as young as you think I am. Our real age difference might surprise you."

Zelda stretched her legs and lay back on her pillow. Tomorrow would be a busy day. She had meetings with Doctor Castillo and several candidates for senior staff positions at the clinic. She intended to pay generous salaries and was looking for the sort of gifted young doctor who usually ended up starting an expensive private practice aimed at wealthy patients, or who might leave Honduras altogether, for Miami, Panama City, even Buenos Aires. Nursing staff were even harder to find and she had finally decided to devote a portion of the clinic building to a nursing training facility that could feed talented well trained nurses into the clinic. She also had a telephone conference with the lawyer for Chad's estate, most of which was held in trust. The transfer to her as trustee was almost complete.

It bothered her a little that Jahaira had not told her she had been married before. Why was she so unwilling to talk about how he died? Was Jahaira gay or heterosexual? For that matter, was she herself gay or straight? Or were they both bisexual?

Really, it shouldn't matter and Zelda was beginning to think that these classifications meant nothing. As these thoughts bounded through her brain she felt the dildo press against her thigh. She couldn't believe Jahaira was still horny after all they had done tonight and that she was not exhausted like Zelda. As always though, Zelda felt herself submit to whatever Jahaira wanted. She climbed on top of Zelda and kissed her hard then scooted up to Zelda's face and straddled it. Zelda obediently began softly, gently licking Jahaira who rocked slowly over her face. For Zelda it would be another tired day tomorrow.

Forty-four
LA CIUDAD BLANCA

Peter woke in complete darkness. His body ached and he felt sure that he must have broken a bone. But as he tried out each limb they seemed to work, and he was shocked to find he had no major injuries after falling almost thirty feet onto a stone floor. The floor was the only thing he could sense. It was stone and it was flat and well worn. The air in the chamber was musty smelling but not entirely stale, as if there were some faint source of fresh air that flowed into it. He could barely see the opening above him. It seemed small and remote. But as his eyes began to adjust to the darkness, the distant light from the opening allowed him to pick out a few details. He could sense walls and barely make out the outlines of carvings that seemed to cover every surface he could see. The chamber seemed to be far smaller than the outline of the base of the pyramid.

He hobbled to his feet and shouted up at the opening. "Help me! I'm okay but I'm trapped down here!" He tried this several times and got no response. On the far end of the chamber he thought he saw a pale blue light. At first he thought this was his imagination but gradually he came to believe the light was real. Since no one answered his calls for help he thought he might as well seek out the source of the light. Who knows, he thought, it could even be an exit.

He slowly made his way across the chamber, occasionally stumbling over pieces of rubble. The blue light came from an opening at the far end of the chamber. As he approached it, he saw stairs leading down from the chamber to a lower level. The blue light was coming from somewhere in this sub-chamber. He carefully descended the stairs. There was just enough light that he could see a few steps in front of him. When he had gone all the way down the stairs he could see that the blue light came from the top of some sort of huge stone chair. He moved slowly towards it, noting the floor was strewn with artifacts. He made out carvings, statuary, clay vessels of some sort and even an obsidian knife. The stone chair was three or four feet off the floor of the sub-chamber with a series of steps leading up to it. Each arm was a carved jaguar figure, while the back of the chair featured a large bas-relief carving of a capuchin monkey face.

"At last you are here," said a soft female voice. A nude young woman emerged from behind the stone chair. The only object she wore was a slender silver necklace with a blue stone carving of a monkey head, identical to those worn by Jahaira and Ophelia, the San Jose whore. "Yes, it is," she said, as if reading his thoughts "there were only a few of these necklaces made here almost two thousand years ago. Now only truth seekers wear them, and, as we know, there are not many of them are there, Peter?" The woman was stunningly beautiful. She could not have been much older than twenty, had long black hair, large dark eyes, pale, creamy skin, rounded hips and lovely breasts. Where she walked light seemed to emanate around her. He could not keep his eyes off the small patch of pubic hair at her groin. She noticed this and laughed. "Of all the qualities I invested in humans, lust has provided me with the most amusement. You supposedly rational creatures compromising yourselves over and over just to satisfy an animal instinct is often so comical. Really, the animal side of you is a source of endless entertainment for me." Peter felt quite sure he must have hit his head during his fall and suffered a concussion. He wondered if he was still unconscious.

"I can assure you, Peter, that I am quite real," said the

woman, once again seeming to read his thoughts, "in fact I am the most real thing in this room, the only real thing in this room to be blunt. You and everything else here are just products of my own creation, nothing more than projections of my thoughts or fantasies. In your language, Peter, the word for me is 'god.' It does not really describe what I am very accurately but there is no other word. I know you are an atheist, Peter, which by the way, makes meeting you a bit more interesting for me, and I really cannot blame you for not believing in the rather drab one dimensional deity your cultural religions have created. I am not anything like that. I hope my appearing to you in the form of an object of lust might demonstrate that. Unlike your Judeo - Christian god, I have no objection to unbridled human lust. As I said, I enjoy the absurdity it often creates. I created you to watch your venality in action as it struggles against the desire of mankind to establish peace and order. I created you for my amusement and you have not disappointed." As bruised and confused as he was, Peter felt his penis stiffen at the site of a beautiful nude woman moving elegantly and sensually as she spoke, the pale blue light playing off the curves of her hips and breasts. Assuming any of this was not just a hallucination, he could not understand why it was happening to him.

"From time to time, using the human concept of time for explanatory purposes, I choose someone to break the pattern. For humans, your brief existence is defined by your inevitable death. That shadow stalks you as you move through life. As you get older the shadow grows longer. Some people are haunted by it. Others seek it out as the solution to an intolerable existence. For many the illusion of an after-life sustains them, at least until death draws close; then they often feel doubt and fear regardless of their faith. I like to see what happens when the shadow is withdrawn. I like to choose contemplative types for whom the absence of death may actually cause more suffering than the onset of death. I enjoy watching that struggle. It has been almost two hundred of your years since I bestowed my 'gift' on another.

Sadly it turned out badly for him. His own excessively clever daughter, who seems to have taken an interest in you as well, betrayed him. She is a human in whom I delight, but if I were you, I would be very careful of her." The blue light seemed to flicker then grow stronger, Peter's erection was rock hard.

"All of the modern religions seem to portray god as beneficent, perhaps a bit strict and intolerant, but the very essence of goodness as humanly defined. That is not at all what I am like. I would have loved Sodom and Gomorrah but I might still have destroyed them just for the pleasure of doing so. A part of the gift I am giving you, Peter, is the realization that these religions are created to sustain hope, to give support to authority and provide a rationale for moral behavior. But they are all false. I am not 'good' as humans define 'good.' I am beyond good and evil. I gave you limited lives and condemned each of you to death to avoid hope, and look what you have done with it. If there are aspects of your world that seem to reflect order, at least in a scientific sense, you must understand that the concept of order is imposed by humans on a universe that is random and chaotic. That order is an illusion, the universe is a maelstrom of randomness, which I set into motion. Humans are beyond hope. You must live and then you are condemned to die. In between, you have suffering; illness, violence, natural disasters, ignorance, bigotry and the humiliating descent into old age as the body decays while you still live. Of course, there are the occasional moments of happiness that keep each of you slogging through your lives in search of more, like the slot machine player whose first jackpot convinces him there are more to be had just around the corner. Your lives are illusions lived for my entertainment and delight. Peter, I can see you are aroused. Come to me, embrace this lovely body and kiss me."

Peter could not help himself. He hesitantly walked towards the woman. With every step she became lovelier. A deep, enticing, musky smell arose from her. She took the last few steps and embraced him. She put her hand behind his head and drew it to her. His hands grabbed her round, naked buttocks. When she locked her lips on his and slithered her tongue deep into his mouth, he felt a surge. Energy coursed through him, leaving him feeling intense pain and intense pleasure simultaneously. He felt as though he would explode. The smell of sizzling electricity burning human flesh filled his nostrils. The feelings became too much for him and he lost consciousness, slipping from her embrace and falling to the floor.

Forty-five
TEGUCIGALPA

Zelda had never been in the kitchen of Jahaira's house before. But she had arrived home early and heard her voice somewhere deep in the house. She passed through the swinging door leading from the dining room to the kitchen and found Jahaira tending a large pot of braising meat. Angelica was at a long marble counter straining coconut milk.

She was surprised at how modern the kitchen was. The meat was braising on the cooktop of a black La Cornue oven, there was a double door Subzero refrigerator, a stainless steel prep table in the middle of the room and dark solid wood mahogany cabinets. An array of copper and cast aluminum pots and pans hung from a rack over the stove. Jahaira went from the pot of braising meat to a battery of mortar and pestles where she started grinding whole spices. The smell in the kitchen was rich and hearty from the meat and redolent of allspice, ginger, coriander, cinnamon and cardamom. A stainless steel bowl of scotch bonnet peppers sat waiting to be chopped and seeded. Jahaira was smiling a contented and very genuine smile, she was clearly at peace in the kitchen.

"*Carina*, you are early tonight. Angelica and I are just making a Jamaican goat curry. How spicy can you handle it?"

"I'm not sure, I've never eaten goat and I usually don't eat spicy, but I'll give it a try, just don't make it so hot I'll cry. I got word today that the messengers the *ciudad blanca* expedition sent to the base camp arrived and they have sent a group out to recall the field team. They should be there in a few days and the whole thing should be wrapped up in two weeks. Everyone can go home and I can stop paying tens of thousands of dollars in bills every week."

"Have there been any casualties?"

"I don't know, I don't think so, I would have heard, wouldn't I? I guess no one really knows what has happened with the field team, they could all be dead for all we know. Why? Are you thinking about VanOwen? Are you still obsessed with that nebbish?"

"Yes, I am talking about Peter and, I suppose, obsessed with him. They are in a very dangerous place and it is possible he might not survive the experience. Well, thanks to you we will soon know his fate. You remember your promise to me?"

"What promise?"

"That in exchange for helping you with the clinic you will help arrange a meeting between Peter and me."

"You certainly did help with the clinic, it wouldn't have happened without you, but I thought you did that because you loved me."

"Well, that may also have been a motivation but it really is important to me to see Peter when, and if, he gets back. Let us move to the dining room and enjoy a cocktail while we wait for Angelica to finish dinner." In the dining room Jahaira made Guaro sours using local sugar cane liquor, lime juice and simple syrup.

"I ask you again, Jahaira, why such interest in Peter VanOwen? You never give me a straight answer even though you want my help."

"Are you jealous, afraid that this grey haired, potbellied man may supplant you in my affections?"

"Maybe a little," Zelda said with a shrug, "but you still haven't answered my question."

"He has something I want and I intend to get it and you

will help me as you have promised," said Jahaira with a tight smile. Angelica came into the room with steaming bowls of fragrant goat curry and white rice. On the side was a small cut glass bowl of homemade pineapple chutney. Angelica brought bottles of cold Port Royal beer with chilled glasses. Zelda found the goat meat surprisingly delicious, tender and a bit gamey, but the curry itself had an after kick of spice that took her by surprise. It took three cold Port Royals to get her through her bowl of curry. Dessert was a chilled bowl of fresh fruit macerated in rum. Zelda worried that eating like this would cause her to gain weight but she had found a gym and the hard pace of her workdays and the relentless nights of sex with Jahaira, at least four or five times a week, had kept her slender and fit. Although she found Jahaira a bit opaque at times about her life and activities, Zelda was happy and fulfilled in her new life in Honduras with her peculiar lover.

Forty-six
LA CIUDAD BLANCA

Peter awakened in a blaze of light, which temporarily blinded him. He could hear movement all round him and muffled voices. "He has been electrocuted," a voice seemed to say.

"He is awake! Peter, can you hear me?" said the voice of Cruz-Madrid. As Peter's vision began to focus, he could see that Aramis was kneeling beside him. "We are going to get you out of here, Peter, no one can believe you survived that fall, where did you encounter electrical current? You look and smell like you have had a severe electrical shock." Peter made a sound but was unable to form a word. He was carefully transferred to a makeshift stretcher that was carried to the upper chamber and placed in a sling raising him to the surface.

He slept for several hours. When he finally got up it was evening. He was lying in a tent on the edge of the camp. He noticed activity throughout the camp, workers were packing equipment and some of the tents had been taken down.

"You saw him, didn't you?" Arias Garcia was standing in the entrance of the tent looking at him.

"What do you mean?"

"*El diablo* is what I mean, the father of lies, the serpent. You saw him below the pyramid. He singed you with his hell fire. Now do you believe?"

"I saw nothing, at least I don't think I really saw anything.

212

I had a bad fall, I probably hit my head and lost it, that's all. No diablo, nothing but a bad dream."

"How do you explain the electric shock you experienced? That is the power of Satan, the fire of hell he subjected you to."

"I have no idea, it must have been some freak accident, I thought I just dreamed it. Arturo, what is going on? It almost looks like they're tearing down the camp. Are we moving or something?"

"No, we are going back. Senor Toeb, our sponsor, died. His widow does not want to continue with the expedition. They have sent messengers to tell us to return immediately. The expedition is over. Doctor DeGroet is devastated."

"Indeed he is," said a gravelly Dutch voice that belonged to the Doctor himself, "this is the biggest find of my career, it is huge and there are many years of work to be done here, but it could change our conception of the history of Central America if we could finish it. Those chambers you fell into, Peter, are amazing, like nothing I have ever seen in Mesoamerica, stylized statuary and bas-relief, beautiful pottery, obsidian tools and some amazing azurite carvings. This was a highly advanced and very unique civilization with a complex religion and culture and we are being told to leave it and go home without even preliminary evaluation. I will make every effort when we get back to find funding for another expedition."

"Is it true that Chad Toeb is dead? He was younger than me and he certainly seemed to be in good health," said Peter.

"He was murdered, quite grisly I hear, throat cut, no one knows who did it. His widow is in charge now and wants to spend the money from the expedition on a clinic for the poor in Tegucigalpa, a tragedy, truly. If you are recovered, we plan to move out the day after tomorrow. You will have to walk, I am sorry but we cannot spare the men for a stretcher. What do you think, are you up for it?"

"I like the idea of going home, I'll give it a try. I think I'm okay, no broken bones or any permanent damage. I am still a little woozy right now but I think I'll be okay."

"By the way, where did you encounter the electrical charge that left you unconscious? We could find nothing in the lower chambers that could have generated such a charge, yet you clearly experienced a substantial electrical shock."

"I don't know, I had a hallucination that ended with a very strange sensation, both pleasurable and painful at the same time. I didn't think it was real."

"Ha, just one more mystery from the lost city of the monkey god."

For the next day and a half, Peter watched as they packed up the camp, taking artifacts and extensively photographing the site. As he ate and began to move about, Peter felt better and began to dream of sitting on his patio in Esterillos watching the bats play in the evening as the waves lapped the shore.

When the day came to leave, Peter gave DeGroet the okay, saying he was sure he could make the hike. They did not ask him to carry a pack this time so even though he was weakened from his experiences he felt unburdened and happy as they began the climb out of the valley. The next few days were uneventful as they retraced their steps back towards the base camp. Peter was tired each night and his bones ached, but the thought that they were on the first leg of the journey home kept him energized.

On the fourth day out of the valley they were travelling on a level stretch of trail, which paralleled the *Rio Platano*. As had happened every day of the journey, Peter fell behind the main group. He was not concerned because the trail was wide and clearly marked here and he knew he would eventually catch up to them. Suddenly, he heard a clatter of popping sounds in the distance; there were shouts and a scream from the trail ahead. Peter summoned up all the energy he had to get his rubbery legs into a fast trot. It was several hundred yards of thickly overgrown trail before Peter trotted into a scenario where several dozen men armed with Kalashnikovs and Uzis surrounded the expedition party. Two of the soldiers lay apparently dead on the ground, the other two had surrendered their weapons, as had Cruz-Madrid. The armed men were raggedly dressed with torn cotton shirts, khaki shorts, rope sandals, long hair and ragged beards. Their leader was a man dressed in cargo pants and soft leather boots. He was middle-aged, clean-shaven, with short cropped black hair flecked with grey and thick glasses with heavy black frames. He wore a pistol belt but the pistol was holstered. "Another guest at our little party," the leader said in Spanish. "It's unfortunate for you that your group arrived just as we are expecting a very large shipment from Peru, quite inconvenient for all of us."

"We are an archeological expedition on our way home, we are no threat to you. Just let us go and I promise there will be no repercussions," said Peter in Spanish.

"A gringo who speaks Spanish, a rarity. Look, I have no doubt that your group are not hunting drug runners but the presence of the army among you makes my men quite uncomfortable. And you can imagine that your assurances, while I am sure sincere, cannot be considered reliable. We have a very nice set-up here and I would hate to have it compromised. Your people are going to have to come with us while we decide on a course of action."

The expedition members were herded off the main trail onto a narrow track through the jungle. After about a mile and a half they emerged into a small clearing ringed with thatched roof huts. The expedition members were all made to kneel together in the far end of the clearing. The first to be separated were Doctor Mellon and Wendy, the intern. Their hands were bound and they were marched under armed guard across the clearing to one of the huts. Within a few minutes they heard screams coming from the hut. A group of the drug runners gathered at the door of the hut while half-dozen others stood guard, training their guns at the remaining expedition group.

The next to go were the two remaining soldiers. They too

had their hands bound and they were marched to the center of the clearing. The leader drew his gun and placed it right at the forehead of each soldier, pulling the trigger. Peter had never seen anyone shot point blank in the head. He was amazed and nauseated at the amount of brain matter that was blown from the skull. He felt his stomach turn and vomit rising in his throat. He realized now that they would all be killed, they had no hope of ever getting back.

Cruz-Madrid was next. "Captain," said the leader "your military has hunted us like dogs. They are the lackeys of the Americans whose people are the very consumers of the drugs they seek to stop being shipped to their country. We want to make sure when they find your body that we have sent a message. As an officer, you no doubt come from one of the elite families in this corrupt cesspool of a country, so for the many years of exploitation and abuse of the poor and indigenous people of Honduras we will offer you a difficult death." Cruz-Madrid was marched to the edge of the clearing, hoisted onto a tree trunk and tied to it, his arms splayed onto extended branches. One of the drug runners unsheathed his machete and hacked at Cruz-Madrid's side. He screamed, his screams merging with those still coming from the hut where Mellon and Wendy had been taken. Another drug runner stepped up and hacked off Cruz-Madrid's ear. His high pitched, hysterical screams filled the air. Peter vomited. Others in the group were trembling. For over an hour they hacked away at Cruz-Madrid until he was covered in blood and mercifully lapsed into unconsciousness. He had screamed in agony at each hack of a machete until he lost consciousness. The screams from the hut stopped but men still lined up outside it. Finally they heard two loud pops. The naked bodies of Doctor Hannah Mellon and Wendy Dirks were carried out of the hut with gaping red holes in their heads and unceremoniously dumped with the bodies of the two soldiers. The leader walked over to the remaining expedition members. Peter noticed that both DeGroet and Selby had wet stains in the crotches of their pants. Arias-Garcia sat calmly with his eyes closed as if in meditation.

"Our methods seem brutal to you, do they not?" said the leader who appeared to be addressing him directly. "Over the years I have learned that brutality is necessary to accomplish worthwhile ends. One has to be strong enough to endure the burden of cruelty. In the 1970's I was a young philosophy student at the University of San Cristobal of Huamanga in Ayacucho, Peru. I had a brilliant professor named Abimael Guzman. I worshipped him and became his disciple. Eventually he left the university to guide *Sendero Luminoso* the guerilla group that came so very close to overturning the corrupt government of Peru. There was a time I can tell you when we even controlled large sections of the barrios in Lima itself. When Guzman was captured, the movement began to falter. We needed him and eventually he turned away from us and disowned us all to get pastries for breakfast and softer toilet tissue in his prison cell. But I learned from Guzman, the need to be decisive and to be unafraid of cruelty when cruelty is called for. We cannot afford to lose this airstrip. We get three flights a week from Peru with the highest quality cocaine. There is no military or police anywhere near. I know you are only scholars who have come into this territory to loot the heritage of the indigenous people. But I cannot afford to have you return to *La Ceiba* to alert the military. Besides, you are all bourgeois asswipes who have lived your lives off the labors of the poor, you will not be missed."

"What about the laborers?" asked Peter, who felt he had nothing to lose by arguing "they are only here to make a few lempiras to feed their families, they are not bourgeois asswipes, just the kind of poor you were supposed to be helping."

"We learned. In Peru when the *Indios* failed to cooperate, when they informed on us, we had to make examples of them too. It was necessary that they be sacrificed. Those who clung to their Christianity and their priests, we crucified them. Those who informed on us, we slit their throats then cut off their balls and stuffed them in their betraying mouths. All of you must be sacrificed so we may continue our endeavor. It is tragic but necessary," he said with a smile. At that, the leader signaled to the guards, who dialed their Kalashnikovs to fully automatic and began spraying them all with bullets. Peter felt one, two, three bullets penetrate his chest with searing pain. Then everything went black.

Forty-seven
TEGUCIGALPA

The woman who entered the back room of Jahaira's *botanica* was attractive. Long, dark hair, large black eyes, late twenties, thick, heart shaped lips. Her ample, shapely hips were clad in a denim dress from Hollister. This one, thought Jahaira, is no typical barrio girl. But when she opened her mouth she spoke the sharp guttural Spanish of the Honduran slums. "They say you are a *bruja*, is that true?"

"More or less. There are many things I can do. How can I help you?"

"I need you to kill my husband, can you do that?"

"Oh yes, or let us say I can make it very easy for you to kill your husband, will that do? Most people these days, when they want a killing, they go to the gangs. That is what they do well."

"I tried that but the local gang leader told me I had not only to pay him but to suck his cock. You do not have a cock so I thought I would try you."

"Why do you want to kill him?"

"He is old and he uses me like a whore and slaps me when he is angry."

"So just leave him, he sounds worthless."

"No, just old and mean. He owns a market in the *Zona Azul*. He is a wealthy man and I am just a girl from *Barrio Rosales*. He saw me and fancied me and my mother made me marry him. If I leave him, I leave a good life. If I kill him, I get everything and I lead a perfect life, maybe with a better, younger man."

"I understand and I must confess I too have done away with an old and no longer useful husband. Very sad, he was handsome when he was young and full of life but he became a burden as he aged and I needed to lose him."

"How can that be when you are no older than me? You are not old enough to have seen a young man grow old."

"Aah, well maybe I just killed him because I was sick of him after all. I can help you. There is a colorless, tasteless powder. It needs to be given in three doses. After the third dose his heart will fail as if he had a heart attack. The doses must be given no more than a day apart. The Honduran police, if they suspect anything, will not be able to trace the drug. Do you understand? The cost is 30,000 lempiras. Does the thought of murdering a man in cold blood not disturb you? It is no small thing to take a human life."

"Yet you say you yourself have killed a husband who became a burden? I have spent my life in poverty being deprived of decent food, education, nice clothes. I have been abused by a father who drank too much cheap guaro and beat me, a mother who treated me like a valuable property to be sold to the highest bidder. I have learned to look out for myself. The world is a cruel place and I have no desire to be a victim so I must be cruel to get what I want. I must be the victimizer. Too bad for him that the old *cabron* was not born a decade or two earlier, was not born a handsome man and was born a cruel bastard, too bad he became so rich. If not for those things I might let him live. But right now he is more valuable to me dead. Give me the powder and I will not live with any guilt *bruja*!" Jahaira smiled, took the woman's money and handed her the powder.

Forty-eight
RIO PLATANO BIOSPHERE

Peter felt himself swimming in a salty ocean. Ahead of him was a woman seated on a stone throne. As he swam closer he saw it was a young Zelda Aronson as she had appeared when she was 18 and that she was nude. He found himself crying as he swam and the tears began to turn to blood. Soon he was soaked with the blood of his tears and he could see that Zelda was laughing. Suddenly he found himself holding the corpse of Cruz-Madrid and his own tears of blood blended with the blood oozing from the mutilated corpse. Perhaps, Peter thought, this is death and hell, both of which for me are inevitable.

He awakened covered with blood next to the corpse of Arias-Garcia, which was riddled with bullet holes. He reached for the wounds in his chest and was surprised to find nothing there. The blood, which soaked his clothes and stained his face, was in fact from Arias-Garcia. He remembered being hit at least three times and could not understand why there were no wounds. He opened his eyes to see a burial detail beginning to haul away bodies and he knew he somehow had to get away. There was a sound from the sky of a twin-engine plane flying low. The burial detail looked up and dropped their shovels, running towards a trail at the edge of the camp to meet the plane and unload its precious cargo. Peter knew this was his only chance. He got up on wobbly legs and lurched towards the jungle on the opposite side of the clearing from where the drug runners had gone. He began running in a panic, tripping over vines and under growth. He ran this way for about twenty minutes when he realized he was completely lost with no hope of getting back to the friendly confines of any sort of civilization. He could not even find his way back to the drug runners if he wanted. He sat down beneath a tall palm and began to cry.

As he sobbed he suddenly felt a presence that threatened him even more than being hopelessly lost. Not more than ten feet away was a jaguar, close enough for him to smell the musky feline smell of the cat. It made a soft mewling sound. Peter thought he had escaped death at the hands of gun wielding drug runners only to be torn apart by a jungle cat.

The jaguar turned and began walking away. After three or four yards it sat and looked back at him and mewled. Peter could not be sure but he remembered a dream where he followed a jaguar to safety. If this seemed insane, and it did, nothing that had happened to him on this trip made much more sense. His choice was to sit here, utterly lost, in the middle of the jungle or to follow a cat. He decided to follow the cat. He got up and began to move towards the jaguar. It immediately got up and began walking.

Peter had difficulty keeping up with the cat but it often stopped and waited for him as he struggled through the brush. When he came to streams he stopped and drank as the cat waited on the other side, always keeping about a twenty-foot distance between them. When the first night fell the cat stopped a few feet away from a huge tree whose trunk had been hollowed out by termites. The cat lay down and seemed to rest and Peter climbed into the tree and immediately fell asleep. The next morning when he woke the cat was still there, waiting for him. The second day went much as the first as they traversed untracked forest. Peter had no idea where he was going but on the third day he heard the roar of the *Rio Platano* in the distance. By the fourth day they encountered a broad, well-marked trail that ran parallel to the river and Peter knew they were going in the right direction. That night the jaguar brought Peter a small dead animal. He tried to start a fire and could not but he was so famished he ate it raw tearing strips of raw flesh from the carcass and choking them down.

On the fifth day the cat disappeared but Peter could follow the trail and could only hope the base camp was where they left it. It took two more days without food before he began to hear voices on the trail. He assumed they were auditory hallucinations brought on by hunger but as he staggered on he could see a trail of smoke in the air and Zodiacs beached on the riverbank.

The base campers saw a dazed, emaciated man staggering into camp. His clothes were tattered and soaked with blood. They could barely recognize him as Peter VanOwen.

Forty-nine
LA CEIBA, HONDURAS

Major Hector Cordoba was the commander for the La Ceiba military district. It was not a very prestigious assignment. La Ceiba was a steamy little Caribbean seaport with drug runners and smugglers on all sides. His men were often outnumbered and always outgunned. The *Indios* and Garifuna would not even talk to the army and the Coast Guard was corrupt beyond redemption. The fucking Americans were always on his ass about drug interdiction but he was always two steps behind the drug runners.

Cordoba was the son of a skilled woodworker in a little town in the northern mountains of Honduras. His father made enough money to send his precocious son to a prestigious military secondary school from which he matriculated to the national military academy. He graduated with honors and received his commission but, as he learned throughout his education, he was not from the right family to expect to rise successfully or receive the most desirable assignments. The fact that his mother was half *Indio*, and it showed in his features, did not help. Although he had risen in rank faster than his classmate, Aramis Cruz-Madrid, it was Cruz-Madrid who had gotten a plum assignment with Special Forces in Tegus while he was stuck here in this piss hole.

Across the table from Cordoba sat a very miserable looking gringo. The military headquarters in La Ceiba was not air-conditioned and only a wobbly ceiling fan created the slightest breeze in the stifling heat. The gringo had been part of some fool expedition into La Mosquitia to find a lost city. He had emerged from the forest at his base camp covered in blood and told his comrades that his group had been caught by drug runners and massacred, including his old classmate Cruz-Madrid and four Special Forces soldiers. That part of the gringo's story was entirely believable. What troubled Cordoba is why had this particular gringo escaped and no one else and how the hell did this guy find his way through the jungle? That part was not so believable. The report from Tegus on this gringo, Peter VanOwen, was that he was clean, no criminal record, no association with known drug traffickers. In fact he had never even been to Honduras before. He was a lawyer at home, retired, living in Costa Rica and brokering wholesale coffee. All in all, Cordoba was inclined to believe this guy, even the unlikely parts of his story. He appeared highly traumatized, physically exhausted. He had obviously lost weight and suffered from leeches and insect bites. But he had no gunshot wounds, just three small, round bruises in his chest just above his heart as if he had been wearing a Kevlar vest which he swore he had not.

The gringo could not pinpoint where they met the drug runners but he could give a fairly good idea of the approximate location with regard to the expedition base camp. The Pech, whose territory this is, would not be cooperative and undoubtedly knew all about the operation. They would be getting presents from the drug runners and possibly selling their young girls to them as concubines. Besides, the Pech hated the Honduran army and with good reason. But Cordoba had a half Pech first sergeant in his unit whose knowledge could help narrow down the location even more. He could get a high level aerial reconnaissance from the Americans, give them some coordinates and, if they found it, some choppers from the air base at San Pedro Sula to wreak havoc. He was not going to put his soldiers on the ground for this one, it was too vague and besides they were always outgunned. No, a few rockets and some fifty caliber rounds should tear the place up pretty good and at least force them to find another location. Military command would support him on this one, after all one of their own; Cruz-Madrid, had been killed and pretty brutally according to the gringo.

Cordoba had resented Cruz-Madrid as an entitled prick, but in reality he had been pretty friendly for an aristocrat and had gone out of his way to praise Cordoba's achievements. These fucking scumbags had to be taught they could not hack up an army officer without retribution. As for the gringo, he would put him on a plane to Tegus and let the poor fool go home.

Fifty
PLAYA ESTERILLOS

Ophelia was sitting in a small *mariscos* restaurant just north of Jaco, sipping an Imperial and eating grilled red snapper for lunch. The restaurant, really just a palapas over a concrete slab, was right on the beach with fishing boats lying on the shore. She was probably eating what they had caught that morning. A group of young Ticos walked into the restaurant and sat down. They were in their early twenties, dressed in designer jeans and white linen shirts. They were probably coming down from San Jose to Jaco for the week-end to gamble and whore. One of them walked by her table and offered in Spanish to buy her a drink. "Why would you do that?" she replied in English.

"Hey, maybe you would like to come with us and have some fun in Jaco?" he replied in heavily accented English. She started to respond when her cell phone rang. She did not recognize the number but she was pretty sure who it was.

"Hello," she answered in English as the Tico guy stood by her table.

"Why are you speaking English?" asked the *bruja* on the other end.

"Well, I am trying to eat my lunch and this guy is hitting on me."

"You should learn how to cook, then you could eat at home and stop getting into trouble at restaurants. Anyway, you will be eating at my table soon, I need you to come home soon, *carina*. Peter VanOwen is out of the jungle and on his way to Tegus. You do not want to be there when he gets home do you?"

"Maybe I do. He liked me a lot. Maybe he will take care of me from now on?"

"*Carina*, he is an old man, plump and ugly, and not that rich, you could do better. Just come back, I will have a plane ticket for you the day after tomorrow. There will be a car at the airport. Leave VanOwen's house clean and locked up, okay?"

"I drank all his rum and beer. Do I need to replace it?"

"No. just make the flight on time. I need your help, *carina*."

"Is Angelica still cooking for you?"

"Yes, of course. We will have *arroz con pollo* the night you return, okay? Love you, baby." The line went dead. The Tico was still standing by the table looking at her with big, wet eyes.

"Why would I want to go with you?" she said in her Honduran barrio Spanish which obviously took him by surprise. "I do not fuck any one for fun and I do not fuck any one for free and I do not fuck anyone cheaply, so you, my child, can fuck off." She paid for her fish and left.

Fifty-one
TEGUCIGALPA

Peter reveled in the luxury of the Marriott. There were clean sheets, hot water, air conditioning, clean towels, color satellite TV and the room service American beef steak he had just devoured. In La Ceiba he had been kept in a military hospital on a narrow cot in a room without air conditioning with only rice and beans to eat. He had been interrogated three times by military intelligence before finally being flown to Tegucigalpa. He had a flight out the following afternoon to take him back to Costa Rica. By tomorrow evening he would be having dinner in his own house.

Peter felt a deep sense of guilt over the deaths of his colleagues and his inexplicable survival. None of it made any sense. His journey through the forest guided by a wild animal seemed unreal and a part of him still believed he was in such a state of shock he fantasized it. His fall into the depths of the pyramid and his hallucination of a beautiful naked woman with a 220 Amp kiss seemed also to be a product of his crumbling psyche, except he had apparently actually encountered an electrical shock and still felt the after effects. His body was badly bruised in a dozen places, including the three circular bruises over his heart which would not go away, his joints ached and he had easily lost thirty pounds during his ordeal on the expedition and his escape from the drug runners. His flesh sagged and as he looked at himself in the full length closet door mirror he saw a gaunt, haunted looking man who looked ten years older than the one who had started on the expedition. He thought of Cruz-Madrid, the amiable, playboy aristocrat and his horrible death. Doctor Mellon and poor Wendy had been raped, brutalized and shot in the head. Selby, whose meddling had gotten him into this nightmare, had been mowed down by gunfire after wetting himself in terror, as had the eminent Doctor Phillip DeGroet. Even Arias-Garcia was dead, after calmly kneeling in prayer as the drug runners set their rifles on automatic. It was his blood that had soaked Peter's clothes and undoubtedly convinced them he was dead. Perhaps what the female deity in the pyramid had told him in his hallucination was true, god was whimsical and cruel with no love for its creations.

His close brush with death had convinced Peter to embrace the life he had left. Not that he meant to change or do anything dramatically different, just that he would more deeply appreciate each precious moment, savoring even the mundane, ordinary aspects of daily life and the small freedoms he had always taken for granted. He liked his solitary life, reading on the beach, trading and roasting coffee, reveling in a quiet and peaceful life free from threats, ambition, jealousy, fear and strife. He looked forward enormously to a return to a life he now appreciated more than he ever thought possible.

As he lay on his hotel room bed watching a "Law and Order" rerun in Spanish on the TV, his room phone rang. "Peter?" said a woman's voice on the other end. "It's Zelda Aronson, how are you?" Peter hesitated before replying.

"I have to say you were about the last person I expected to hear from."

"I know and that is part of the reason I called. I feel really bad about what I said that afternoon before you left on the expedition. What's happened to you and to me, too, has kind of put all of that into perspective. Look, I'm sorry if I hurt your feelings, maybe it was just the shock of seeing you after all these years, maybe some guilt about how we parted back in college, anyway it was harsh and I really didn't mean it. You were not a bad guy and not a bad boyfriend. I also heard about what you went through back in the jungle. In a way I feel responsible because I pulled the plug on the expedition and put you guys in the position where you were vulnerable to being attacked. Was it as horrible as it sounded?"

"Worse, it was unimaginable what they did to the women and to poor Captain Cruz-Madrid and then they just let loose with a volley of automatic weapons fire on the rest of us. I have no idea how or why I survived. But you shouldn't feel responsible. It was only sheer bad luck that we were passing through just as they were expecting a shipment of drugs. There was no way you could have known."

"Thank you, Peter. I still have very mixed feelings about my involvement. Did the expedition actually find anything valuable? I guess you are the only one left who can answer that question."

"Yes, they actually found what must have been a magnificent city two thousand years ago, a completely unknown culture very sophisticated and artistically mature. Someone has to go back and continue the work. But I understand that you lost your husband. I am so sorry, it's difficult to understand something like that happening back home."

"Yes, it was a shock."

"I also understand you pulled the plug on the expedition because you're funding a clinic here in Tegucigalpa in a poor barrio. I think that's wonderful. Really, in the end, archeology has to take a back seat to the needs of people here in the present."

"I'm glad you understand, Peter. Look, would you like to get together for a drink some time?" Peter felt a thrill surge through his body as if the prettiest girl in the class had just passed him a note.

"Well, I'd love to but I'm going back to Costa Rica tomorrow afternoon."

"How about tonight if you're up to it? I can send over a

car to pick you up."

"Yes, yes I'd like that, what time?"

"I'll have the car there by six."

Peter felt energized by the invitation and got off the bed to shower and dress carefully. He knew there was very little chance of anything happening between him and Zelda but he could not help thinking they were both now single and this meeting might spark a renewal of an attachment that had been long dead. While a part of him knew this was utter nonsense, he could not help a soaring feeling of hope.

The car arrived promptly at six, a dark sedan with no markings and a driver in a light cotton jacket with a shoulder holster peeking out from underneath. The ride through the evening streets of Tegucigalpa was as unsettling as he remembered it from his night with Cruz-Madrid, only this time he was not drunk. As always, the poverty was disturbing, but even more so since his encounter with the drug runners were the small clusters of young men in sleeveless white T-shirts and baggy khakis. These were the street corners where the drug runners recruited. Here and there acrid smoke rose from trash fires by the curb, many houses were squat cinder block squares with corrugated metal roofs and gaping openings where windows should be. They entered a district, which looked vaguely familiar to him. The streets were narrow cobblestone lanes lined with tall rickety old houses having arched windows covered with masonry grates in abstract designs. The roofs were red tile and many of the homes were three stories. They pulled up in front of a house that looked very familiar with a wide mahogany door. The driver gestured for Peter to get out. He was not sure but he felt as if this was the house where Jahaira beat and sodomized him. But he could not be certain, and any way what would Zelda be doing in Jahaira's house? Maybe she had just taken a place in the same or a similar district. He felt reassured when he knocked and Zelda herself answered the door. She looked lovely in a long sheer cotton, black sheath dress with her hair pulled back loosely. She was still the elegant, long legged, raven haired beauty he had always desired, even at her age. The anteroom into which he stepped had a familiar feel. There was the same broad mahogany staircase and the same sober oil painting of an early nineteenth century prelate on the wall. Could these be standard décor in old Honduran houses?

Zelda obviously tried to hide her dismay at the way he looked, and greeted him warmly. She took him into a great room with a fireplace and two carved wooden chairs that convinced him finally that he was in Jahaira's house.

"I've been in this house before," he told her.

"Yes, I know. It belongs to my new friend Jahaira who helped me get the clinic started. She said she had met you before. I'm staying here now."

"Did she tell you what she did to me?"

"Well, I know she has worked as a prostitute, so I assume it was something sexual."

"She hurt me, she drugged me and sodomized me and she beat me badly enough to draw blood!"

"Peter, I have a hard time believing she would do anything like that. The Jahaira I know cares about the poor and unfortunate. She is wise and kind and gentle. Besides why would she do that to you?" As she spoke, a tall black woman Peter recognized from his last visit came in carrying a tray with two glasses of gold liquid in tall sweating glasses. Peter, remembering his last visit, looked appraisingly at the glass set down in front of him. "It's just fresh squeezed passionfruit juice with a little sugar in it, I wasn't sure if you would be up for an alcoholic beverage." Zelda smiled at him and drank hers. Peter hesitated and finally drank. It was smooth and refreshing, not too sweet but with a seductive aftertaste of passionfruit. "Tell me about the expedition, if it isn't too painful, after all you are the only witness." Peter winced at that but responded.

"The Pech guides took us to the white city, not the same place as the National Geographic expedition found, we passed through that site and it was definitely interesting but it was not the principal city of this civilization. That site, the real *ciudad blanca*, was deeper into the mountains in a large valley. There were hundreds, perhaps thousands of structures and a huge, intricate pyramid with a deep subterranean chamber which I managed to fall into." He was beginning to feel tired and he wondered if coming here had been more than he could handle.

"What did you find down there?"

"I'm not really sure. A lot of carvings and artifacts, I must have hit my head and hallucinated. I found myself talking to a naked woman who claimed she was god. A very strange and uuh, yeah very strange, I'm not sure ... " Peter could not stay awake he fell back in his chair and lost consciousness.

When he awakened he was lying strapped to a gurney by heavy canvas restraints with metal buckles. He was in a cellar room filled with jars of dried herbs, small cages of insects and snakes and several large worktables on which were piled large leather-bound books and what looked like an obsidian knife. Zelda and Jahaira were standing across from him. Zelda looked concerned.

"Welcome back, Peter. You have no idea how happy I am to see you again. You have had quite a journey and I want to hear all about it," said Jahaira.

"What he said about you hurting him, was that true?" asked Zelda.

"We had a sexual tryst, he likes it rough, so I made it rough. Perhaps we miscommunicated."

"You are lying, Jahaira," said Peter, almost sobbing, "you attacked me and you sodomized me. My ass bled for days."

"I have been known to lie. In my profession lying is often necessary, but I would never lie to Zelda, not to my wife."

"You're what!" Peter suddenly realized that the plain golden ring on her left hand was not the large purple diamond she had worn when he first met her at the Marriott. "You two are married?"

"Yes," said Zelda, "for more than two months now. I started seeing Jahaira even before Chad died. Peter, I'm sorry for the deception but I was fulfilling a promise I made to Jahaira a long time ago to help her lure you here. She knew you would never come on your own unless I asked you. Jahaira, this is wrong, he isn't a bad man and you're holding him prisoner against his will. Let him go, I don't want to see him hurt."

"*Carina*, I promise not to hurt him, I promise only to help him and when I am finished he will be free to go if he so desires. Aren't you supposed to be at the clinic this morning?"

"Yes. Can I trust you to do the right thing and not hurt him? I would never forgive myself or you if you did."

"You have my solemn word, *carina*. And I promise you that nothing I do to him will hurt him or affect your feelings about yourself or me." Zelda nodded, looked guiltily at Peter strapped to his gurney and walked to the stairs leading to the ground floor.

When Zelda was gone Jahaira looked at Peter and smiled. "What you saw in the subterranean chamber was real Peter, more real than anything in this room. Do you not feel a change in yourself? Those round bruises on your chest what are they from?"

"I don't know. Please, let me go, I have a flight to catch tomorrow and I really want to go home. Can't you just leave me alone?"

"That flight is today, Peter. It is the morning of the day after you shared passionfruit juice with Zelda. When the time comes, I will give you the choice of leaving just as I said to Zelda. Those bruises are from bullets, are they not? Did you not wonder why you did not die when all of your *compadres* did?"

"I don't know, they must have missed, that's the only explanation."

"You know they did not. Those bullets struck you point blank and you did not die or even experience a wound. Do you know why?"

"I have no explanation, I don't know what happened."

"I was born in 1807. In those days Tegus was not the capital and Honduras was not yet even a country. As I have said, my father was Hector Cristales, who was, at the time of my conception, a parish priest and a scion of a wealthy and powerful family, one of the very first Spanish families to settle Honduras. My mother was a profoundly beautiful woman from a family of modest means who was seduced by my father when she went to him to seek help for her depression. The Cristales family gave my mother a small stipend and eventually, this house, which was their very first Tegus town house, when they realized that she was pregnant with Hector's child. When I was fifteen my mother committed suicide. I was a precocious girl who had learned to read, play the piano and speak several languages. My father was gone then. He had taken a journey to *La Mosquitia*, visited the Garifuna and the Pech and, very much like you, *la ciudad blanca*, where he had an experience not unlike yours. I was nineteen by the time he returned to Tegus. I went to confront him about my mother's death for I blamed him above all for seducing and abandoning her when she came to him for help. When I met him I sensed something strange about him, something different. He was impressed with me, even as I reviled him for my mother's death. From then on, once or twice a week, we met and he taught me what he had learned from the Garifuna and the Pech and most especially in *la ciudad blanca*. He knew more than he realized and I was able to glean from him more than he knew he was teaching me. I noticed as the years passed that he did not grow older as other men did. As I researched the old stories of the Pech and those my father told me, I realized that he was not the first to meet the great deity in the white city. My father had been given the gift of immortality. For a man like my father, who was of a philosophical, self-examining nature and a man of his time, immortality was a gift he did not relish. He was afraid of the future and he was grounded in his mortality.

"I decided to take the gift away. I studied and puzzled over how to do it. To take the gift, it would be necessary to kill my father, but he was immortal and could not be killed, but if I killed him would not the gift go away? Would the deity be angry if I took what it had given? I found the way. It was always there in the old Pech stories of the sacrifices in *la ciudad blanca*. I immobilized my father and I cut his heart from his chest and devoured it while it was still beating. Indeed, my father died and I have lived ever since. I was twenty-seven when I did it and I have remained twenty-seven all these years."

"Even if I believed you, and I'm not sure I do, you can take my 'gift.' I'm like your father, I have no desire to live forever, I've had enough problems in this life. It has been a struggle. I don't want to live forever in this old man's body with its aches and pains and debilities. Do whatever you want to take away this gift you say I've been given. If you have to kill me please just do it without pain."

"You do not understand, Peter. I do not want what I already have. What I want is a companion who can live the years through with me. I have seen so many loved ones age and die before my eyes. What has been unendurable is the loss and loneliness. Your gift solves my problem."

"I don't see how. We hardly know each other and based on what I know of you I have no desire to spend eternity with you. Besides, why would you want a worn out old man as a companion?"

"All very good points. I think that by the time I am ready to release you, and I will release you, you may be more amenable to our companionship. While I think that intellectually you would be a very good companion, I do have a solution that may leave both of us, or at least me, happier. You will see, Peter." She approached the gurney picking up a hypodermic needle on the way over. She swiftly and expertly injected Peter with it and he quickly faded back into sleep.

Fifty-two
RIO PLATANO BIOSPHERE

The leader relaxed on a hammock reading Rousseau's *Discourse on The Origin and Basis of Inequality Among Men*. The next shipment was due tomorrow night. Until then he and his men had little to do. Rereading the Rousseau text on the development of a truly natural human being within a truly equal society, something which required nothing less than the complete reformation of modern and traditional human society, left him feeling nostalgic for his days as a revolutionary with *Sendero Luminoso*. These days he was just a drug runner. He still had dealings with *Sendero,* which often supplied him with some of the highest quality cocaine. But *Sendero* had withered to a tiny group of hard line holdouts who, these days, did little to advance the revolution. They occasionally raided a rural police station or assassinated a local mayor but mostly they just collected cocaine from the local farmers and sold it to people like him. The capture of and ultimate betrayal by Guzman had poisoned the movement. He longed for the days when they could field thousands of rifle bearing guerillas, controlled whole districts and seemed on the verge of collapsing the government in Lima.

The distant rumble was a familiar sound. He found it difficult to believe what he was hearing because he had never felt the security of the airstrip to be endangered. Surely the Pech would not have betrayed them? They were the only ones who knew the location. The archeology expedition was all dead and had no working radio gear. With *Sendero* they would be ready when the soldiers came. Aerial defenses and an escape route were always prepared. But they had nothing of the sort here and their only escape was into a jungle, which would surely kill them if they stayed too long.

When the first rockets hit the airfield the leader jumped out of his hammock shouting orders to his men. In the sky above he could see two rickety old American Huey helicopters with mounted rocket tubes. Three more rockets exploded in the vicinity of the thatched roof huts setting them on fire. His men were running for the jungle beyond the airfield, he decided he might as well join them.

As they crashed through the underbrush they found themselves running directly into repeated heavy caliber volleys, which tore through the trees and brush. A third Huey appeared, this one carrying a fifty caliber machine gun, and had cut off their line of retreat. They were running directly into its field of fire. The leader felt a large slug hit his shoulder and he fell from the impact. The initial pain was unbearable. All around him his men were falling too. He thought briefly, as another bullet crashed through his back and into his lungs and the life began slipping from his body, that the shipment would have to be delayed.

Fifty-three
TEGUCIGALPA

Zelda found Jahaira's treatment of Peter disturbing. She really did think of Jahaira as having a kind soul, which was inconsistent with the way she had tricked then confined the broken old man he seemed now to be. What did she want from him? Why would she need to hold him against his will? Was Peter telling the truth about what Jahaira had done to her? She felt guilty about her part in the deception. When she called him she could hear the eagerness in his voice at hearing from her and she found as she spoke the things Jahaira had advised her to say to him she really meant them. Somehow, after all these years, Peter still adored her and she liked that. It felt good to be adored but she knew she had taken advantage of his feelings in luring him to Jahaira for whatever purpose she had with him. Somehow, Jahaira realized far better than she the extent and depth of Peter's feelings for her.

She never entirely got used to the ride through *Barrio Rosales*. Once they passed the army roadblock, the neighborhood became more and more desolate with tumbled down plywood and cinderblock shacks, dirty children playing in the street and a vague odor of organic decay pervading the air. Yet this was precisely the clientele who most needed the services her clinic provided, which is precisely why she was driving through this morass of human misery. The traffic, as always, was crawling through the narrow streets. Many of the intersections completely lacked traffic controls and the few that did were ignored. She did not notice the yellow Suzuki motorbike until it drew up right next to her sedan. The driver and passenger both peered into the window and grinned maniacally at her. She turned away just as the passenger produced an Uzi from under his jacket and began spraying the car with bullets. The sedan careened off the road as the driver slumped over. Zelda felt pain in her chest and found blood spurting out her mouth. As the car smashed into a roadside fruit stand she gasped, choking on her own blood, and quickly suffocated to death.

Fifty-four
TOEB CLINIC, *BARRIO ROSALES*

Doctor Castillo had a full day ahead. The clinic had just opened, he had several excellent young doctors on board but they were badly understaffed with nurses and trained medical technicians. Then there was the matter of Zelda Toeb's brutal murder. He had no idea what that meant for the future of the clinic. Now that wretched Cristales woman insisted on seeing him. She was waiting for him in the reception area and he decided he had better get their interview over with so he could attend to the more important business of running the clinic.

She entered his office wearing a striking orange and black dress, hemmed just below the knees. She wore a black veil pinned to her hair as if she were in mourning. For the first time Castillo noticed she wore a plain golden ring on her left hand. He was sure that had not been there before. "Thank you for seeing me on such short notice, Doctor, I promise not to take too much of your very valuable time." Castillo thought he must have imagined a hint of sarcasm in that last comment.

"What can I do for you, *senorita?*" he said brusquely.

"It is *senora*, actually," she said wagging her ring clad finger in front of him." Zelda and I were married several months ago in California."

Suddenly Castillo understood. He never really believed that MS13 had killed Zelda because of the clinic. They had no problem with the clinic, their own families and associates had been using it and they had never asked for protection money. But if Zelda and the Cristales woman were married, Zelda's death would likely mean her surviving spouse would inherit a substantial fortune. He looked at Jahaira with surprise and fear.

"Whatever you may be thinking about me, Doctor, let me assure you I will continue to fund the clinic and I want you to continue as medical director. Zelda would have wanted that. Besides, I believe in the work you are doing here, having been a *curandera* for this barrio for so many years. I know how badly your services are needed. So rest assured, your work will continue. However, I will be leaving Honduras very soon. After I have lived here for a few years I always feel, shall we say, conspicuous, and I think if I am gone for a while people will forget me and when I return I can start fresh with a new generation who does not know me and will not ask questions."

"*Senorita* Cristales, or whatever your real name is, were you responsible for the death of Zelda Toeb?"

"Doctor, you know very well that MS13 killed Zelda, as do the authorities. Why would I kill my *esposa*? I wish you luck in your work here. My attorney will handle the financial affairs and he will know how to contact me if you need anything. *Adios*, Doctor, I doubt we'll meet again."

Fifty-five
LOS ANGELES

Miriam sat on her terrace overlooking the Pacific Ocean, scanning the Los Angeles Times. On the back page of the "California" section she found an article that caught her attention.

"SECOND AMERICAN FOUND DEAD IN HONDURAS

The body of Peter VanOwen, former Senior Deputy Los Angeles County Counsel, was found in a trash dump in a slum of Tegucigalpa, the Honduran capital. His body had been mutilated with a gaping wound in his chest and was missing his heart. He was the second American found dead in the last five days. On Monday, the body of Zelda Aronson/Toeb, widow of software magnate, Chad Toeb, was pulled from a car, which had been sprayed with bullets in the streets of the same district in which VanOwen's body was found. Authorities said Aronson/Toeb's murder appeared gang related. VanOwen was sixty-two years old and a resident of Costa Rica. He had a long and distinguished career in the County Counsel's office and, at one time, was considered a candidate for the top job. VanOwen is survived by two daughters, Aileen, 24 and Leia, 22."

The story did not come as a surprise to Miriam as she had been called that morning by Honduran authorities who reported that Peter's body had been found. They did not mention the mutilation. She could not imagine who would do such a thing or what it might mean. She found herself mildly annoyed that the article failed to mention Aileen and Leia's respective careers. After all, any publicity was valuable and they both could use a boost. After getting off the phone with the Hondurans she immediately called both girls. Leia had little reaction. It was years since she had seen her father and, undoubtedly, she was unsure how to react to such strange news.

Aileen's only comment was "Well, I guess now we own a beach house in Costa Rica."

But Aileen was wrong. Later that day Miriam received a call from an Arturo Camarosa, a Honduran lawyer, who told her that her two daughters had been specifically disinherited by name. Peter's entire estate, such as it was, including his Costa Rican beach house, went to someone named Jahaira Cristales. Probably, thought Miriam, a Costa Rican whore.

Fifty-six
TEGUCIGALPA

Peter's body felt very strange upon his awakening. He felt as if he must have slept for days. He was strapped into a bed in a bedroom with several large arched windows covered with curtains. His first thought was that his joints no longer ached. He felt flexible and lithe but also somehow more compact. As he looked around the bare room he could feel whatever anesthesia had been used on him slowly begin to wear off. His chest felt strange as if it had suddenly become padded. Then with a shock he realized he could not feel his penis. Jahaira, the bitch, had castrated him!

He reached down to touch his groin and did not recognize the small, smooth hands in front of him. He looked around for a mirror and found none but he knew something profound and terrible had happened to him. He was conscious of the fact that he felt no pain in his groin area, which he would have expected after a castration. Instead, although there were no longer penis and testicles, the feeling down there was one he had never felt before and could not describe. He squirmed in his bonds but he was firmly held.

A half hour after he awakened, the door to the room opened and Jahaira walked in. "What have you done to me?" he wailed, but the voice that came out was one he had never heard before, at least not from his own mouth.

"I have solved the problems we discussed earlier and I

must say it was quite difficult," she said in Spanish, "now, respond to me in Spanish."

"Please tell me what you have done to me," the Spanish was his heavily accented correct version but the voice was feminine, low and husky for a woman perhaps, but definitely a woman's voice.

"Aaah, I have indeed succeeded. Your Spanish is not that of a native speaker, it is that of Peter VanOwen."

"Of course it is," said the female voice "who else's would it be?"

"Well, I would have been very disappointed if it was the Spanish of a native speaker like Ophelia Morales. Peter, I have given you a great gift to go along with the deity's gift. I have taken your old, decayed, unattractive and infirm body and given you a healthy, beautiful twenty-five year old body. Jahaira opened a drawer in the nightstand and pulled out a hand mirror holding it up to Peter's face. The reflection showed a pale, young woman's face with large pale blue eyes and jet black hair. It was a face he had seen before except the pageboy haircut had grown out to long, thick tresses. He was filled with horror, he was no longer himself he had become a stranger and one of a different gender.

"The world will no longer know you as Peter VanOwen. In fact, Peter VanOwen is officially dead. It was necessary to sacrifice your old body to affect the transfer but it was Ophelia who really died. Now, you will be, officially and legally, Ophelia Morales, a street whore from San Pedro Sula with no education, no money, no property, no prospects of any kind. If the truth were known, Ophelia Morales is also guilty of the murder of Chad Toeb, a punishment I am sure you would prefer to avoid."

"What! That whore killed Chad Toeb?"

"No, *carina*, you did," said Jahaira laughing. "I will make you a proposition, Ophelia," she said, emphasizing the name, "you will become my *relacionado*, you will follow me and do as

I say and I will see that you live comfortably and prosperously. I will not hurt you and I will treat you with respect but you will be mine in every way. If you choose not to stay with me then I will let you go, just as I promised Zelda I would, but you will have no identity other than Ophelia Morales, not a lempira to your name, no property, nothing. Even the real Ophelia, who was tough and could make her way on the street on her own, chose to come with me. You are just an old gringo who could never survive on the streets of Tegus. The beauty that allowed Ophelia to survive would soon make you a target for brutality and exploitation."

"I don't know," said the feminine voice coming from his face "how can you expect me to give up my freedom, my whole identity?"

"You are not giving up anything, you have already lost it. By the way, our mutual friend, Zelda, was murdered in an unfortunate incident. I am told that MS13, the gang that controls *Barrio Rosales* where Zelda's new clinic was located, was angered by her refusal to pay protection money. In retaliation they gunned her and her driver down on the street. As her surviving spouse I inherit her entire estate."

Fifty-seven
CAFÉ LOUISE
BOULEVARD SAINT-GERMAIN
PARIS, FRANCE

Jean-Phillipe saw the women come into the Café Louise two or three times a week, usually around ten in the morning. They would order café-crèmes and brioche and sit for an hour or so and watch the crowd move by on the Boulevard Saint-Germain. He noticed them simply because they were two of the most beautiful women he had ever seen. One was dark skinned and dark haired, with a compact and curvaceous body Jean-Phillipe appreciated. She was friendly and vivacious, smiling and laughing. She spoke very good French but with a pronounced Spanish accent. The other was even more beautiful, like a young Liz Taylor, very pale skinned with long jet black hair and huge, pale blue eyes. She was quieter and spoke little French. She moved with an awkwardness that seemed strange in such a beautiful woman. She had trouble walking on the four inch platform heels she often wore. She seemed subdued and a bit depressed. They spoke to each other in Spanish or English and somehow Jean-Phillipe decided they were from South America somewhere. Clearly they were wealthy, for they were always dressed in clothes by Thierry Mugler, Gareth Pugh, Alexander McQueen or other expensive designers. He heard they had taken the entire top floor of a handsome old beaux-arts building on the Boulevard Saint-Germain just down the boulevard from the café.

Jean-Phillipe initially assumed they were normal heterosexual girls because they were both exceedingly feminine in their clothing, hair and makeup. The dark one, Jahaira, even flirted good-naturedly with him. But he had more than once seen Jahaira reach beneath the table and caress the thigh and genitals of the other. One day he had even seen her grab the pale girl by the head and give her a hard, erotic kiss. Jean-Phillipe could only conclude, to his disappointment, that they were a couple.

The pale girl, Ophelia he thought her name was, only seemed to come alive when they engaged in the kind of literary or philosophical discussion that he had problems keeping up with, especially since it was usually in English in which he was only moderately competent. He knew they talked about Sartre, Camus and Simone De Beauvoir, whose old haunts were only a few blocks away on the Boulevard Saint-Germain, Kant and others. Ophelia loved Proust, whom Jahaira provocatively mocked as bourgeois, self-indulgent and onanistic. Jahaira seemed to be a strong proponent of Nietzsche while Ophelia did not seem comfortable with her enthusiasm but Jean-Phillipe did not really understand most of their arguments.

After an hour or so they would finish their café-cremes and leave. Jahaira, the dark one, had a jaunty bounce to her step. Lovely Ophelia, teetering on her platform heels, walked dutifully behind her, head down.

Epilogue

Ophelia hated the stifling atmosphere of *Le Caveau de la Huchette*, the Latin Quarter jazz club Jahaira insisted they visit tonight. There were too many bodies on a warm night, too much cigarette smoke and too much noise in the cellar-like room. She hated, as always, the stares of the men as she walked into the room, mentally undressing her and imagining the various sex acts they would like to perform with her. It was a feeling she could never quite get used to and always made her feel uncomfortable and violated. They sat at a table close to the stage, Jahaira with her arm casually but possessively around Ophelia. Occasionally her fingers played with Ophelia's nipple. She was sore from their almost nightly rough sex, which inevitably involved imaginative ways to humiliate her while pleasuring Jahaira.

Four musicians came onstage, to Ophelia's relief, as the crowd quieted down. There was a young white piano player, a middle aged black standing bass player, a tubby young black tenor sax player and a tall handsome young black man on trumpet. They started with a version of Charlie Parker's "Salt Peanuts" in which the trumpet player took the first solo and wowed the crowd with quick, tonally perfect improvisations. The sax player followed, he lacked the speed and dexterity of the trumpet player but gave a credible cover of the Parker solo. The bass player and piano player did their things, neither had the virtuoso skill of the trumpet player but the music was fine. Their second number "I Cover The Waterfront" featured a brilliant solo by the young trumpet player. Ophelia realized he reminded her very much of Clifford Brown who also recorded a memorable solo of that same tune while he was in Paris. At the end of the tune, Ophelia, as most of the crowd, stood up to give him a standing ovation.

"*Mesdames et Messieurs*," said a voice over the sound system, "*donner s'il vous plait un accueil a Leia VanOwen*." Peter VanOwen's older daughter stepped out on the stage. Short, elf-like, with long brown hair and large green eyes she looked more beautiful and confident than Ophelia had ever seen her. She wore a black skirt with a flowered print, sleeveless top and very little make-up. Her first number was Billie Holiday's "God Bless the Child." Her voice was stronger and more controlled than Ophelia remembered it, but then she realized the last time she, or that is Peter, had heard her was in her high school musical play.

She sang the sad, cynical lyrics about crass obsession with money and family alienation at a slow tempo with a mournful catch in her voice. Had Peter VanOwen been here he would have been proud of the little daughter on the stage struggling to express herself in a dying art form, he too had loved. Had he been here perhaps he would have regretted his abrogation of fatherhood. But Peter VanOwen was not in the room.

Ophelia looked away from the stage and found she was crying, the tears flowed faster down her cheeks as the song continued. She looked over at Jahaira to see her looking directly back at her, a tight, crooked smile on her face.

About the Author

R. V. Wadden Jr. is a retired lawyer with a Masters in Literature from U.C.L.A., splitting his time between the Los Angeles area and his house in Playa Esterillos, Costa Rica.

VISIT OUR WEBSITE
FOR THE FULL INVENTORY
OF QUALITY BOOKS:
http://www.roguephoenixpress.com

Rogue Phoenix Press

Representing Excellence in Publishing

Quality trade paperbacks and downloads

in multiple formats,

in genres ranging from historical to contemporary romance, mystery and science fiction.

Visit the website then bookmark it.

We add new titles each month!

www.ingramcontent.com/pod-product-compliance
Lightning Source LLC
Chambersburg PA
CBHW051943220626
47052CB00004B/771